MILANA ROBERTSON

Angel in Black

Contents

Dedication

To my very Russian family, whose intimidating presence once had people asking if you were in the mafia.

To my husband, who endured my endless medical questions without alerting the authorities.

And to my daughter, who napped just long enough for Mommy to write love stories with a little too much spice.

Note to Readers

This novel contains content that may be distressing to some readers. Please be advised that the story includes references to:

- Kidnapping
- Violence
- Explicit sexual content
- Attempted sexual assault
- Organized crime and mafia activity

Reader discretion is advised.

1

Lena

Tonight, the hospital hums with chaos. The fluorescent lights overhead intensify my pounding headache until I have to squint to see straight. I glance at my watch and note I have one more hour in this shift. It is my fifth twelve-hour day this week, and it is going out with a bang. Today alone brought six open abdominal surgeries, two compound fractures, and a suicide attempt by gunshot. The bullet hit the skull but somehow missed the brain. On nights like these, adrenaline is the only thing keeping me upright.

A gurney screeches as it's wheeled in, carrying a man in his late fifties, pale and unconscious, blood spreading across his abdomen like a virus. I swiftly move around the horde of nurses and doctors and dip into the break room. I finally exhale, my body drooping with exhaustion. *No, not yet, Lena. Just one more hour, you can do this.* I love working in the trauma unit; it works for me. I crave the fast pace of it, the thick tension when you know every second counts. Once you're in the storm, you don't get out until you're struggling to breathe, choking on the madness, and damn, I love it. Unfortunately, even I have my limits. Well, my body does anyway. My mind never stops working.

I hear Amanda, the charge nurse for this evening, barking orders outside the room, and I mentally prepare for her to detect me with her *whoever is taking a break is screwed radar*. Because screw me if I need to take a moment to breathe. She is the reason my twelve-hour shifts sometimes become fourteen-hour ones. I hear her high-pitched voice reverberating through the halls, landing right in this room with me.

"Ah, there you are! Listen, Bea is stuck in room 204. Apparently, Mr. Anderson took out his catheter again, so I need you to head up to Med Obs and help out. They are severely understaffed tonight, practically drowning in patients."

I look down at my watch again, *shit*. The medical observation unit is the only place in this hospital where it feels as though the minutes are dragging their feet through wet cement. I plaster on a fake smile and agree to go, as if it were ever a choice.

Once I get to the unit, I hear the low murmur of people talking and nurses rushing in and out of patient rooms. It's nothing like the mayhem upstairs, but I welcome the noise. I take a look at the patient charts and notice a familiar name. I take the chart and make my way to his room, which is coincidentally the same room he's always in.

"What is it this time, Jackson?" I ask, a smile dancing on my lips. This kid has been in the ER five times in the past six months. His appetite for danger, specifically dirt bike riding, is almost impressive, if it wasn't so alarming.

Jackson beams when he sees me. "Fractured clavicle."

"Wow!" I act impressed. "A new one for your collection, huh?"

"Already added it to the list," he retorts, a little too enthusiastically. I'd probably be worried if I were his mom, but since I'm not, all I can do is give him a fist bump.

"Alright, let me take a look at it." I don my gloves and peel back the navy-blue hospital gown. Splotches of deep purple and blue bleed out of the area that is covered in thick bandages. I can see that it's still swollen and angry, but the alignment is already doing better. I touch it lightly to make sure there's circulation, and he flinches.

"Sorry," I mutter. "Just making sure you're not numb there."

"No offense, Lena, but you kinda smell," he says after a while, crinkling his nose at me.

I take in the pungent smell of antiseptic mixed with what has to be at least three different kinds of bodily fluids, and I cringe. I can't believe I didn't notice before.

"You saying you don't like my new perfume?" I ask with a smile, and he laughs.

All humor dies when I hear the overhead speaker call a code blue on this unit, only a few doors down. I leave a wide-eyed Jackson and run over to room 119. With it being so close, I'm the first to arrive other than a petite young nurse, who was probably the one who called the code. She leans over the barrel-chested man and checks his pulse with shaky hands. Even from here, I can tell he's fading, his lips turning an unnatural shade of blue.

I look at the nurse's badge and see her name is Katie. "Hi, Katie, you did great calling in the code. I'm going to start compressions, and I need you to be my partner in crime and start doing pulse checks," I tell her while readying myself above this man. I don't wait a second longer and go right in, starting the compressions, making sure they are sharp and deliberate.

This isn't my first code, but it looks like it is for Katie. Her eyes are glassy, and her stance unmoving. I don't blame her, though. This is Med Obs, this kind of thing doesn't happen here. All the scary stuff usually happens in my unit. I wonder how desensitized I've become to all the blood and gore. What, if anything, can make me look as terrified as Katie right now?

I feel a rib crack under my hands and internally cringe. It's such a strange sensation, feeling human bone breaking under you. You'd think it takes more force, but even my 110-pound frame can do it with the right amount of pressure and adrenaline. If this guy makes it, he'll have a lot of pain breathing, but I can't think about that. I can't hesitate or slow down even for a second because if I did, I may as well stop altogether.

Footsteps echo in the room as Doctor Riddick and his team surround the man, and me still on top of him. Pads go on his chest. "Charging," someone says. "Clear." I lift my hands for a heartbeat as the shock snaps through him, then I'm right back on his chest. My hands are starting to cramp, the color draining away from them into a paleness, *just a little longer, Lena.* I've only ever lost two patients since working here, and this guy will not be a third. Despite being a trauma nurse, I do not handle loss very well, never have, really, since childhood.

Tension fills the room like smoke as one of the nurses cracks open a vial of epinephrine and injects it straight into the man's IV. We keep working, and then the stark charging sound of the defibrillator fills the room. I move off the man swiftly, a second before I hear "Clear!" and then we all hold our breath waiting for any sign of life. The man's chest heaves as the bolt of electricity runs through his body. The silence ringing so loudly in my ears. I'm back on his chest a moment later.

"Pulse!" one of the nurses declares. All eyes turn to the monitors, and the steady sound answers us. Normal sinus, just how we like it. The room itself feels like it sighs in relief. The man's chest rises and falls steadily as the team prepares for the next phase. The code is over, but I can't help but think for how long?

"How did you get here so fast? You're supposed to be upstairs," Riddick says.

"I was only two rooms down, heard you guys needed some help," I say.

"Amanda sent you?" he asks, crossing his arms.

Richard Riddick is one of the only doctors in this place who gives a damn about his staff. He's one of those doctors who doesn't quite look like a doctor but more like a linebacker. He towers over me in his six-foot-three stature, dark blond hair covering his head in one of those casual but messy hairstyles. He'd be swoon-worthy if I ever had time to swoon.

"Well, I had a whole hour left on my shift, so I had to make every second count," I say sarcastically.

He rolls his eyes. "Say no next time, it's easy. I do it all the time."

"Say no and miss out on all this fun? Chocolate pudding *and* a code blue all in one day?" I tease as he swats me away.

"Go home!" he calls out. I smile and head back toward Jackson's room.

"You okay?" I ask, standing next to the door frame. I know sometimes he gets a bit jumpy when codes are called. His mother passed away three years ago when he was just eleven years old, so every time a code is called, I can see the panic in his eyes.

"Did you save him?" he asks, his expression sullen.

"Yes, we did. I promise that guy will not be having any more codes for at least ten minutes." He doesn't smile. I sigh. "I'm sorry. I know it's scary, but I want you to know that we have some pretty great nurses and doctors here who will do everything in their power to save anyone who comes through those doors."

He gives me a half smile. "So, he's okay?"

"Yes. He's okay."

When Bea comes to relieve me, I look at my watch and sigh. Somehow, two hours have passed since coming down here, with one hour left on my shift, and now I'm an hour over. I don't even know why I'm surprised anymore. I don't remember the last time I left my shift on time.

"Sorry, Lena, I know you have that date tonight," Bea says while I hand her the charts for this evening.

Shit, I completely forgot about that. "It's fine, I guess I'll just have to reschedule," I say, half joking.

She crosses her arms. "You better not! You need to get out more; you're always working, and frankly, I need someone to live through. My life isn't any more exciting than yours," she says.

I laugh. "Fine. I'll do it for you, but I can't promise he won't run away from me. Have you smelled me lately? I didn't notice until Jackson pointed it out!"

"Lena, we all smell like that upstairs. My cat won't even go near me anymore." We laugh, and then she pushes me toward the elevator. "Go get your shit and go home. Tell me everything tomorrow!" she orders with a grin.

Once I get my stuff, I make my way to the garage and into

my white Toyota Camry.

"Hey, buddy, I've missed you," I say to my car as he roars to life. I drive home in silence, feeling the weight of the day heavy on my body. Once the high from working in such a fast-paced environment wears off, you're left with nothing in you.

I love my job, but I've always wanted more. A small part of me wished I had enough courage to go to medical school and become a doctor. Being at the forefront of all the action and decision-making is everything I've been wanting since starting as a nurse.

I pull into my apartment complex, the iron gates greeting me as they open. I follow the row of palm trees to my apartment building, marked forty-two, and park in my designated spot. My apartment is located on the second floor of this building, which I absolutely detest because after a long day like this, the last thing I want to do is climb a flight of stairs. As soon as I open the door and see my queen-sized bed waiting for me, looking so fluffy and inviting, I start to contemplate whether I should get dressed for my date tonight or skip it altogether. I'm not sure I could get the stench of the hospital off my skin, even if I scrubbed it raw.

My mother found me my "perfect match" while cutting his hair at her barbershop. She told me, "Lena, I can always tell how a man treats his partner by the way he treats his hair, and this man's hair is better than mine!" I smile at the thought. My mom has taken it upon herself to find me a partner; she's been worried that I will end up alone with a bunch of dogs. I have to remind her that, unfortunately, I don't even have time for one dog. As I get up to change, a thought enters my mind: *he better not have nicer hair than me.*

I look at myself in the mirror, my short black hair slightly curled, nude lipstick, red flowy midi dress with black heels. I give myself a once-over. I look damn good, considering I haven't worn anything but scrubs in months. My stomach gurgles as I pace a little, going toward the door and back.

"Lena, you are not agoraphobic. Get the hell out of this house. You deserve to have some fun." I give myself a mental fist bump and step out the door. Once I get downstairs, I'm greeted with roses the size of my face, and I can only assume the man holding them is my date.

"Brandon?" I ask, walking toward him.

"Lena?" he asks back, looking a little confused.

"Uh, yeah, that's me." I smile. "You look confused." I let out a breathy laugh.

"Oh, sorry! I was expecting…" He looks afraid to say the words.

"Someone blonde?" I finish his sentence. He looks uncomfortable for a moment, like he doesn't know what to say. I guess my mom didn't show him a picture of me.

"It's okay, I get that a lot. My dad is pretty handsome, though, so I'm not too mad about getting more of his genes." I chuckle, trying to lighten the mood.

My mother and older sister Stella both have blond hair and blue eyes, while my brother Danny and I both have dark hair with dark eyes. But like I said, I'm not mad about it.

"You look beautiful," he says and ushers me to the car.

We ride in polite silence, both of us not knowing what to say. I get up the courage and very covertly peer over at him from the corner of my eye. He is definitely someone my mom would pick out. Don't get me wrong, he's gorgeous with his sandy brown hair perfectly styled. He's clean cut, lean in all the right places, and of course, blue-eyed. He wears a blue button-down shirt that clings to every muscle in his body. He looks like my mother pulled him out of *GQ* magazine. I don't know what it is, but I just want to straddle him and mess up his hair, unbutton his shirt, and see his eyes widen in surprise. I smile inwardly because I can already see my mom disapproving of me messing up his perfect hair.

Once we get to the restaurant, he holds the door open and pulls out my chair. I make a mental note: chivalry is not, in fact, dead.

"I hope you like Italian," he says. "Your mom didn't give me much information on what kind of food you like."

"I can pretty much eat anything, but since I'm Russian, I'm genetically programmed to like Russian food the most," I joke.

He grins and asks, "So, have you always wanted to be a nurse?" as we sit down.

I take a moment to think about his question. I honestly can't think of a time when I didn't want to be in healthcare. It was just a question of what in healthcare I wanted to do.

"Yes and no," I admit.

"From what I hear, being a nurse is a stressful job. Your mom said you're looking into switching careers?"

I almost spit out my water onto his very chiseled face. Now, where would my mother get that idea from? Oh, right, these atrocities just come to her. I'm sure her intentions are good, and she is just worried that this man, and all men really, will hate to have a partner who works like crazy and barely comes home. I get it. But shouldn't he like me, for me? She also could've told him I have plans on becoming a doctor, but of course, she wouldn't want to intimidate him. I mentally pound my head on the table a few times and begin a game I like to play when I'm out with guys my mother chose for me. It doesn't happen often, but I'd say three times now. I call the game: *how much did my mom tell you, and how much of it is true?* Let's see how many points Mom can rack up this time.

"Actually, I love being a trauma nurse. It's long hours, but I'm basically saving lives." I chuckle. "Do you know how many karma points I've collected this week?"

He seems taken aback by what I said, but then a boyish smile creeps up, and he laughs. "Way more karma points than a job in insurance," he says.

"I'm going to have to agree with you on that one," I smirk.

We end up ordering three different pastas and share all three. When we polish off everything on the table, he motions to the dessert menu.

"This is the part where I say I'm way too stuffed and can't possibly eat another bite," I tell him. "But that would be a lie because I always have room for dessert."

"I am so glad we're being honest because if we're ordering dessert, we need to order double. I don't share well when it comes to sweets," he winks at me. Well, at least he has a good sense of humor.

I nod, "Two of everything it is!". We scarf down two tiramisu cakes, two cannoli the size of my head, and two coffee gelatos.

"So, you're from New York originally, right?" he asks. "It must've been so cool to grow up in the city. Your mom made it sound like a dream, the ideal place to raise a family. I don't know why you guys would leave." He chuckles. "Not that I'm complaining."

And here it is, another point for Mom. I would never describe New York City as the ideal place to raise a family. Probably not even the ideal place to raise a dog. Many people seem to be impressed when I say I'm from New York, and I've never understood why. Maybe because my childhood was less of a dream and more of a nightmare. I grew up in the heart of the Russian community, Brighton Beach, Brooklyn. It's our own mini-Russia. It's where the air smells of pierogi all the time and where you can escape to the beach in a heartbeat. That's not the part that makes me want to forget I ever lived there. It's the fact that anyone can go missing, and no one will ever question it. So, when people ask me how it was growing up there, I just say "it was interesting," and that seems to do the trick.

Brandon smiles. "I bet. I've always wanted to go but never had the time or opportunity."

"Actually, today marks my tenth year of living in Phoenix. I'm no longer a city girl, I think I've officially become a Phoenician," I smile. "I get cold when the temperature hits seventy-five and always have a farmer's tan; those are the qualifications, right?"

"Wow, then yes, on behalf of all Phoenicians, we accept you as one of our own," he teases.

When I turned seventeen, we moved all the way across the country to Phoenix, Arizona, and I could not be happier. After my parents decided to separate, my mom packed our bags, and we left. No looking back. Maybe that is why I agreed to this date in the first place. She has always told me to find someone steady and dependable.

We finish our drinks, stealing quiet glances at each other. He checks off all the boxes. Boxes I did not even know I had. Loyal. Reliable. Safe. So why am I more excited to go home and sleep than to keep this date going?

* * *

When we arrive at my apartment, he walks me to my door, and we stare at each other, not knowing who should make the first move. I'm not opposed to kissing on the first date; I actually prefer it. People can fake politeness and interest, but no one can fake sexual chemistry. I guess you can call me impatient.

He steps closer, and I have to crane my neck to meet his gaze. His eyes are fixed on my lips. His tongue sweeps across his bottom lip, and heat blooms in my chest. I take a step toward him, imagining the taste of him, the feel of his mouth on mine.

I all but throw myself into his space, giving him every green light to kiss me. He smiles, lifts his hand, and cups my cheek with a touch so soft I melt where I stand. *Kiss me*, I chant over and over in my head.

He leans in, hovering just above my mouth before finally closing the distance. The kiss is slow, deliberate, and intimate. Our lips move together in perfect sync. No teeth, no tongue, and no awkward tilt. His hand slides to the small of my back, his touch feather-light. I feel his smile against my mouth, and I smile back.

"I had a wonderful time, Lena, please let me take you out again," he says, his eyes shining in the moonlight.

My smile widens. "I'll have to clear it with the boss, but I think she'd approve," I tease, knowing my mother will definitely approve.

We exchange phone numbers and promise to go out on another date soon. When I finally head inside my apartment, I can't help but feel… nothing. No butterflies, nervousness, or jitters about the kiss or seeing him again. Maybe I'm just out of practice. Maybe I've become cynical and secretly want to end up alone with seven dogs just like my mother predicts. As I push those thoughts away and walk toward my room, kicking off my shoes, I hear the doorbell ring, and my heart begins to race. Does he want to continue the date? Am I okay with that? As I make my way to the door again, I feel more excitement now than I have the entire date. When I open the door, my thoughts of getting lucky disappear, and I'm forced back into reality.

My brother Danny stands in front of my door, looking like he's been to hell and back. If he presses the doorbell any longer, he'll probably break it.

When he sees me, he sighs with relief. "Lena, I've been calling you all night. Where the hell have you been?" He brushes past me. He stops in the middle of the living room and turns to me with a disgusted look on his face. "I forgot about your obsession with pink. You need help, Lena," he says.

I roll my eyes. Do I have an unnatural obsession with the color pink? Yes. Is my entire house decked out in pink decor? Yes again. Am I ashamed? Not even in the slightest.

"What do you want, Danny?" I ask, closing the door.

"Have you heard from Dad?" his question slams into me.

My face contorts into a look of confusion, and I walk over to him. His usual light brown eyes are tinged red, the kind of red that you get when you've stayed up all night looking at your phone. His brows are drawn, and his chocolate brown hair is even more disheveled than usual.

"Uh, no, not in a while," I say. Now that I think about it, it's been days since he's called. Even though we don't see him much since we moved, he does make it a point to call us several times a week.

"I haven't heard from him in a week. Something must've happened," his jaw tightens.

"Danny, calm down. Dad is probably at his favorite spot in Atlantic City. You know he doesn't pick up the phone when he's there," I say, trying to calm this tugging in my chest.

"Yeah, I know, but he's never there for a whole fucking week, Lena," he paces up and down my living room, burning a hole in my rug.

I've never seen him so worried about my dad before. He's usually the one trying to calm *me* down. My brother is the youngest in the family, and he's taken on the 'man of the house' role pretty seriously since our parents split. Sometimes I wanna shake him and say it's okay to be a stupid teenager. It's okay to need someone to look out for you for a change. His voice brings me back before I can reach out and bring him into a hug that would probably freak him out.

"I've even called Erik, but he hasn't seen him at the casino or the barbershop in at least a week. Babula called and asked if I've heard from him. She's really worried. I had to lie and tell her he's at the casino."

"Dan, Grandma is always worried about him. He lost all her money," I say, rolling my eyes. It's probably for the best that he didn't tell my grandma he thinks my father is missing. She had surgery recently, and stress would slow her recovery.

"Lena," he says with a serious tone and starts rubbing his head vigorously, "you don't understand. Ugh... he borrowed more money recently...." He closes his eyes and breathes out a sigh like he's been holding his breath for a long time.

"He always borrows money and then loses it. It's what he does," I shift in my seat, not really liking where this is going.

"Not from these people. He told me not to tell anyone,

especially you… but I think maybe they took him or something. He told me not to worry because he had a plan to win the money back, but I don't think he did, Lena."

"Who took him? What do you mean?" Slight panic rises in my voice.

He finally sits down and puts his head in his hands. "The Volkhov. He told me he was tight on cash, and Babula needed money for her hip. That was months ago. What if he couldn't pay them back? I know you know who I'm talking about."

In this moment, I feel the room shrink, making me slightly claustrophobic. I'm instantly transported back to my home in Brighton, sitting on my doorstep because I forgot my keys again. Dima, the boy next door, comes out of his house and reflexively reaches for a cigarette. I look at him. He's slender in all black; he has sunken, dark eyes, and when he sees me, he smiles. The kind of smile that's reserved for innocent little girls who know nothing about life. The smile that catches me off guard every time, because boys like Dima don't smile often.

"Want one?" He extends his arm to give me a cigarette. That's when I see the mark. The letter V is tattooed in Russian on his forearm. It's not big, but it's noticeable, and by its placement, I think he wants it to be noticeable. I focus on the tattoo and don't even remember taking the cigarette.

"Alright! Tight ass isn't as tight!" He smiles and then takes off, rounding the corner of our block. A few minutes later, my mom found me with that cigarette in my hand, and the rest of the evening I spent in my room thinking about "how not to be a delinquent and how much my parents have done for me". Since then, I've tried really hard to repress this memory because even at that young age, sitting on that doorstep, I knew what that meant, and I knew it wasn't good. I just didn't know that was the last time I'd see Dima.

"Dan, are you sure? Is there anyone in New York who can find him somehow? How do we even contact these people?" My head spins with questions that strangle me slowly with each answer that comes into my mind. The answer is we don't. No one goes looking for those people unless they have a death wish or they have nowhere else to go. I'm not there yet, I can't be. There has to be another way.

"I'm getting a flight tomorrow, and I'm going to get him back. That's the only thing I can think of doing," he replies.

"Danny, slow down. Have you even called the police? You're only seventeen, I'm not going to let you go anywhere." I'm almost yelling at him now, feeling the weight of the situation.

"Erik and I have called the police several times, and each time they tell us we need to file a missing person's report, and each damn time I tell them I already did! This is serious, Lena. The police will not help us with this."

His words go back and forth in my mind. This isn't a fucking movie. How can the reports keep disappearing?

"I'll go," I say, the words not at all confident. Danny almost laughs, like me, going isn't even an option he ever considered.

"They will eat you alive, Lena. We'll have a better chance if Stella goes, but she hasn't talked to Dad in months."

Being the middle child, I've always felt like the weakest of the three. My sister had to grow up fast because she had us to take care of. Dad's absence forced my brother to grow up before he was ready. And me? Apparently, it's laughable that I would be the one to do this.

"Dan, I'll fly out and ask around about Dad. I'll find him, I promise. Just don't do anything stupid. Dad wouldn't want you to get involved in his shit," I pray he doesn't mention *me* getting involved in Dad's shit. Honestly, I think my dad would hate it even more if I were the one to find him. His pride and guilt would prevent him from accepting it.

He looks at me long and hard, like he's waiting for me to back out. I return the stare and reassure him that I would do this. That I *can* do this.

2

Lena

It's been a full day since I last talked to Danny. Now I'm sitting in front of my computer, two hours deep into chewing my lip while I read over the leave of absence paperwork. Danny wasn't too happy about me not already being in New York, so I had to remind him I couldn't just teleport there. The next flight wasn't until tonight, so that's the one I booked. Plus, I can't just leave without telling anyone. I have a job, friends, and a mother who would kill me if I left without telling her. I mean, she'll probably kill me anyway after finding out, but this way will probably be less painful.

I scroll through the leave options. Childbirth, nope. My own serious health condition, nope. Caring for a family member with a serious illness… does kidnapping count? Probably not. The last two involve a family member being called into active duty. Nope and nope.

God, I hate lying, but something tells me that "my dad was possibly taken by the Russian Mafia and I have to find him myself because the police probably work for them" would not be considered a valid excuse.

Caring for a family member with a serious illness will have to be the one. I check that box and move on to the next part, fifty signatures and my soul. I pray they don't ask me for proof of illness. I submit the paperwork and begin to pack my bags. Usually, if it's approved, you get up to twelve weeks off, but I'm really hoping to just go for a week or so. That should be enough time to find my dad, give him a piece of my mind, and get the hell out of that city.

The sound of my phone ringing startles me, and I look down at it, hoping it's not work.

It's worse.

"Hi, Mom," I say, face-palming myself. She definitely knows I'm leaving.

"When were you going to tell me?" she asks in her mom voice.

"It just happened last night, Mom. I didn't have any plans on going, but I have to," I tell her. I'm wondering if she found out from Danny and how much he actually told her. *Shit*, I wish he had warned me at least.

"I know it happened last night. I set it up!" Her voice is smug through the line.

Um… well, now I'm thoroughly confused. "What?"

"What do you mean, what? The date, Lena." There's a pause, like she's waiting for me to catch up. "When were you going to tell me you two kissed?" Her voice jumps an octave.

I let out a big sigh. She's talking about the date, not me going to New York. Wait. Let's roll that back. How the hell did she know Brandon and I kissed?

"How do you know that, Mom?" My voice sharpens.

"Brandon's hair appointment was this morning, and I happened to have asked how it went," she says, like it's the most normal thing to do.

"Do you know how weird it is to have your mom know everything about your love life before I even get to process it myself?"

"Oh, come on, I'm just excited for you. Now tell me how it went." She sounds giddy.

I can never stay annoyed with her for long. She means well, and hearing her excitement over a date I went on is actually kind of cute.

"It went really well, Mom. He seems like a really nice guy." I try to match her enthusiasm.

There's a pause, and I can almost hear her frustration through the line.

"Then why don't you like him, Lena? He's educated, has a great job, and have you seen his hair?"

"Yes, mom, I know, and I didn't say I didn't like him."

"Then what is it? You're twenty-seven and alone. I just want you to at least start thinking about settling down."

She means well. She means well. She means well. I chant these three words over and over again until I no longer want to scream.

"I don't know what to tell you, Mom. I didn't feel a spark, I guess. And plus, I don't have time to date right now anyway," I say, trying to ease into the other huge thing I need to tell her. God, this wasn't even the huge thing, and I'm already exhausted.

"Lenachka, let me tell you something, sparks can come and go. Maybe they're not there initially, but they can come later if you just give someone a chance. And what's this about not having time to date? When will you have time then? When I'm dead?" she says dramatically.

Great, and here comes the guilt trip. I am preventing her from seeing her daughter find her partner and be happy, and eventually give her grandchildren. I am an awful daughter. I roll my eyes.

"Mom, I'm going to New York tonight, and I can't think about you hating me for not seeing Brandon again. I mean, I might see him again. I just want to decide when and *if*, without you pressuring me."

Silence comes through the line, and I check my phone to see if we're still connected.

"Mom?"

"How much trouble is your father in?" her voice softens. This woman has a sixth sense or something.

"I'm not sure. Danny thinks something happened to him. He hasn't been picking up his phone either," I say, intentionally leaving out the bit where my father borrowed money from the mafia and is probably kidnapped.

"Erik can't find him?" she asks.

"No, Mom. And it isn't his responsibility. He can't just drop everything and go around looking for him."

She's quiet for a moment. "Do you want me to go with you?"

I smile. It's nice, in a way, that Mom still worries about Dad, even after everything. "No, Mom, I'll be okay. I'll find him and then come home. And if I can't find him, then I'll go to the police," I say. Only half of that is a lie.

"I know you're strong, Lena, but you don't know what happens to people there. Mothers lose their kids in the blink of an eye. I will not lose my baby, too." Her voice is stern and serious, and it sends goosebumps prickling up my back. I've heard those words before, but not from my mom. They belonged to Dima's mother, the night she came pounding on our door two days after he went missing.

I was the last one still sitting at the dinner table, pushing stuffed peppers around my plate. Everyone else had finished. I once got food poisoning from them, and ever since, the smell alone makes me gag. As soon as the knocking started, I jumped up. We all did. My mother glanced at my father as he rose from the couch and went to the door. The house fell silent, except for the creak of the stairs as my sister sneaked down to see what was happening.

The door opened, wind rushing in and scattering my father's newspapers across the carpet. I bent down to gather them, but my mother's hand shot up, stopping me.

"Jana, is everything okay?" my father asked. I craned my neck to see our neighbor, the woman who had lived next door all my life. She was soaked from the rain, trembling, her hair hanging like a wet rag across her forehead.

"Dima hasn't been back in two days. Have you seen him?" she asked, sniffling. My father turned to my mother, who only shook her head.

"Come in, Jana," my mother said from the couch. In all the years we had lived there, she had never once invited a neighbor inside. Not for holidays, not for anything. When Jana stepped into the house, my mother motioned for me to leave, as if she already knew the conversation wasn't meant for my ears. But I did what most teenagers do. I climbed to the top of the stairs and sat with my sister, hidden but listening.

"Giorgiy, please tell me you've seen him," Jana pleaded. I couldn't see my father's face, but when her voice broke into a sob, I knew he'd shaken his head.

"Did you call the police?" my mother asked. Her tone was soft, gentler than I'd ever heard when speaking about Jana or her son.

"Yes, over and over. They say they filed a report, but when I call back, they tell me it doesn't exist. I've gone down to the station three times and been escorted out like I'm the criminal." Her voice cracked with desperation. I could picture her wide blue eyes, the ones that had always smiled at me on my way to school, now raw with panic.

My father sighed heavily. "I've seen his tattoo, Jana. I know you have too. It's not my place to say, but we both know what happens to boys who wear that mark."

A thick silence settled over the house, the kind that makes you afraid to breathe.

"He got it as a joke. It wasn't real. He wasn't part of that." Jana's voice was hysterical now, and I found myself edging up one stair toward my room. My sister pressed a finger to her lips, warning me to be quiet.

"Jana, please," my mother began. "I know—"

"You don't know a single thing about my life or my son." Her footsteps pounded toward the door, and when it opened, I caught a glimpse of her face. Her eyes met mine, a single tear slipping free as she gave me a smile so broken it split my heart in two. Then she was gone.

When the door closed, my mother spoke. "We can't stay here any longer, Gresha. Not in a place where mothers lose their children and the authorities do nothing. I will not lose my babies, too."

That night, I lay awake, listening to the pitter-patter of rain on the window and the faint, lingering cry of a mother calling for her son echoing down the street.

"Lena, just promise me you'll call and update me." My mother's voice pulls me back to the present. I promise her I'll send regular texts from New York, and her tone shifts from worried to almost cheerful. She even seems glad I am taking time off work. Leave it to Mom to find the silver lining in a search and rescue mission.

3

Lena

The plane smells like plastic. Plastic that has been cleaned with Lysol and left to dry. A last-minute flight calls for a last-minute seat smack in the middle and right next to the bathroom at the end of the plane. The snoring coming from the large man next to me tells me I will not be getting any sleep for the next five hours. It's fine, I don't think I could fall asleep even if I had the row to myself. I keep trying to come up with some sort of plan, but all I can think about is that I'm going back. I'm *actually* going back.

I told myself I wouldn't return to New York until I was stripped of my memories of it, but of course, here I am, going back to create new ones. In the last ten years, I've never considered going back, not even visiting my dad or grandma. I've never said that out loud, never even tried to explain it to anyone, because I know how it sounds. I'm ashamed to say that I just couldn't see my dad like that, alone in that house without us. I feel an enormous amount of guilt for leaving him, but also relief for getting out of that place. It's an odd feeling that I never intended to deal with.

The plane ride is rough, shaking with turbulence, reminding me where I'm going and my journey ahead. I know what lies ahead, and I know it can't be good. I keep thinking about when Dima vanished. I was only fourteen, but even then, I knew it had to be because of the Volkhov. We weren't best friends, but it's hard not to get to know someone when they live next door to you your entire life. He was the kind to dabble in drugs, steal cars, and offer you cigarettes. He was far from perfect, but it was just him and his mom. I knew in my bones he wouldn't have left her. I knew it by the way he argued about her working too much, not getting enough food, or going out to get some sunlight. He loved her, I knew that for sure. It's why every time I saw him, I couldn't help but smile.

Sometimes in my dreams, I hear his mother running up and down the streets, calling his name. I went through a million scenarios in my head about what could have happened to him, but I always come back to the same truth. This place isn't normal.

The bad things here were never accidents. People spoke in hushed voices about the evil that lurked on every corner. Everyone knew the gangs owned every inch of New York, and nothing happened without them knowing. I saw it in the pitying stares neighbors gave his mother. I saw it when not a single cop came to take a statement. I saw it in the way she unraveled, knowing she could not do a thing about her missing child.

I could not live in a place where someone could vanish and no one would even blink. That is why I am glad I am the one going and not Danny. This place and the people in it will not destroy another boy's life.

* * *

I arrive at JFK at 4:36 a.m. without a ride or a place to stay. I didn't even tell my grandmother that I would be in town. I didn't want to worry her and tell her I was there to find my dad and possibly get him out of a bad situation. I'm not sure she'd be able to handle that kind of news.

The doors from the baggage claim open, and a wind of humidity hits me right in the face. I can already feel the ends of my short hair start to curl and cling to my neck. I'll take Arizona's dry heat over this any day. Once I get into the cab, the weight of the situation comes crashing down on me. What the hell am I doing here? I close my eyes for a minute and breathe in and out slowly.

"Where to?" asks the cab driver, snapping me out of my near panic attack.

"Sheepshead Bay, please, the Sleep Inn." It was the only hotel I could find in the middle of everything I needed. Close to my old house and all the places my dad frequently visited.

"First time in New York?" I see the driver looking at me through the rear-view mirror. His bushy gray brows cover most of his eyes, and the wrinkles in the corner tell me he's smiling. I start to feel my body relaxing. Distraction, it's exactly what I need.

"No, I used to live here, just visiting family."

"Yeah, I kinda figured." He meets my eyes again.

"How's that?" My brows slightly shooting up in question.

"Well, for starters, you're not already taking pictures as the tourists do." He grins. "And no one requests to go to Sheepshead Bay unless you're from there." He gives me a throaty laugh that fills the entire car, bouncing off the walls.

Dread settles in the pit of my stomach. He's right, no one in their right mind goes to Sheepshead Bay for vacation. When I don't see his eyes in the rear-view mirror anymore, I lean from my seat to get a glimpse of his license. *Jacob Baranov. Of course, he's Russian.* For a second, I contemplate covertly asking him if he knows anything about the Volkhov, but all the movies I've ever watched come flooding into my brain and tell me that I shouldn't. No one asks about the mafia group that runs Brooklyn, right? No one talks about them, and I'm assuming no one will willingly share information about them with someone they don't know.

When we arrive at my hotel, I hand the guy a twenty and take my bags to the main lobby.

When I get in, my phone buzzes in my pocket.

Stella: *Made it safe? Or do I need to call the NYPD already?*

Me: *I'm fine. Checking in now.*

Stella: *Fine = not dead, or fine = actually fine?*

I roll my eyes and shove my phone back into my bag. I guess Danny told her why I'm here. Or she beat it out of him, I vote's the latter.

"Name and card, please," the slender lady at the front desk asks me without looking up from her computer. New York hospitality right there.

"Uh, Lena Petrovna." I hand her my card. "I don't have a reservation or anything."

"Single or double?" she asks, still not looking at me. Her long nails clacking on the keyboard.

"Single is fine." While the receptionist types viciously on the keyboard, I take a look around the hotel.

There is nothing special about it. It has hunter green-toned walls and low ceilings. There is a water cooler in the corner with no cups, and the main lobby has three brown leather chairs, all cracked and weathered. The lighting is dim, casting a deep yellow glow over the entire place. The receptionist's voice floats back into my consciousness, and I hear her say, "The elevator is down the hall," while holding out a hotel key.

"Thanks," I say and head toward that general area. When I reach the elevator, I press three and wait for the doors to close, feeling the exhaustion ripple over me.

"Excuse me! Please hold the elevator!"

I quickly hold out my arm to stop the doors from closing. I swallow down the irrational fear of the elevator closing on my arm and taking it right off.

A woman in her early thirties runs into the elevator and quickly darts her hand out to push the button for the doors to close.

"Sorry," she tells the man outside the elevator in a sarcastic tone. She puffs out her bangs and looks at me, smiling. "Girl, I just could not do another minute with that man! I had to endure walking two blocks with him staring at my ass," she rolls her eyes.

"Glad I can help," I smile.

"Andrea," she says, extending her hand.

"Lena. Nice to meet you." I shake it. Everything about her screams she was born and raised in New York City, from her accent to her skin-tight running clothes. I never understood why people woke up at the butt crack of dawn to exercise; it's like self-inflicted torture.

"It's nice to see a young face around here. I've only seen fifty-something-year-old, the creepy ones." She fake shudders.

"How long have you been here?" I chuckle.

"Ah, well, my apartment flooded a month ago, and my

landlord is taking his sweet ass time getting the floors re-done, so I've been staying here," she says.

"That sucks. What happened to all your stuff?"

"It's still there. I only live a few blocks away, so I go there often. I mainly just come here to sleep. I'm not paying rent until he fixes the floors, and my hotel room is cheaper than my rent, so I'm not mad about it."

"Oh, nice, it's kind of like a stay-cation then."

"Yeah, kind of, except you get creepy middle-aged men ogling you more than usual."

We laugh, and the elevator dings when it gets to my floor.

"Well, I'll see you around then. I'll be in town for…" I don't know how to finish that sentence. Until I find my dad? Until I find the Volkhov, and if they don't kill me, then I'll see you around?

"I'll just be around," I end up saying.

"Sounds good. I'm in 504 if you need me."

I leave the elevator and head to my room, 311. As soon as I open the door, I'm overwhelmed by its musty smell. The room and everything in it have a staleness to it, as if it hasn't been aired out or dusted in years. It has a corner chair and a single bed with a TV across from it. That's about it. It's no Hilton, that's for sure. I drop my suitcase on the floor and fish out a change of clothes. Right now, I need a shower and a nap.

As I stand beneath the running water, I wait to feel something other than uncertainty and fear, but it never comes. I'm afraid that whatever I dig up in these coming days, I might not be able to dig my way out of.

4

Lena

When I wake, it takes me a moment to remember where I am. Yesterday is a blur, returning in waves. One minute I was coming back from a date, and the next I was in New York.

I sit up in bed and rub my temples. I need a game plan for the day, or I will end up wandering in and out of casinos, asking if anyone has seen my dad. I should probably start with my uncle Erik. He will know more about what my dad does day to day.

I put on a pair of ripped jeans and a pink tank top. I almost look like I'm sixteen with my short hair and stature, so I put on a thick layer of eyeliner and lip gloss to compensate for it. I take the elevator to the lobby and text my dad. It couldn't hurt.

Me: *Hi, Dad. I just got into town. Please call or text me when you can. Danny and I are worried about you.*

After that, I send my uncle a text

Me: *Hi Erik, can we meet up somewhere today?*

Erik: *Of course, Lenachka, come to my work. Do you know* *where it is?*

Me: *Yes, I'll see you in about an hour.*

As I walk to the subway station, I take in everything around me, feeling nostalgia wash over me. My senses are overwhelmed with the smell of fresh bagels, the cars racing past, and the people walking in an unnatural, fast, and focused way. The thing about New Yorkers is that they all at some point, develop tunnel vision. I think of it as an art form. These people weave in and out of busy streets, all while staring at their phones, and they don't get run over. It's truly mind-boggling. I could stare at a person for twenty minutes if I wanted, and they would never notice. I guess living in Arizona made me slow down in a way.

When I get into the station, I take a seat and wait for my train. I used to play this game where I'd look at all the people around me and try to guess their emotions. Since New Yorkers excel at stoicism, it's a challenge to say the least.

I glance to my right and see a mother and her teenage daughter, arms weighed down by what look like fifty shopping bags. The daughter is turned away, smiling at something on her screen. The mother watches her, and I can almost feel the longing in her gaze, a quiet hunger for her daughter's love and attention.

To my left, I see a homeless man sitting a little too close to the yellow line leading to the train tracks. I've seen it before. It's when you finally come out of that tunnel vision fog and look around to see if anyone can really see you. If they'd even care. Almost like he's testing himself or others to see if anyone would tell him to scoot back. I think the emotion is a mixture of despair, vulnerability, and a little bit of hope.

When I look straight ahead to the other side of the tracks, I see something else entirely, *someone* else. My breath catches in my throat, and I swear everything around me dims and falls away into nothing except for me and this angel in black. He is wearing a black suit with black loafers, sitting down with his head bent low as he rests his forearms on his thighs. His dark hair perfectly parted, not a single thing is out of place on this devastating man. *Look at me,* I beg, needing to see more of him. As if he'd heard me, he looks up and straight into my eyes. I feel my heart pick up its pace as his gaze bores into mine. His piercing green eyes dance with the light above, entrancing me further. Everything about him is breathtaking, from his strong jaw to his out-of-place appearance. I don't know how long I stare at him for, but I just can't take my eyes off him. I'm mesmerized, and to look away would mean leaving him alone, which my body just won't let me do right now. Loneliness is his emotion. For a moment, his features soften, and it almost feels like we share the same sadness.

I'm forced to snap out of this trance I'm in when I hear my train approaching. His eyes instantly go from soft back to hard, and all I want to do is walk over the tracks and into his arms. His gaze follows me as I get up. The closer I get, the closer he leans in. My heart speeds up as I watch him get up slowly and walk toward me, still staring. As the train passes and stops, the cool air hits me like a slap in the face. *Get it together, Lena.* I let out a shaky breath and get onto the train, still feeling his gaze all over me.

5

Lena

"Lenachka! How are you?" My uncle stops cutting his customer's hair and walks toward me with open arms. "Hi, Uncle," I smile, letting him hug me.

I haven't seen him in ten years, but it feels like I just saw him last week. Like, no time has passed. Maybe the connection you have with family withstands time. Or maybe he just hasn't aged. Let's hope I have those genes too.

"Sit tight for ten more minutes, I will be finished soon."

I sit at the corner of the barbershop, across from a little table with a chess set. This is where my dad came to play with Erik almost daily. Every time I'd call him, he was right here, passing the time and betting he'd win the next round. When we moved away, my dad chose to stay in our same apartment, and eventually, the memories of us kind of got the best of him. He ended up picking up a few bad vices, specifically gambling, and let's say he owes a lot of people a lot of money.

"Lena! It's so nice to see you. How have you been? Danny?"

"We've been good. Arizona has been good for us," I smile, and begin to feel homesick. He nods and takes a seat next to me. "Erik, have you heard from my dad?" I get to the point, anxiety creeping back in.

"Ah, not for a while, Lenachka," he says grimly. "He does this sometimes. Maybe he is with a woman? You know it happens." His thick Russian accent makes the words sound heavier.

"Erik, he would never disappear without telling one of us, especially if he's leaving for that long. You know that," I lean forward, searching his face.

"Yes, yes…" He rubs his beard. "I know, Lena. I don't know what to do anymore. I went to the police station when Danny told me he hadn't heard from your father either. I looked the officer in the eye while he took down the report, and when I went back, that same officer looked at me and said no report was filed. How can this be?"

I suddenly feel sick. Hearing him say that he went in person to file a report and it suddenly disappeared just confirms that something dangerous is going on here.

"What do you know about the money he took from the Volkhov?"

Erik instantly looks around the barbershop and answers in a hushed tone, "I don't know much, Lena. He asked me for the money, but I didn't have that much. You know, it was thirty thousand dollars, so he said he would find another way. I told him this way is dangerous, but he said he knew one of them, that it was okay." He looks almost hopeful when he says that, and I nearly believe it.

"Did he say who it was?"

"No, he didn't. He said it would be better if I didn't know."

"Erik, do you know how I could find one of them? Maybe I can talk to someone and see if they've seen him."

"Lena, are you *crazy*? Your father would never forgive me if I let you do something like this. Do not go looking for them, and do not go poking around. We have to just keep looking for him elsewhere and hope he turns up. He will turn up, I know it." His eyes are stern and scolding, reminding me of my dad.

"I just need somewhere to start. He mentioned a person that he met whom he could trust, who he felt was okay, right? Maybe I can find that person. Please, uncle, is there a place where I can start looking for him? I just need something, anything," I plead.

"I don't know, Lena. I don't know these people. He might've met them in the casino, he goes there often, you know."

I press him further with my eyes, but when he looks at me, it's like he's aged right in front of me. He looks old and tired, like this has been eating at him, too. While we've been starting over in Arizona, he's been here holding down the fort along with my grandmother. Guilt sweeps over me, and I stop asking. Whatever this is, it's been affecting him longer than it's been affecting us.

"I'm sorry. I know this is a lot. I know my dad has been a lot since we left."

"Lenachka, you are always welcome here. Please don't carry the guilt for your parents. They made their choices. You're just a kid." He smiles and takes my hand. "Come visit me again, yes?"

I smile back and nod. "Yes."

* * *

As I approach my hotel, I daydream of the man I saw at the

train station. I picture him walking to my side of the tracks, stepping in front of me, and placing his palm on my cheek. I close my eyes from the warmth of his touch. I picture his thumb tracing over my lips, and I open my mouth instantly, inviting him in. I remember his eyes, hard but alluring. Eating me whole.

"Hey, girly!"

I instantly snap out of it and realize I almost walked into the side wall of the hotel. Maybe this is why New Yorkers are so oblivious to their surroundings. They're too busy daydreaming.

"Ah, hi… Andrea." I give an awkward wave, embarrassed by my thoughts. I've never felt this way before, borderline obsessive over a man I've never even met.

"You looked like you were about to walk into that wall if I didn't say something!" She chuckles.

"Yeah, I was a little spaced out for a second. Thanks for saving my face," I feel my cheeks reddening.

"It's all good, we all have those days." She smiles. "Oh, let me introduce you to my boyfriend, Roman." She waves at someone approaching the hotel. "Babe! Did you get the champagne glasses? I forgot to tell you!"

"Yes, yes." A man in his early thirties dressed in all black stops next to Andrea, holding bags of what look like household appliances. I crane my neck to get a good look at him. He has to be over six feet tall. His short, dark blond hair is styled into a faux hawk, and every piece of exposed skin is covered in tattoos. He's also big, like the kind of big that spends his entire life at the gym. The two of them make one hell of a power couple. He bends down to kiss her, and she giggles.

"Babe, this is my new friend Lena." She gestures toward me.

"I finally met someone at this damn hotel who isn't over fifty!"

He kisses her forehead and then glances at me. "Roman," he says. "I'd shake your hand, but I'm afraid these bags wouldn't make it if I set them down."

"Lena," I give him a nod. "It's totally fine." I reach out and open the hotel door for them, and we all walk toward the elevator. As Roman reaches to press the button with his finger, I see something I haven't seen in years. Something that just brings me a step closer to my father.

I see the tattoo on his forearm.

6

Lena

I can't stop looking at his tattoo the entire elevator ride. I can't believe I just found my way in. All I need to do is find a way to bring it up. I know I can't just come outright and ask if he's a member of the Russian Mafia who runs the very city we're in right now.

"How long have you guys been dating?" I ask instead, wondering if she knows who he really is.

Andrea looks up at him, smiling, waiting for him to answer.

"Ah, eight months now?" he says.

"Yes!" she squeals. "You passed the test, babe." She stands on her tiptoes and kisses his chin.

"You guys are adorable and also extremely intimidating," I grin, and we all chuckle.

"Do you have a guy back home?" Andrea asks me.

"No, I don't really have time to date," which is entirely the truth.

"Perfect! Then you must come out with us tonight. We're going to this super exclusive club. Roman's best friend Lev is adorable and newly single!" She nudges me with her elbow.

Roman stiffens beside her. "Baby, I doubt Lev is looking for anything… serious right now." He eyes me, waiting for me to back out.

My first instinct is to get a spontaneous stomach flu and get out of this immediately, but this is my only chance to get some answers about my dad. I swallow the urge to run and say, "okay, sure. Except I don't really have anything to wear." I packed enough clothes for two weeks without needing to do laundry, and none of them are even remotely club attire.

"Girl, I got you. Come up to my place around eight, and we'll get you all sexy," she winks.

I chuckle and say my goodbyes when we land on my floor. I start to contemplate all my routes in going about this. I could ask Andrea about the Volkhov, but what if she knows nothing about it? It would be really weird of me to press her on why her boyfriend has that damn tattoo if she doesn't even know what it means. However, if she does know something about it, would she even tell me the truth? Would it ruin my chances of getting close to them? I go back and forth in my head while in the shower, through my corner deli dinner run, and on my way to Andrea's room. I knock twice and step back like whatever's in there might snatch me up.

"Oh, good, you're here! Come on in, don't mind the mountain of clothes, uh, everywhere…"

I walk in and look around. She wasn't kidding. Her clothes are scattered on every piece of furniture, and I'm not sure I could find a place to sit even if I wanted to.

"It's okay, this reminds me of my sister's room when we still lived together." I smile, remembering all the years my sister and I shared a room. Stella is actually really similar to Andrea in that she is insanely confident… and messy.

Andrea shuts the door and goes straight to her closet. "I've got the perfect dress for you! I haven't been able to wear this baby since Roman and I started dating. He doesn't let me," she pouts.

"Uh, can I just say that I don't really go out anymore? I've pretty much only worn scrubs for the past two years," I confess.

"Then that's more reason to put this bad boy on! Here, take a look," she holds the dress out to me.

At first glance, the dress looks like a miniature disco ball. I almost laugh at how *not me* this dress is.

"I know she might look intimidating initially, but just try it on. I promise it grows on you."

My brain says no thank you, but my hands seem not to understand that thought. I reach out and take the dress from her, heading into the bathroom. I strip off my clothes and then immediately regret my choice of underwear. Let's just say that my underwear covers more than this dress does. I decide to ditch the underwear and very hesitantly open the door.

Andrea's eyes widen, and she begins to whistle when I step out. "Oh my god, Lena! This dress looks better on you than it did on me! Take it off, I changed my mind!" she jokes.

I turn to look in the mirror. God, I look… sexy. It is black and shimmery throughout and stops a few inches below my ass. It has a slit that goes up my side, leaving nothing to the imagination. The dress hangs on two thin straps and plunges into a cowl neck in the front and back. I don't even recognize myself.

"Andrea, I don't know if I can pull this off," doubt creeping into my mind.

"Girl, you're pulling it off already! A little red lip and you're good to go!"

We're ready as soon as I finish my makeup and Andrea straightens my hair. The whole time we're in the elevator, I feel utterly naked. I feel like I should be carrying pepper spray, but to be honest, I wouldn't know where to hide it.

Roman meets us outside the hotel, leaning against his white Audi. His eyes go straight to Andrea's aqua dress, with mesh going all the way up her side. She does a little twirl, and he whistles at her while she does it.

"Babe, how gorgeous does Lena look!" she asks him. I blush, wishing I had brought a jacket.

"You both look great. There's a good chance they'll let us in now," he teases.

When we get into the car, the smell of leather and men's cologne hits my nostrils, making me instantly nauseous. The engine revs and Roman speeds off, making everything I see through the window a blur of lights. I look over at Andrea in the passenger seat. She's practically giggling with how fast he's going, almost like she loves the danger. It makes me think she knows everything about him and just accepts it. When I think I can't handle another second of this car, smell, and all of it, we finally arrive.

At first glance, it just looks like an old apartment building. Brown, worn down, nothing that screams club. Roman leads us to the side of the building, and we take a few steps down into the basement. We weave through corridors, and I try to memorize the way we came in, but I soon come to a realization that I wouldn't be able to escape this place even if I tried. Maybe that's the intention. We finally stop once we reach two heavy metal doors, and I half expect a fighting ring behind them. The two large men by the doors look us up and down, and a part of me wishes they'd turn us away. They don't. Instead, they just nod at Roman and open the doors. As soon as they do, I'm instantly blinded by bright lights that shoot out in every direction like lasers. We walk in, and my eyes widen in awe. This is not just a club but a club on steroids. It has naked women dancing in cages, half-naked acrobats hanging from the ceiling, and three stories of dance floors. The bass climbs up through the floor and pounds in my chest. Andrea looks back at me and basically helps me pick up my jaw from the floor.

"It's amazing, right? I've only been here once, and I looked exactly how you do now," she shouts over the music. She holds out her hand, and I take it, holding on to her for dear life. Roman leads us to the second-floor bar and orders us a drink.

"Stay here. I'll be right back," he tells us. Andrea grabs his hand before he leaves and brings him in for a kiss. They smile at each other like they've just communicated something to each other, only they can understand. It's so cute I almost forget he might've been the one who kidnapped my father.

Once he leaves, I scan the entire second floor and notice it's smaller and more intimate than the first. I look over to where Roman is and see a group of men sitting in the corner of the room. There are bodyguards all around them, and I wonder if they are also part of the Volkhov. A woman is dancing for them on a pole, their private little show. I try not to gawk.

"Who are those guys?" I ask Andrea.

"They're like his brothers. Roman works with them some-times," she says, shrugging. She's either naïve to all of this or she's a great actress.

I see Roman pull a guy and point toward us. The man,

who I assume is Lev, looks me up and down slowly and says something to Roman. They both walk in our direction, and I brace for what I might have to do tonight.

"This is my friend Lev," Roman tells me. His tone is indifferent, and he seems just as unsure of me as I am of him.

"Lena," I say, extending my hand.

Lev smirks and shakes my hand. "Russian?"

"Uh, yes?" *Shit.* I probably should've given them a fake name, but then again, I didn't know Andrea had any connection to the Volkhov when I met her.

He shakes his head in approval, which makes me feel gross. He's looking at me like I'm a snack ready to be eaten. I guess I look the part. I squeeze my thighs closer together. Why did I think going out without any panties on would be a good idea?

"Oh my god, I love this song! Let's go dance!" Andrea pulls me toward the dance floor. "Follow my lead, and he will be eating out of the palm of your hand by the end of the night." She winks at me.

When we reach the dance floor, she spins me around and grabs my hips from behind. I feel her body flush with mine, and we sway slowly at first. She looks at Roman the entire time, teasing him. I can't help but smile. We have only just met, yet it feels like we have been girlfriends for years. It feels good to have someone I can let my guard down with.

I close my eyes and let the music carry me. For a moment, I am weightless. All the shit I came here for slips from my shoulders, and I can finally breathe again. When I open my eyes, I see *him*. He stands leaning against the wall next to the stairs with a cigarette in his mouth. My body stops swaying, and goosebumps begin to slowly spread wherever his eyes travel. Normally, I'd hate this, being watched like I'm some prey to be caught and eaten. But with him, I want him to chase me down, pin me to him, and devour every last bit. I finally catch his gaze and hold it. His eyes narrow, and I feel hands grabbing my waist, bringing me close. I turn my head and see Lev. He takes my hips, and I sway against him, still looking at the angel in black. I don't know why, but my body decides to put on a show for him, to make him feel what I feel when he looks at me. I let Lev's hands explore my body. I turn and snake my hands up and around his neck, bringing my dress a little higher. I close my eyes for a second and let my head drop back, imagining him still watching, his hands touching me, holding me. When I look back, he's gone. I don't know what I expected, for him to throw me over his shoulder and claim me? I stop dancing and look around, feeling naked once more. I shake off the embarrassment and remind myself what I'm here for and what tonight should be about.

"I'm hot. Do you want to go get some air?" I say into Lev's ear.

He smiles and takes my hand, leading me downstairs. Once we reach the metal doors, he says something to the bouncers, who open them for us. We turn left, passing couples who are one piece of clothing away from having sex. Great, he thinks I asked to come out here so we can hook up. We end up stopping a little further down the hall. He turns to me and comes in close, backing me up until I'm pressed against a wall. I suddenly feel his weight, the way he invades my space. He's tall and slender but muscular. His hazel eyes tell me he wants to continue what we were doing on the dance floor. I begin to realize that while I was putting on a show, I was also leading him on. I try to move around him, but his arms stretch out, caging me in. I can see his face coming closer to mine, and I know what he wants to do. I turn my head right when I feel his breath on my mouth and see the same tattoo that Roman has, the letter V tattooed in Russian.

"Uh, nice tattoo," I say, trying to sound more sexy than scared.

He glances at it. "It's my most recent one, but I have others I can show you." He leans in a little closer to my neck this time, blowing lightly like it's some sort of trick to get my panties off faster.

"Yeah? What does it mean?" I press.

His lips stop at my ear. "It means family. Brotherhood."

Bingo.

"I heard about the Volkhov. Is that tattoo for them?" I try sounding less like an undercover cop and more like a groupie, but I'm not sure I'm succeeding.

His lips go back down to my neck. "Would it make you wet if it was?"

God, this guy is something. I mentally roll my eyes and try not to gag. As soon as I open my mouth to press him further, his mouth covers mine, and his tongue slips in uninvited. I press my hands to his chest and push, but he doesn't seem to get the hint. I then push a little harder, but he still doesn't budge. I close my eyes and think this is it. No one would hear me even if I screamed, but I will not go out without a fight, that's for sure. Right when I'm about to knee him in the crotch, cigarette smoke clouds my vision. This seems to have caught Lev's attention because he moves away from me so fast it takes me a second to understand what happened. I look from him to wherever the smoke comes from, and my heart catches in my throat.

"Artyom, I didn't see you there. Did you need me?" Lev asks, looking uncomfortable as he adjusts his pants.

The hallway grows smaller by the second. I feel like running, but at this point, I'm unsure if my legs would run away or straight into his arms. He is more intimidating up close; everything from his broad shoulders to his perfectly tailored suit screams dominance. He towers over Lev and me, scowling, not saying a single thing, like he's intentionally letting us stew in our fear. As soon as he finishes his cigarette, he lifts his hand and waves Lev off, like he couldn't be bothered to speak to him. Lev quickly takes my hand and begins to lead me out. My stupid mouth almost opens to protest, but Artyom beats me to it.

"She stays," he says.

Lev instantly stops and looks at me hesitantly, an apology written in his eyes. He drops my hand and walks away with his head bent low. My breath catches again, and the room starts to spin. I'm afraid to look at him again. I give myself a mental rundown of the situation: Lev and Roman are part of the Volkhov, Lev answers to this man, and he almost shit himself just now in his presence… so I'm going to go out on a limb and say that this man, Artyom, is someone important in the Volkhov. Maybe he's the one who calls the shots. He's no angel, he's the devil, and I've just caught his attention.

"Are you following me?" I say, trying to sound more confident than I really am. He eyes me and then pushes off the wall, coming closer and stalking around me like a predator.

"This is my club," he says matter-of-factly, continuing to circle me. "How did you find this place?"

"I came here with some friends." I try to catch his gaze, showing him I am not scared.

"And who are your friends?" he asks from behind me.

"Roman and Andrea." The names seem to catch him off guard.

He comes around to face me, close enough that I can imagine swimming in the green of his eyes.

"What is your name?" His voice is low and deep, a delicious rumble that scratches an itch I did not know I had.

"Lena," I say. I'm not sure if I want to give him my last name just yet. I need to fully think things through. I can tell him who I am right now and possibly get killed, or I can get more information from Lev or Roman, gain allies, and then have them lead me to the person in charge. I just don't know how much time my father has left, and I can't do this right now in a shady club where there's nowhere to run, with a man I can't trust myself with.

"Your little dance got my attention, *kroshka*," he says. My cheeks involuntarily blush at the endearment. It came out so organically, like he was saving it just for me.

Snap out of it, Lena, he's bad news.

"I wasn't dancing for you," I say, standing a little straighter. I see a hint of a smile tug at his lips.

"No?" he mocks.

"No," I lie. "Actually, you interrupted my date." *Look who grew some balls.*

I watch his eyes harden for a fraction of a second.

"Is that what that was?" he asks. "You looked like you were begging for someone to save you."

"I can handle myself just fine, thanks," I spit out.

"I don't doubt that," he steps so close my chest touches his. For a second, our hearts beat in unison. Fast and erratic. Does he feel what I feel right now? He takes his finger and traces my lips, and it takes everything in me not to open for him. "Next time you let a man touch you like that in my club, I'll break his fingers and send them to you," his voice low and almost intimate, but the threat is sharp. His words go down like a shot of whiskey, burning everything inside of me. With that, he turns around and leaves.

I let out a shaky breath and sink to the floor. What the hell just happened?

7

Lena

After fifteen minutes of breathing exercises, I get my ass up and go back into the club. I need to find Andrea and tell her I want to go back to the hotel. I've had enough for one night. I need to think of a plan for how I'm going to go about finding my father, a plan that does not involve the devil I just met.

I walk through a sea of people, practically dry humping each other, and spot Andrea dancing solo with a drink in her hand. I let out a sigh of relief and tug her arm, trying to get her attention.

"Lena!" Her eyes go wide. "You naughty girl." She winks.

Oh god, she thinks I was getting it on with Lev this whole time. Great. I let out a nervous chuckle.

"We just talked," I shout over the music. "Actually, I'm really tired, I'm going to call a cab, okay? You stay!"

"I'm over dancing alone anyway, let's go," she takes my hand. We begin to walk toward the metal doors, but then she stops, takes a drink from a short man wearing tight leather pants, and downs it. We both look at him and watch his face contort into confusion, but before he can respond in any way, we burst out laughing and haul out of there. Once we get through the doors, we lean on each other, panting and laughing.

"What was in his drink?" I ask, genuinely curious.

Andrea makes a face. "Water," she laughs. "What a waste."

"What now?" I ask, wondering how we're getting back to the hotel.

Andrea reaches into her bra and pulls out her phone. "I always find a place for my baby," she says, kissing her phone.

"I would've too, but I couldn't even wear underwear with this dress!" I laugh.

"And that's why Roman won't let me wear it anymore." She winks at me. She dials a number and holds the phone to her ear. "Lena and I are ready to go home, Roman," she says with a bite.

"No, I'm tired of dancing alone. You promised you'd spend some time with me, but of course, it's bros before hoes. Well, this hoe is going home, so either you drive us or we're hopping on this guy's bike and going home with him." She turns to me and rolls her eyes. This girl has some very big lady balls. She turns the phone off and huffs out an exasperated breath.

"I swear, every time we go out, he has some business with the boys. I'm so fucking tired of it," she complains.

I give her a side hug. "Hoes before bros?" I ask, hoping to lighten her mood.

Andrea chuckles and squeezes me tighter. "Thank God you're here."

A moment later, the door swings open, and a large man dressed in a suit comes out and approaches us. My first instinct is to back away because this man looks exactly like those I saw standing around in the VIP area with Roman.

However, Andrea doesn't seem fazed at all.

"Did *you know who* send you, Alec?" Andrea asks, narrowing her eyes at him.

"Roman is a bit inebriated at the moment, but Mr. Volkhov wants to make sure you ladies get home safe, so he sent me to drive you home," he says.

"That son of a bitch got drunk without me," she puffs out. "Remind me to thank Art the next time I see him."

My heart begins to race again. "Who's Art?" I ask as we walk through the corridors.

"Oh, that's the club owner, his name is Artyom, but I've always just called him Art," she replies.

My legs almost give out right then and there. This means I was talking to the mafia boss all along. The man who might have my father locked away somewhere is the same man I've fantasized about since the moment my eyes landed on his, the other day. I feel bile rising in my throat, and it takes everything in me not to throw up before we get outside. As soon as Alec opens the doors, the musty night air meets my face, and I double over and throw up everything I ate today, which, in retrospect, wasn't that much.

"Shit, Lena! Are you okay?" Andrea tucks my hair behind my ears.

"Yeah, just had one too many drinks," I lie. I didn't have a single drink all night.

"Well, let's get you home." She ushers me to the car with its door propped open for us.

I hesitate for a moment. "You know him, right?" I ask her.

"Who? Alec?" We both look at the man already behind the wheel. I nod slowly. "Alec is good people, trust me," she says. "He's taken me home a few times already."

I watch her slide into the back seat, and then I warily slide in next to her, feeling the leather groan after me.

I prepare myself for more of Roman's driving, but to my surprise, he goes the speed limit the entire drive and avoids all the speed bumps. I look over at him, trying to read him.

"He's like a hot dad, huh?" Andrea whispers to me.

I guess I wasn't being very covert about analyzing him. She's not wrong, though; this man can have any girl he wants call him daddy. He has salt and pepper hair throughout and a jaw that could make Superman jealous. The thing that makes me wary of him is how stoic and calculated he is, like like he's trained. At what, I don't want to guess.

We pull up to the hotel, and I all but kiss the sidewalk when I fling myself out of the car. I hear Andrea mutter something to Alec about giving Roman hell for her, and then I hear her shut the door. "You're not going to puke again, are you?" She approaches me.

I laugh. "No, I think I got it all out the first time." We walk into the hotel and make our way to the elevator.

"Thanks for coming out with us tonight. It was fun having another girl there. It's usually just me and the guys."

I smile. "It was fun, thanks for inviting me." The elevator doors open, and we get in.

"I know I'm mad at Roman right now, but I promise he's a good guy," she says.

I don't even know how to respond to that. Is he a good guy? All I know about him is that he's a part of the infamous mafia that runs Brooklyn. That makes him a dangerous man, but can he also be a good guy? I just don't know.

"I have zero doubts he loves you; it's almost gross how much you guys love each other." I mean it. The few times I've seen them interact, it was adorable, and it felt sincere.

Andrea smiles and hugs me. "Let's go out to dinner tomorrow night, the three of us. It'll be nice for you to see the Roman I know."

The elevator dings and opens on my floor, which means I have no time to think about my answer. "Uh, okay, sure. What time?"

"Meet us downstairs at seven. We'll take you to our favorite Italian spot."

"Sounds good!" I say as the doors close. I walk to my hotel room, feeling my body droop. This search and rescue mission is taking a lot out of me.

In my hotel room, I throw myself on the bed and curl into a ball. Pictures of my dad tied up and held prisoner invade my mind. Then pictures of him being tortured and killed take over, and I can't hold back the panic attack that rolls over me. Mascara-streaked tears roll down my face, soaking the white pillowcase. I lay there crying until my swollen eyes force themselves shut, and I drift into darkness.

8

Lena

I wake to my phone ringing. When I look at it, Danny's name is lit up. I sit up way too fast and give myself a head rush. "Ugh", I groan.

"Hello?"

"Any updates?" he asks impatiently. No hello, how are you, glad you're still alive…

I roll out of bed, take a deep breath, and dive into everything that happened last night.

"Yeah, sort of," I say, my voice groggy.

"Tell me you've found him," he says.

"More like I've found the people who might've taken him."

"Are you serious? How?" He sounds taken aback. *See? I'm not completely useless.*

"I went to their club last night and met the boss," I say, only then realizing how incredibly insane it sounds.

"Lena, tell me you're joking." I kind of wish I were.

"I met a friend here at the hotel who happens to be dating one of them. They took me out to a club, and while I was fishing for information, I kind of accidentally met with the boss, who I didn't know was the boss until after meeting him," I say, trying really hard to leave out the part where I flirted with him and he threatened to dismember any man who touched me. Not sure that would go over well with Danny.

"Shit. Does he know who you are?"

"No. I had to give him my real name, though. I don't think he knows who I am. I just don't know what to do now." I sigh.

"Do not go back to him, Lena. It's too dangerous. Stay with your friend and her boyfriend, and try to gauge whether they know anything about Dad."

"I have dinner with them tonight. That might be a good time to bring up Dad," I say. "Danny, Erik said Dad had someone he trusted who convinced him to borrow from you-know-who. Maybe I can spend some time trying to find that person today. Do you know who he might be talking about?"

"I don't know. He never told me about anyone like that; he doesn't really have friends. But if he did, they'd be at the casino. Maybe start there?"

"That's a good idea. I'll go and ask around." There's silence between us for a moment. I can tell he's worried; the stress between us is almost palpable.

"There's still hope, Danny. I'll find him." I'm not sure I completely believe myself, but hope is all we have left.

By the time we hang up, it's 9:00 a.m., and I get a doomsday feeling, like I'm running out of time and should already be doing something to find my dad. I get dressed and head out of the hotel, looking up the casino my dad frequently went to. Unfortunately, it is nowhere near where I am now. Once I reach the lobby of the hotel, I instantly freeze when I see Roman sitting on one of the leather chairs. He's focused on his phone, and his leg is jumpy like he's nervous. He's probably waiting for Andrea, and I'm thinking he's still not off the hook for yesterday. Right when I decide to just keep walking like I didn't see him, he looks up and we make eye contact. His leg stops jumping, and he just stares at me.

"Hey," I say awkwardly.

He looks at me a little longer before saying, "Lena," and gives me a nod. Something about this seems off, like he's being careful.

"Waiting for Andrea?" He nods again. "She still pissed?"

He sighs. "Yes. But never for too long."

"That's good. She's really amazing. You got yourself a keeper." I don't know why I'm so nervous right now. I can feel my pulse beating faster with each nod he gives me. He dips his chin and gives me a small smile, clearly not the chatty type.

"I guess I'll see you both at dinner. I kind of have to go." I wait until I see him nod once again and push through the doors to go outside. The air does nothing to clear the tension I'm still feeling. Does he know something? Did I screw up somewhere and give myself away? I nervously chew my lip all the way to the train station, thinking of all the possible reasons why Roman was so weird just now.

By the time I reach the casino, I give my mind a break and just tell myself he's feeling shitty about last night and has other things on his mind. Things that have absolutely nothing to do with me or my dad. Yep. That's what I'm sticking to for the time being.

The doors screech when I pull them open, and a pungent cloud of smoke hits my nostrils right away. This casino definitely has no smoke alarms in its vicinity, or they'd be blaring right now. I walk in and try to adjust my eyes to my new environment, blinking a few times to get a good look at the place. It's underwhelming in how simple it looks. I've only ever been to the casinos in Las Vegas, so I guess my expectations might've been a little too high. The building itself is quite large, but when you walk in, the number of slot machines and gaming tables in it doesn't do it justice. There is at least five feet between each slot machine and only two poker tables as far as I can tell. I walk toward the bar in the far right corner and try not to stare at the people who are hypnotized by their slot machine, inserting coin after coin. I understand the appeal of Vegas casinos, the lights, the fancy-looking people, the different sounds, and the excitement it brings to be in a place like that. However, this place just looks like your last resort in life. A place you go to with your last paycheck, risking it all just to survive one more month. My chest tightens when I think of my dad being here.

"What can I get you?" the bartender asks me.

"Um, I'll have a gin and tonic," I say.

"Coming right up."

I give him a polite smile and watch him make the drink. He takes his time making it, not like there's a line behind me. He's an older man, probably a little older than my dad. His gray hair covers his entire head and most of his beard. There's a softness to the way he moves, which makes me oddly comfortable. If this man has been around a while, then I can imagine my father talking to him, maybe even befriending him?

"Anything else?" he asks, handing me my drink.

I decide to go for it. "Actually, I was wondering if you've seen my father. His name is Georgiy." I take out my phone and show him a picture. The man's face tells me he knows my father without even having to look at the photo, but he glances at it anyway.

"He's missing?" he asks.

"Yes. My family is really worried."

"I haven't seen him here in a while, which is unusual for him."

"Is there anything you can remember about the last time you saw him? Maybe something he said or the way he was acting?" I lean in a little, urging him to talk without pushing too hard.

He seems nervous for a moment, not meeting my eyes. "I don't remember," he finally says. For someone who works in a casino, he doesn't have much of a poker face. I can read him like a book. He knows something, and he feels guilty for knowing it. The question here is, how the hell do I get him to tell me?

"Can you please try to remember? Any small detail might help. I just don't know what to do anymore. The police told me to check out the places he goes to frequently, and I couldn't think of the name of this place until today." He might not be afraid of me, but maybe he'd be afraid of the cops getting into his business. Just because the police have completely checked out of helping us doesn't mean I can't still use them.

I watch as the man's face changes into full-on panic mode. *Gotcha.*

"Listen, I don't know where your father is. He comes in here frequently and we talk sometimes," he hesitates. "He told me about his financial struggles just like many other people here, and all I did was give him a number. That's all."

Shit, shit, shit!

"Whose number?" I ask, finishing my drink in one swallow.

His eyes narrow at me, like he's had enough of my questions. "Look, I'm sorry about your dad, but I've told you all I can, now please go," his voice sharp.

The liquid courage now coursing through me has no intention of leaving. "My father trusted you." Some friend he is. Delivering him to the devil.

"He's also an adult. No one forced him to do anything," he says in a harsh whisper. "I'm sorry," he adds.

I push off my seat and storm out, intentionally not paying for my drink. He doesn't call after me. I'm seething by the time I get outside. Tears spill out of me like a waterfall, and no matter how much I want to blame them on that asshole, I can't because he's right. My father is an adult who is fully capable of making his own decisions. He took the number, knowing whose it was, probably set up a meeting with them, and took their blood money. All on his own. And here I am trying to save him from his own actions.

I make it back to the hotel with a total of five blisters and an enormous headache. Getting back took hours because of some issue with the train tracks, so I thought I'd just take the bus, but, of course, I just missed it and had to wait forty minutes for another one to show up. God, I miss my car and the ease of getting around. I arrive grumpy, tired, and in a terrible mood, and on top of all that, I have to haul my ass into the shower and get dressed to go out again. At least there will be food. Pictures of pasta fill my head, and that alone gets me back into my room without collapsing.

After showering, I pull out the only nice dress I packed just in case my dad wanted to go out for dinner and put it on. It's an orange mid-length dress that flares out on the bottom. I tighten the spaghetti straps and smooth them out, looking at myself in the small bathroom mirror. I look tired; dark circles surround my eyes, and my skin looks paler than usual, almost ghost-like. I slather on some more concealer and blush, pretending it helps my appearance, and head out once again.

As the elevator dings open to the lobby, I see Andrea and Roman already waiting for me. When she sees me, her smile widens, and she runs over to me, giving me a tight hug.

I hug her back. "You look amazing." When I look over at Roman, his eyes have hardened as he watches us, creating a huge knot in the pit of my stomach.

"I am so glad we are doing this. You're going to love the food there. It's our favorite spot!" she beams.

I follow them out of the lobby to the white Audi parked out front. Just as Roman opens the door for us to get in, another vehicle pulls up next to his, a black Lexus SUV. I hear Roman let out a low groan, and then he slams the door shut. I stare in awe as Artyom swings the door open and strolls toward us with unshakable confidence. He's dressed in a black dress shirt that is unbuttoned at the collar with his sleeves rolled up. It's supposed to look casual, but this man radiates elegance and power. I try not to ogle, but I can't help it. I'm drooling over this man, and I don't know how to stop.

"Art?" I hear Andrea say. "Don't fucking tell me you need Roman for something because we're about to be late for dinner, and you don't want to see me hangry."

I almost laugh because this right here is a person who definitely doesn't know who she's talking to. *Andrea, I freaking love you.*

"Andrea." Artyom gives her a tight smile and a nod, and then looks at Roman, giving him one of those half-handshake, half-side-hug pat things that guys do. He then turns to me, his gaze traveling up and down my body. I get the sudden urge to go back to my room and hide. "I actually came here to take Lena out," he says casually.

My mind has to be playing tricks on me because I think he just said he wants to take me out. Like on a date? Or like kill me, take me out? My eyes widen, and I look at Andrea, who looks back at me, wiggling her brows.

"Lena, I didn't know you already met Art."

"Uh, we met briefly last night," I say, remembering our conversation outside of his club. Artyom meets my eyes again, and I can tell he's thinking of our last conversation as well. "Would you hate me if I went?" I ask, but I don't think I have a choice in the matter by the looks of it. I start making a plan in my head. I'll make sure he takes me somewhere public and then bring up my father at some point. It's now or never.

"Girl, go have fun." She winks at me. "Catch me up tomorrow."

We hug, and then Artyom leads me to the passenger side of his massive car. He holds the door open for me, and as I get in, his scent fills my mind once again, clouding every red flag I see.

"Where are we going?" I ask once he gets in and starts the car.

"It's a surprise."

I look at him warily. "I don't really like surprises."

"Then you're not going to like this one," he says flatly, turning from the main street into a neighborhood of town homes. My eyes turn to the window, scanning familiar houses. My heart pounds in my chest as he pulls up to a house and parks in front of it. *My* old house. The one my father lived in before he disappeared. My mind goes a mile a minute, not understanding what is happening or what's about to happen. All I know is that he found out about me. I had completely underestimated him.

"I rarely make house calls, but you've impressed me, Petrovna," he says.

I look out the window, refusing to meet his gaze. "Well, I'm not impressed at all," I say, my voice shaking. It's taking everything in me not to fling this door open and run for my life.

"No?" he asks. "This is the house you grew up in, the very house we took your father from. You now live in Arizona, alone in a one-bedroom apartment. I'm not a huge fan of pink myself, but by the look of your place, it seems like you are. Your brother Danny is also very impressive, a total of five missing persons reports in a matter of days."

My head whips around to look at him, stunned and speechless. I try hard to hold back my tears, begging myself not to cry in front of him, but when I open my mouth to speak, the tears start to spill.

"Is my dad alive?" I ask, my voice low.

"Do you have the money he owes?" he counters.

More tears stream down my face because that's something I completely overlooked. I hadn't even thought about the money he owes. I was so focused on finding him, I didn't think about what would happen after I did. When I don't answer, he leans over and cups my cheek, swiping at a tear with his thumb. I close my eyes, waiting for fear to take over, but it doesn't come. Instead, my body leans into his warmth. After a moment, he pulls away, and I'm left cold and trembling once again.

"I don't do well with people wasting my time, Petrovna," his eyes narrowing.

"I'll get you the money. I just need some time," I say, wondering how many times he's heard that one before.

"You have twenty-four hours," he finally says, and starts the car. We drive in silence except for an occasional sniffle from me. We don't look at each other again until he pulls up to my hotel. I instantly reach for the handle and tug on it, but it doesn't budge. I try again, and nothing. My heart hammers in my chest as I turn to look at him.

"Twenty-four hours, Lena. Tell me you understand."

I nod because forming any words without crying is just not possible for me right now. I hear the doors unlock, and I climb out of the car as fast as I can, speed-walking to the large double doors of the hotel. Once I'm in, I let out a shaky breath and keep walking toward the elevator. Paranoia rises within my chest, my eyes darting from side to side, wondering if he has someone watching me at all times. Waiting for the command to come and kill me.

I get into the elevator, repeatedly pushing the button to close the doors. When I'm on my floor, I race to my door like someone is hunting me, but something in front of my door brings me to a stop. It's a large brown paper bag. I approach it slowly, holding my breath. I picture severed fingers in the bag as a warning of what he's capable of. I lean down and pick it up, feeling the warmth underneath it. I look both ways down the corridor and then swipe my key card, opening the door. I set the bag down and open it, spotting a receipt from an Italian restaurant resting on top of two takeout containers. Holding my breath, I lift the lids. The scent of penne alla vodka hits me, and I exhale, feeling a flicker of relief softening the tightness in my chest. I then pick up the receipt and flip it

over, wondering where this came from. And then I see it.
I'll see you soon, kroshka.

9

Lena

I stare at the clock until my eyes burn, until the neon glow reads 6:00 a.m. and the city starts to rise. I've spent the entire night coming up with a plan on how I'm going to get thirty thousand dollars in twenty-four hours. The first thing that comes to mind is my savings account, which took years of hard work and many hours of night shifts. The next idea that pops into my mind, one I wish didn't with all my heart, was my grandmother's heirloom ring. There's nothing in this world I wouldn't give to get my dad back, but that doesn't mean it doesn't hurt to give it up. My grandmother gave me her ring when I turned thirteen. It's been in my family for generations. My grandmother felt proud to pass it on to me. With glossy eyes and a smile, she took my hand and slipped it on my finger. It was a true honor to receive it.

I walk over to my suitcase and fish it out of the hidden compartment. I never travel without it. I have an irrational fear that my house will get broken into, and it will be stolen, along with all the memories it holds. I wish I had left it at home this time.

I pick up the phone and dial Danny. I can come up with a good chunk of money on my own, but definitely not all of it.

He picks up the phone after only one ring, which is impressive since it's 3:00 a.m. in Arizona. "Did you find him?" he asks, sounding just as stressed as I do.

"Yes, kind of. They definitely have him, Danny, and they want thirty grand in twenty-four hours… well, it's more like sixteen hours now," I chew on my lip nervously.

"Fuck!" He pauses. "How much money do you have? I can probably get five thousand for my truck. Max has been begging me to sell it to him for months."

"I have some savings I can take out, and, um… Grandma's ring," I say, tears stinging my eyes.

"God, I'm sorry, Lena, I know how much you love that ring. Is there something else? Do you think Mom would help?"

"No, Danny, don't involve Mom. She's been through enough. I'll pawn the ring and wait to take out my savings once you send me what you have."

"Okay," he sighs. "Give me a few hours."

"I'll wait for your text," I say.

We hang up a few moments later, and I instantly start looking up pawn shops in my area. Thankfully, there is one within walking distance from my hotel. I quickly change my clothes and run out the door without even looking in the mirror. Today is more of a casual, "I just woke up and threw on some sweats" kind of day. It's also a "I'm not sure if I'm going to make it till tomorrow" kind of day.

Once I'm out of the hotel, I walk to the pawn shop, nervously looking around. The feeling of being watched is overwhelming. There's something so vulnerable in not knowing whether someone is watching your every move. Not knowing if I should run or hide.

I reach the pawn shop and pull the door open, and I'm greeted with a loud chime and a skinny gentleman with a fedora. His eyebrows shoot up when he sees me, like I need an appointment to be here or something.

"You need something, sweetheart?" he says in a thick New York accent.

Obviously, I need something, or else I wouldn't be here.

"Yes, I want to see how much I can get for my ring," I say, taking it out of my pocket and showing it to him. I hold it out, the emotional weight of it heavy in my palm.

He reaches out to take it, and I almost close my hand, my chest tightening, screaming that I should be protecting it and not giving it away.

He holds it up, examining the antique gold band, the smooth oval cut of the natural emerald gemstone. I could cry at how beautiful it looks in the light. The green hue reminds me of someone I don't want to think about right now.

The man finally looks up at me, still holding the ring, and smiles. "I'll take it off your hands for nine hundred, it being real gold and all," he says.

I stare at him, my face blank. *Alright, let's play.*

"It being a real emerald and all, I'll take no less than two thousand," I say, my face stone cold. "You know as well as I do that this is an heirloom ring that costs well over what you're offering. If you don't want it, I'll be happy to take it to the shop around the corner."

The man's face drops, and he looks at the ring one more time. "Fine, two thousand. Just because I hate the prick around the corner."

I bite back a smile. I walk out of the shop feeling bittersweet.

I have two grand in my pocket, but I know I've let my ancestors down. I let my grandmother down. That ring will never be passed down in this family again, and it's all because of my father.

I take out my phone and text Danny.

Me: *Any progress?*

Danny: *Yeah, I just sold the truck and my guns. I guess I'm back to taking the bus.*

Me: *Take my car while I'm gone. The keys are with Mom.*

Danny: *Thanks. I'll send the money over in a bit, going to the bank now.*

I start walking toward the bank, which is about a twenty-minute walk from here. By the time I get there, Danny should already have put the money into my account. Ever since I started working, I've been saving to pay off my loans, buy a house, and take my mom to Paris. We've been imagining the day we see the Eiffel Tower together since I was about ten years old. She always said it was her dream to go, so it became my dream, too. I guess that dream will have to wait a little bit longer.

Once I get to the bank, my hands start to shake like I'm about to do something illegal. *Get it together, Lena. You're not stealing, this is your money... that you're about to give to the Russian Mafia in exchange for your father. But let's not think about that last part.*

I walk in and go straight to the little station on the left where they have all those little withdrawal slips. After messing up my name twice, I decide to just go up to the teller and go from there.

"Next," a woman in her early twenties says in a very high-pitched voice that just screams trainee.

"Uh, hi," I say, approaching the window.

"How may I help you today, Ms…?"

"Petrovna," I finish. "And I need to take some money out of my savings account."

"Great, we can definitely make that happen," she smiles. "Can I see your card, please?"

I take my card out of my wallet and pass it to her through the open slot in the window.

"Thank you, Ms. Petrovna. Just give me one moment." She swipes the card and starts typing on the keyboard. Every time she stops, my heart begins to race like I'm about to be caught or something. I have to keep reminding myself that I'm not doing anything wrong here. We've tried the cop route, and it didn't work, so now I'm having to take care of it myself, which means draining my life savings and handing it over to gangsters.

"How much would you like to withdraw today?" she asks.

"Um, all of it please," I say. "And the eight grand in my checking account."

She looks up from the screen and stares at me, almost as if she's waiting for me to say more. "You currently have twenty thousand dollars in your savings account," she says.

"Sounds about right." I shift on my feet, getting a little antsy.

"Just give me one moment. I need more clearance for an amount that large. Please bear with me, ma'am." She passes me my card and leaves.

I wait there, fidgeting with my card, running my finger over each side until it starts to burn. How long could it possibly take for them to get the money? It is a bank, after all, shouldn't they have, like, a big safe with millions of dollars in it? Or is that just in the movies? The sound of footsteps snaps me out of my spiral of thoughts and into the present.

"Thank you for waiting, Ms. Petrovna. I just need to do a few things on my end, and then you will be all set," she says.

I let out a breath and feel a fraction better. A minute later, she hands me a large yellow envelope and has me sign some papers. I make a signature that doesn't even remotely resemble my name and nod a thank you. I stuff the envelope in my bag as best I can and try hard to focus on getting back to the hotel and not on the fact that I'm carrying thirty thousand dollars in my purse and anyone at any time could just snatch it away from me. Hell, if Artyom has someone watching me now, they could take the money and kill me. That thought has me nervously checking my surroundings like a crazy person. By the time I get back to the hotel, I'm covered in sweat, shaking like a leaf in a storm.

"Lena!" I hear a voice behind me, and I clutch my bag reflexively, looking panicked. Andrea runs up to me, trying to catch her breath.

"Hey," I say, loosening my strong hold on my bag.

"I've been calling your name for at least a block! You good?" she asks.

Shit, I've been so stuck in my paranoia, I didn't even hear her calling out to me. "Sorry," I mutter. "I was kind of distracted."

"Is everything okay?" she asks, worry spreading over her face.

I want to tell her everything that is happening with me, everything that I'm feeling, because keeping this shit to myself is making me crazy. "No, my dad isn't doing well. It's why I'm in New York, actually." Which isn't a total lie, just depends on how you look at it.

"Oh god, I'm sorry, Lena." She takes my hand, squeezing it. I almost want to cry at how much I need this. "Wanna come up to my room and chat?" she asks. I just nod, because if I say anything right now, I think I might burst into tears. She hooks her arm through mine, and we walk to the elevator and ride it up to her room. It looks just like I last saw it. Clothes scattered everywhere except for one side of her bed, which is where I decide to sit. I must look utterly pathetic because she comes over and hands me a drink of amber liquid. As soon as I smell it, I know it's whiskey. I take a big gulp, feeling the warmth travel all the way down to my toes.

"Thanks," I say, truly meaning it.

"Do you want to talk about your dad?" she asks.

Not sure how much more I can tell her at this point, I shake my head. "I don't think I can talk about it without crying."

"Okay, well, whenever you need to, I'm here." She smiles. "Now, tell me everything that happened on your date last night. You owe me!"

I groan. "Nothing happened. We just drove around and talked."

"You drove around and talked? What happened to dinner?" she asks, shocked.

"We... uh, just couldn't stop talking and lost track of time, I guess," I say. I am such a liar, and I hate it.

"Well, he'd better take you out again on a proper date with pasta and shit." We both chuckle. "Now that I think about it, I've never seen Art with a woman before. I've actually never even seen him out of that club!"

I hate that I like hearing that. "I can kind of see why. He's extremely intimidating," I say.

"He is, right? He's hot but scary hot, you know?"

Uh, yeah, I know exactly what you mean.

"There was this one time when Roman was MIA doing

whatever the hell he was doing with his guys, and some dude started hitting on me, like aggressively. Asshole followed me into the bathroom, the door barely closed behind him before Art came in."

"What happened when he came in?" I ask, on the edge of my seat.

"Art asked me to leave, in that calm but demanding voice, so I got my ass out of there. Even though I wanted to give that perv a piece of my mind."

"Okay, that's pretty badass," I say, totally hooked. And then I remember this guy is the devil who kidnapped my dad and pretty much ruined my life. My sanity is gone, my savings are gone, and my father is gone.

Andrea gives me a suggestive smile.

"Don't you dare say I got myself a keeper." I roll my eyes.

"What? I thought maybe you liked him?" she teases.

How do I even answer that? He became everything I thought about since the moment I saw him, but I also hate him because no matter what I feel, he's a dangerous and heartless man.

"He's not my type. I go for the golden retriever guys, not the broody ones so much," I say.

She laughs. "Well, when you're ready to come to the dark side, I can give you some advice." She winks at me.

I check my phone, and my heart begins to race once again because it's already 7:00 p.m.

"Hey, I should probably get back to my place and take a shower. I'm seeing my dad later," I say, hopeful.

"If you need me, I'm here, girl. Give me your phone, I'll give you my number."

I hand her my phone, and she types it in. I send her a quick text to make sure she has mine. After our goodbyes, I head for the door.

The elevator dings as I reach it, and the doors slide open to reveal Roman staring back at me.

"Hey," he says, scrunching his brows. He's probably wondering what the hell I'm doing on this floor.

"Uh, hey," I say awkwardly. "I was just talking to Andrea."

He scratches at his jaw and nods, like he doesn't know what to say to me. I know he knows, and I just can't stand the awkwardness between us anymore.

"Roman, I need to go back there. Tonight," I say.

"Are you sure?" he asks, getting out of the elevator.

"Yes. I have everything."

"I can pick you up at nine." He moves away from me.

I nod and step into the elevator. Before it closes, I ask, "Does Andrea know?" Because she's the only safe thing in my life right now, and I think I would crumble if I didn't have that semblance of safety.

He looks down at the floor. "No. I'll tell her when the time comes."

As the elevator shuts, he looks back up at me. There's something in his eyes that is begging me to keep Andrea out of this. I won't drag an innocent person into this mess, but I have a feeling she'll find out sooner rather than later.

10

Lena

As I sit in Roman's car without Andrea, it starts to feel wrong. Like we're lying to her. I look over at him and wonder if he's sharing my guilt. By the way he's gripping the steering wheel, I'd say he at least feels a little weird about it.

"Do you ever think about telling her the truth?" I ask, the silence killing me.

It takes him an entire minute to respond, which makes me regret asking him. It's really none of my business, and I shouldn't care whether he tells her or not. But I like Andrea, and she deserves to know who she's dating.

"No." He pauses. "I like to keep those two lives separate. When I'm with Andrea, I'm just Roman, not Volkhov. And I like it that way. It keeps me sane."

I suddenly feel sad for him. "I understand," I tell him, even though I still think he's wrong to keep his identity from her. "You don't think she suspects anything?" I ask, honestly curious. Andrea seems entirely capable of seeing what's right in front of her.

Roman sighs and grips the wheel tighter. "Sometimes I think she does. When there are things I can't explain or people I can't introduce her to, she looks at me in a way that says she knows, but she never questions it or pushes me to explain. I think that's why we work so well."

A match made in heaven, I think to myself. They'd be adorable if he didn't work for the devil.

"I'm sorry about Lev," he says. "He shouldn't have left you like that."

"I don't think he had much of a choice."

"He's sort of new… to the Brotherhood."

"Yeah, he told me his tattoo is new." I roll my eyes.

"God, he's so stupid." He closes his eyes in frustration.

I smile. I guess he's not so bad. Even though he's a gangster.

As we approach the brown building, Roman meets someone outside and throws them his keys. We walk through a series of corridors, the basement smelling like mop water and metal. We cut left then right, and stop at a smaller metal door, paint chipped around the handle. He knocks twice and backs up. Alec opens the door and nods us in. Warm air and cigarette smoke hit me when I enter the room. A brown leather couch sits against the wall closest to the door, and two oversized chairs face a mahogany desk. Behind the desk, I see *him*.

He's writing something down and doesn't even look up when he says, "Leave us."

Roman looks at me like he's waiting for any sign I'm okay with this, and even though I'm not at all okay, I give him a nod. When the guard and Roman leave, the silence feels heavy in the room. I stand there, looking at him. He's just as he was when I met him: dressed in a black dress shirt, unbuttoned slightly, black slacks, and black loafers. His dark brown hair is neatly parted to the side, clean-shaven, but there's something more relaxed about him than when I last saw him. He looked tense and threatening that night. Today, there's a calmness about him; he's almost approachable. As I step forward, his eyes look up, and I can feel the hair on my arms begin to rise. His green eyes flood my mind with the possibilities of a truce, but all that comes crashing down when he begins to speak.

"So, you've come to save your dad," he says, his voice flat. He puts his pen down and leans back in his chair.

"I brought you what he owes." I am not about to play his stupid game.

"Let's see it," he says, crossing his arms.

I take the cash from my bag and put it on his desk in front of him. "Thirty grand. It's all there. You can count it if you want."

He looks at me and then at the stack of money. "I don't doubt it's all there," he says, rubbing his chin. "But you're not as smart as I thought if you think this will cover it."

My stomach drops. "What do you mean? This is what he owes, isn't it?" I blink at him, stunned.

"Yes, this is what we gave him, but what about the interest? This was a loan, like one you get from a bank, not from a friend, *kroshka*."

There he goes using that nickname again, distracting me.

"I gave you your money. I took out my entire savings and pawned my grandmother's ring! I have nothing else to give!" Tears sting my eyes, but I push them away. I'm far beyond crying. I'm furious. My hands begin to shake, and it takes everything in me not to scream.

He looks at me long and hard and then gets up. My eyes follow him, narrowing. "Petrovna, you're forgetting who you're talking to. You wouldn't be here if you didn't have something I wanted." He comes so close to me that I can smell his aftershave. He smells like the woods after it rains, earthy and clean.

"What do you want from me?" I ask, desperation creeping into my voice.

"The physician who attended to my men recently passed away in an unfortunate accident, and I need a new one." His eyes are trained on mine, waiting for my reaction.

My mind draws a blank for a moment, then I start to understand what he's getting at. I suddenly get the itch to run. Run away from him, this place, and New York altogether. "I'm only a nurse," I say, knowing it won't make a difference.

"You'll work as my doctor until you pay the interest off. You will be available whenever I need, and you will do *whatever* I need."

"How much has he... accrued?" The word sticks in my mouth.

He turns the ledger toward me. "Your father borrowed $30,000. Three percent a week, fixed on the original, not compounded. Nine hundred due each Friday. Twelve weeks, $10,800 accrued."

I swallow. "If I keep paying, when am I done?"

"You don't buy your way out, you work it. Every Friday, I add nine hundred to cover the interest and twenty-five hundred against the debt, if you answer every call and keep my men alive. Do that for twelve weeks, and you're free. But if you cost me, I'll take it out of your total. Fall short, and I'll make new terms."

I stare back at him in disbelief, knowing there is no way out of this. Because what are the alternatives? I say no, and he kills my father? I say no, and he kills us both?

"Will you let me see my dad?"

He moves away from me and walks toward the door. When he opens it, he says something to the guard and then closes it. "I will send my men to get your stuff. Your position starts immediately."

I open my mouth to speak, but nothing comes out. I take a step toward him, but my legs won't move. I feel utterly paralyzed. The next thing I know, I'm weightless in his arms, diving into the green of his eyes.

11

Lena

“Lena! Lena! Wake up, honey.” I hear my dad's voice clear as day. But he can't be here. I must be dreaming. When I open my eyes, I'm lying on the brown leather couch in the office, and I see my dad hovering over me.

“Dad?” I sit up instantly and grab his hands, making sure he's real. “Dad, you're here! Are you okay?”

He kisses my hands. “I should be asking you that! Lenachka, how are you here?”

“I got them the money,” I say, pulling him in for a hug.

“Lena, you shouldn't be here. These people are dangerous,” he whispers. “We need to get out of here.” He looks around and sees Artyom lingering by the open door. I instantly see the fear in his eyes.

“You may leave, Mr. Petrov. We don't need you anymore,” Artyom says, his calmness unsettling.

My dad gets up without a single protest or question and pulls me up. “Let's go, Lena. Don't say a word to them.”

My heart begins to sink. What I'm about to do is going to break him. A sob breaks out of me, and I cling to my dad, not wanting to let go. "I can't go with you," I cry.

"What are you talking about? Let's go. They're letting us go!" He pulls me off and tugs on my arm.

"I'll repeat myself once more, Mr. Petrov. *You* may leave. Your daughter will be taking your place."

My dad looks at me, horrified. "Lena! What did you do? What did you do to get me out? You said you gave him the money, right?" He shakes me for answers. For once, I'm glad Artyom is here. I just can't seem to get the words out. How do I tell my father I've sold my soul to the devil for him?

"She gave us what you borrowed, but the interest accumulated, and your daughter will be working for me until she can pay me everything you owe," his voice flat.

"Take me, take me! Let her go! Take me, I will work for you, I'll do anything!" he begs over and over again.

Artyom stays there staring at me, his eyes telling me his patience is wearing thin. I get up the courage and finally speak, "Dad, Dad! It's okay. I'm okay, I promise," I say, wiping my tears and putting on a fake smile. "No one hurt me, and it won't be for long. I've given him most of the money already. All I have to do is what I already do. I'll work as his nurse to pay the money back. That's all!" I say, trying hard to convince him and myself.

He grabs my shoulders, his eyes going wide. "Lena, it's not just working for them; it's committing crimes for them! You will be working for bad people and stitching them up illegally! How could you be so stupid? I don't want this for you!" He's screaming now. Screaming at me. At my decision to come save him. My tears stop, and something twists in my chest, my face hardening. I'm in this mess because of *him*. I didn't want this for myself either!

It's like Artyom saw this change inside me, and a second later, he calls his guard to take my father away, keeping me from saying something I'll regret later. I stand there while my dad is taken away, kicking and screaming. I know he loves me. I know he's scared for me, but at this moment, I can't help but hate him.

Artyom closes the door and walks toward me. He closes the gap between us, wipes a tear off my cheek, and then I feel his large hand cupping my face. I close my eyes, feeling utterly deflated.

"He's right," he tells me. "Everything he said is true." He moves away from me and stands leaning on his desk, arms crossed. "By now, you should already know what we do and who we are. You'll work for me until you pay off the interest, and then you will be free to go, Ms. Petrovna."

I hate how calm and nonchalant he is about all of this. I want to scream at him, to try running and fighting until I can't anymore, but I know that'll get me nowhere. It'll prove I'm a scared little girl, that I'm weak.

"How do I know you're actually letting my father go? How will I know he's safe?"

"You won't," he says. "I guess we'll just have to trust each other."

My face heats in anger. For him to think I would ever trust him is laughable. "I want to call my father once a week to see that he is unharmed."

"Unfortunately, phones can be traced, and calls can be monitored. You get the idea." I cross my arms and seethe, shooting daggers at him. "Any other questions or demands?" he asks, making an exasperated sound.

I let out a sigh. There is nothing I can demand that he will give me. There is nothing I can say to get him to let me go. So, I give up for now.

"Where will I be staying? And working?" I ask, trying to show more composure.

"My guard will show you to your room. It's in this building. Your operating room is also here, in the basement. I'll show it to you tomorrow." He pushes off the desk and strolls around to sit in his chair, the leather creaking behind him. I stare at him, dumbfounded as he begins to shuffle through paperwork like he's done with me and I'm inconveniencing him by still standing here.

I stalk toward his desk and slam my palms on it, leaning down. "And just out of curiosity, does what you said to me at the club about no one touching me also apply to you?" I don't know what came over me, but I wanted to do something that would catch him off guard.

He looks up and pauses before answering, his face hardening. "When I touch you, *kroshka*, you'll actually like it."

I push off the desk. "In your fucking dreams," I snap. "And stop calling me that." I can't keep hearing him call me that because I can't afford to feel confused about him. We stare at each other for a minute. When neither one of us says anything, he picks up the phone and calls his guard to take me to my room, which is starting to feel more like a dungeon.

Alec comes into the room a second later and politely ushers me out. I'm silent at first, but the further we go, the more questions I have.

"What is this place?" I ask. I know it's a club, but without the crowds of people and loud music, it just looks like an abandoned building.

"It used to be an apartment building that was bought many

years ago to hold meetings and such, but since Artyom took over, he turned it into a club, as you remember."

"Then where would I be staying?" I ask as Alec guides me into the elevator and presses number eight.

"There are still a few apartments left in this building for members to stay in if they need. Yours will be on the eighth floor in the right wing."

I scoff at staying in a place that has wings. What is this Beauty and the Beast? More like beauty and the devil, who I have no intention of saving. We stop at a brown door with the number 813 written on it. As I walk into the apartment, I immediately notice it only has a one-way lock from the outside. I swallow hard. If he intends to keep me locked up in this room until he needs me, then that's fine with me. I don't plan on socializing with criminals. I stand at the entryway and look around. I may have underestimated this building. It's honestly more extensive than I expected. It has an industrial feel, with exposed piping going through the entire place. When I walk into the main room, my clothes have already been hung up and put away for me, as well as a few clothes I haven't seen before, primarily black, small, and lacy.

"Did you bring my clothes here?" I ask, confused. Has that much time passed since I got here?

"Yes. As soon as you entered the building."

I roll my eyes. Of course, I didn't actually have a choice with any of this. I stare at the California king bed in front of me and wonder why the hell I need something this big, and then the panic starts to creep in. What if this isn't a guest Artyom? *Get a grip, he said he wouldn't allow anyone to touch me.* Maybe all the rooms have a California king bed for… orgies or whatever they do here.

Alec leaves, and I go to the door to see if it's locked, and yep, it is. I go into the room and look for my bag, and when I find it, I get just the tiniest amount of hope they didn't take my phone, but of course, they did.

I don't even bother changing out of my clothes as I slide into bed, wrapping myself up like a burrito. If anyone comes in, they will have a hell of a time trying to get to me like this. I stare at the clock on the wall opposite the bed until I can't keep my eyes open any longer. As sleep takes over, I let go of everything: my father, the money, Artyom, and this prison.

12

Artyom

ight years earlier
    The clinking of glasses snaps me back into reality. My cue to down another shot. It's been two years since my father passed away and today is his memorial. As I sit at the head of the table, people from the Brotherhood take turns saying something along the lines of "he built this empire from the ground up" and "he was more than just a boss." I stopped listening half an hour ago. My mind is elsewhere today, and I can't shake the anger rising inside of me every time someone looks at me like they're waiting for me to say something about my father. As their new boss, I should say something. I know I should, but I just fucking can't. I can't even come up with some bullshit. Alec keeps putting his hand on my shoulder every few shots I down, his own way of telling me I need to get my shit together and say something.

Alec has been my father's right-hand man ever since I can remember, and now he's mine. Before my father passed, he told me it's customary to pick out your own right-hand man when the time comes. He basically told me to let Alec go. To this day, I'm not sure if he meant to kill him or replace him. Because if there's one thing I know for sure, there's only one way someone leaves the Brotherhood, and it's in a body bag. The day after my father died, I approached Alec and asked him to be my partner. He let out a breath, almost like he was holding it in, and nodded. That day was the first time I saw any emotion on his face, and it almost looked like gratitude.

As I look around the room of people who came to memorialize my father, I see the old and new members, all of whom were incredibly loyal to my father. I inherited all of this: the Brotherhood, the devotion, and the fealty. I am their boss, and they would do anything for me. That should make me feel something, shouldn't it? I guess anger is an emotion I've been feeling a lot lately.

"He was unlike any man I have ever met. He loved this family fiercely, and we all felt it." The words drift past me, blurred by the soft clinking of cutlery and glass. With each toast, I get angrier. I feel my blood boiling over until I see my hands tremble in my lap. I slide out of my chair and head outside. A minute more in there, and I would've exploded. As soon as the cold air hits my face, I feel a fraction better. I close my eyes and inhale, trying my hardest to keep my composure. I hear the door shut behind me, knowing who it is before he speaks.

Alec is the only one who knows me better than I know him. Which is saying a lot since my father made sure I knew each member like the back of my hand. I know each person's strengths, weaknesses, family life, personal life, and everything in between. Alec, however, lives and breathes the Brotherhood, so I guess that's why we understand each other.

"He should be here," he says.

Fucking Alec always knows what I'm thinking. I nod, taking out a cigarette. My brother Ivan wanted nothing to do with the family business. He made it clear that when I took over, he would not watch me turn into our father. That little shit thinks I had a choice like he did. He thinks I could walk away and defy my father. Ivan is eleven months younger than me, and because of that, I was the one chosen to take over. I was born and bred to lead, to live for the family business, while Ivan got to live out his life enjoying the freedom of being whoever he wanted to be. What I didn't know was that he'd drop off the face of the earth and I'd never see him again.

I'm not sure if it's the pressure to be like my father or the pressure to be better, but I feel like I'm being consumed by rage lately. Or maybe it's because Ivan isn't fucking here.

"I can call him. We don't know; maybe something came up."

I take a deep pull and exhale, the smoke distorting my vision of him. "Nothing came up, Alec." I know Ivan like the back of my hand. He is choosing not to be here.

We stand here a while longer until I'm numb from the cold, and I can no longer feel a single fucking thing. The door swings open again, and I see Rob in my periphery light a cigarette next to me. He's been in the Brotherhood for just a few years. I remember my father picking him out like he was choosing clothes from a catalog. "This one is a tough one. We need those," were his exact words. He was right. Rob is as tough as they get. I didn't always like him, though. He was broke with a family to take care of. People like that become desperate. Desperate enough to seek out any extreme way to make money, and then when they get it, they suddenly grow a conscience. He's proved himself, though. I made sure of it.

"This sucks more than my old man's funeral," he tells me.

I almost laugh. "Five years now?" I ask. He raises an eyebrow like he's impressed I know that, and then nods. "My younger brother Mike doesn't even remember him. He has no idea how lucky he is."

Now it's my turn to nod; that's something we have in common. I hear his phone chime, and he gets it out, looking at it, the screen illuminating his dark features.

"Shit," he mutters. "Roman is at the club." I look at him, confused, and then it dawns on me.

A few weeks prior, Rob asked me if I would meet with one of his friends. Said he wants in the Brotherhood. One of my rules is don't recommend friends to join the Brotherhood. Because once there's a falling out, they always want to leave. It's unspoken, but everyone knows you can't just leave. I guess I was distracted when I said I'd meet with the guy.

"It's not the time, Rob," Alec says, clearing his throat.

"It's fine," I say, needing to think about anything other than my father or Ivan. "Give him the Myrtle location."

Rob and Alec are quiet for a moment, waiting for me to say I'm joking. Myrtle Ave. is where Brooklyn becomes Queens. We have a business there we collect from, but because it borders so closely to a rival gang, there's always some kind of bloodshed, either on our side or theirs. I only send my most experienced men to collect. If Rob wants this guy in, he's going to have to prove himself, not only by getting out of there alive, but by showing me I can trust him.

"Tell him he's there for ten grand." He'll be given twenty grand, and the rest is up to him. I can see it on Rob's face. He's nervous. That's another reason I don't take friend recommendations. If Rob were to intervene in any way, it wouldn't be good for him. Rob nods once and leaves, walking down the street until I see him get into his car.

"Find out everything there is about this guy," I tell Alec. "Follow him, and if he can't hold his own, take care of it." Alec nods. "Do you need a ride before I leave?"

"No, I'll take the train."

"You know you can't do that anymore, Artyom. You're the boss now. It's not done," he says, like I don't already know that.

"I'll call a cab," I lie. There's something about taking the train that helps me clear my head, something so peaceful and normal about it. Something I'm no longer allowed to have.

13

Lena

I wake up to the bed dipping next to me. When I open my eyes, it's pitch black, and the clock on the nightstand tells me it's four in the morning. I stay still, frozen, afraid of turning around and facing whatever is next to me. Whoever it is sits there, not moving for what feels like an eternity. I want to turn around, but my body won't let me. I feel paralyzed. The bed dips lower, and I assume whoever it is is lying down now. I hear a sigh, and then there's more silence.

Horrific scenes loop behind my eyes. My stomach roils; I grip the blanket and stare at the wall for hours, my left arm buzzing with pins and needles.

Once the clock says 6:00 a.m. and I see the faintest light squirm its way into the room, I gather whatever courage I have left and quietly sit up, slide my legs off the bed, and stand, taking the blanket with me. When I turn around, I see Artyom. My eyes go wide. He's sleeping in my bed, still dressed in his black suit, still flawless as ever. His body is so still, I almost get the urge to see if he's even breathing. Even in his sleep, he owns the room, terrifying but alluring in every way. It takes me a minute to snap myself out of it and convince my feet to slowly inch out of the room. When I almost trip on the blanket, I unravel myself from it and let it fall to the floor. I tiptoe out of the room and let out a sigh when I finally reach the bathroom. To say I look awful would be an understatement. I lean over the sink, staring at my reflection. Dark circles surround my eyes, and my hair looks like it dried into a giant nest on my head. My stomach churns with dread. I dread any time I need to spend with him, but mostly, I dread this feeling in the pit of my stomach, between my thighs, and in my heart whenever I'm around him.

I think of a game plan for my stay here while I shower. I need to lie low until I can pay back the money, and I need to somehow get in contact with my family. I need to know my father is safe.

As I wrap a towel around myself, it hits me that while I was trying to get the hell out of that room, I forgot to bring a change of clothes with me. "Shit," I whisper. I stare at the crumpled pile of dirty clothes I slept in and contemplate putting them back on. I cringe and decide to risk sneaking into the room and grabbing anything clean I can find to put on. I open the door and quietly walk out, looking both ways down the corridor. Silent for now. I creep toward the room and peek in, my eyes going straight to the empty bed. I sigh, relieved. He must've left when I was showering. Maybe he doesn't want to see me as much as I don't want to see him. I open the dresser and get my clothes out, dropping my towel in the process.

"Yet again, you have my attention, Ms. Petrovna."

I whip around as fast as I can and see him in the doorway, staring at me. His eyes are gems, cutting into me, shredding any confidence I might've had. I use my hands to cover myself, but I'm not leaving much to the imagination. I look at the towel at my feet and almost reach for it. However, reaching for it would mean I'd need to remove one hand from either my breasts or my crotch. I can feel my cheeks heat with embarrassment.

"I thought you left! Why are you even here?" My cheeks burn.

"You're in my room."

"Why am I in your room? I thought I'd have my own place! And can you turn around, please!" My heart pounds as I watch him stare at me, something primal passing in his eyes.

"I said you'd live in this building, and you are." He leans against the door frame. His face gives nothing away, but his eyes are devouring me.

He is having too much fun watching me squirm, and I'm tired of playing his game. My eyes narrow at him, and I'm not sure what comes over me, but I stand straight, no longer trying to cover up. I let his eyes roam over my body while I get dressed, sliding on the black panties I'm sure he picked out for me, the black lacy bra next. My insides are mush, lava coursing through my veins, screaming for me to be done with this. Artyom doesn't even flinch. He just stands there watching like I'm putting on a private little show for him. I roll my eyes and continue dressing like he's not even there. I put on a pair of jeans and my most oversized T-shirt. Purposely trying to look unappealing. When I'm done, I walk toward the door, not looking in his direction.

As soon as I reach it, he grabs my elbow, stopping me. "If you like putting on a show, I can get you a pole next time," he says, letting go of my arm and moving past me like he's angry with me. A smile tugs at my lips, and I think I won that one. I stride out of the room, head held high, and walk into the entryway of the apartment.

"Put your shoes on. I'll show you to the operating room," he says.

We put on our shoes silently, me with my worn-out sneakers and him in his black Tom Ford loafers. Once we stand, he towers over me, letting me feel his presence. For a moment, I let it penetrate me, his scent, his alluring eyes, and the sheer size of him. Before I can stop myself, I'm doe-eyed in front of him, hypnotized. I wait for him to make a noise, to move or call me out, but he just lets me take him in. He knows what his presence does to people, and that thought alone snaps me out of it. I clear my throat and peel my eyes away from him. A moment later, I hear the door open and see him standing next to it, ushering me out. As I walk past him, I hold my breath, because I just can't trust myself when I'm this close to him. I'm beginning to accept that my reaction to him is involuntary and there isn't much I can do about it.

When we arrive at the elevator, Alec is already waiting for us. "Good morning, Alec," I say, smiling at him. Keeping him close might help me in the long run here. Plus, he's not the worst.

"Ms. Petrovna," he says back. What I like about Alec is that he's always consistent. He's polite but not kind. He's not threatening, but at the same time, there's a quiet kind of danger that radiates from him. He doesn't hide it like Roman does, which makes me feel a little more comfortable, almost like I'm not in for any surprises with him.

"Thank you again for telling me a bit about this building. I wouldn't know how to get around if it weren't for you." He opens his mouth to answer, but stops when he sees Artyom's annoyance. He gives me one of his tight smiles.

"Can Alec show me around instead? He's much better company than you are." I guess it's push-his-buttons o'clock because I just can't keep my mouth shut.

The elevator dings, and we arrive in the basement of the building. Alec walks out first, and then I follow. As I step forward, Artyom grabs my wrist, stopping me. He closes me in, pinning me against the elevator wall. My heart feels like it will jump out of my throat the way he's looking at me. He's either going to kiss me or rip into me. Either one scares the shit out of me. I'm about ready to beg for forgiveness when he begins speaking, his tone so hard, I'm crushed instantly.

"Tread lightly, *kroshka*. It would be a shame for Alec to be replaced."

My mouth opens in utter disbelief, and I stare at him. He wouldn't... would he?

He traces his finger along my bottom lip. "You're going to have to open a little wider for me, sweetheart," he says in that same tone.

I quickly regain my composure and push past him. Horror sweeping over me. The horror of what he just did to my body. The lust that is rapidly replacing all the fear.

I catch up to Alec as he takes out a set of keys while approaching a large double set of metal doors, kind of like the ones that lead to the club. The doors creak open to reveal a tired, makeshift operating room, if you can even call it that. Flickering lights above a stainless steel table, cracked, bubbling linoleum on the floor, and the thin bleach-over-blood smell coating the entire room. I've been in some rough-looking OR rooms as a student, but this one looks like it's being held together by tape.

I scope out the room and come across a variety of surgical tools. The instruments look ancient: dinged forceps, a retractor that's seen better days, and sutures scattered around. Not hospital grade, that's for sure, but it's enough to save a life, or lose one. This room was built especially for this, to operate illegally. I stare at it in disbelief.

"How did your last doctor die?" I ask.

"An unfortunate accident," he says, avoiding eye contact.

"Yes, you told me, but what happened?" *Please, please, please tell me it wasn't gang-related.* A car accident or something would be great. Not for the guy, of course, just for my sanity.

He pauses, clearly not wanting to talk about it. "He was shot," he says finally.

I look at his face, and something looks different. His calm demeanor changes into something solemn. I instantly remember how he looked in the train station. My body involuntarily calmed, feeling sorry for the devil in front of me.

"When did he die?" I ask.

"A few days ago."

I'm a little taken aback at his answer. "When I first saw you in the train station?" I turn from him, suddenly unable to look him in the eyes when the memories from that day come flooding back. This would explain why he looked so broken. The way my eyes couldn't leave his, and the way he stared at me like he could devour me, and I'd enjoy every second of it.

"As far as I know, we've never met before that day at my club," he says, his tone cold.

I turn around, confusion written on my face. "I saw you at the train station, and I'm pretty sure you saw me," I say, quieter now.

"I don't take the train, Lena. I have people who drive me." His eyes are hard, clearly done with this conversation.

I feel myself getting redder with embarrassment. Either he's messing with me, or he doesn't remember me, which is even worse because I certainly remember him. I remember everything about him.

"Right, my mistake then." Dropping the whole thing.

He immediately changes the subject. "This is where you'll be working whenever you're needed, night or day. This is where you'll go. You'll tend to my men like your life is tied to theirs. Do you understand me, Lena?"

"I'm a trauma nurse, not a doctor. You can't expect me to operate on your men, not if you want them to live," I retort.

"I'll ask you again, do you understand me?"

I close my eyes, feeling the pressure of the world. Of this world. "Yes," I whisper.

"Good girl. I'll leave you here for a bit. Whenever you're done, tell Alec, and he will take you back upstairs to your room." He waits until I nod, and then he leaves.

I stay here for hours. Looking at books and logs that the doctor left. His logs date back seven years. This poor man was sucked into this life of crime for seven years. I read all about what he had to do for these men and the kinds of operations he had to perform. It's mostly gunshot wounds and stabbings. Only a few broken ribs, noses, and dislocated shoulders. I don't even notice Alec bringing me all the takeout boxes. They appear, and I inhale them like I haven't eaten in months.

When I finally hear the door open, Alec enters. "Ms. Petrovna, I've received orders to take you back upstairs."

I rub my eyes, suddenly feeling the strain. "What time is it?"

"It's eight p.m. You've been here all day."

Shit, that means he's been waiting for me for hours. "Sorry, Alec," I say and walk toward the door. "Is *you know who* upstairs?"

"No, he's at the club tonight."

"Great, I'll get dressed and go there too," I say, trying to hide my excitement. This could be my opportunity to see Andrea or Roman. To somehow get a message to my family.

"I'll have to clear that with the boss," he tells me.

"Alec, did he tell you not to bring me there?"

"No," he says, but his expression reads that he should've.

"Well then, I'm sure it's fine, and you'll be there to watch me. What will I do? Run away? I'm here working off a loan. I can't run away," I say matter-of-factly.

Once we get to the room, I look through the new clothes bought for me, taking out the most revealing of them all. Whoever picked these out has an affinity for the color black. I put on a black leather miniskirt and a mesh top with a black lace bra underneath. It's not nearly as sexy as the dress I wore the other day, but it's definitely not something I would wear outside of a club. With my plan to get a message to my family in mind, I feel some hope spread its way into my chest. The guilt I've been feeling for disappearing and how I left things with my dad has been eating away at me. I need him to know I'm okay.

I follow Alec to the club entrance, passing all the people dressed as though they're going to a sex party. The bouncers nod at Alec and open the doors. They don't look at me like they did the first time I came here. In fact, they don't look at me at all.

Once I get in there, I stare at the place in awe once again.

This club is like Cirque du Soleil but kinky. It's hard to look away. Alec puts his hand on my upper waist and ushers me to the second floor. The club seems more crowded this time, with people covering every inch of this place and making me feel slightly claustrophobic.

"Stay on the second floor, Ms. Petrovna." No explanation, just a command.

I nod, not really wanting to get lost in the sea of people. He drops me off at the bar. When I look over at the VIP area, I see more men gathered there than last time, with more guards. They have two women dancing, and one is sitting on Artyom's lap. I feel my face getting warm and instantly feel like an idiot. Why is my body reacting like this? I turn to face the bartender, needing a drink.

"Can I get a shot? And put it on his tab," I say, pointing to Artyom, rolling my eyes at the woman trying to get his attention with her boobs.

The bartender doesn't even look confused, just nods and hands me a shot. I take it down fast, loving the burn that goes down my throat and lands in my stomach, incinerating the ball of stress from the past few days.

"Another one, please."

I turn from my seat and look out to the dance floor, scanning the sea of people practically dry humping each other. Andrea should be easier to spot with her long blonde hair and amazingly long legs. The lady practically looks like a supermodel. My eyes stop at a woman swaying in the middle of the dance floor, and my heart does a flip in excitement. I make my way toward the dance floor, pushing people aside as best I can.

Once I reach her, I put my hand on her shoulder. "Andrea!"

I shout, almost giddy with anticipation. The woman turns around, and I stare in confusion. The beautiful blonde lady is actually a beautiful blond man in a very tight dress. I press my lips together to keep from laughing.

"Sorry, wrong person!" I shout, turning around before bursting into laughter. I can already picture telling Andrea, she'd probably laugh and find it absolutely flattering. I miss her.

Once I get back to the bar, I reluctantly turn back to Artyom's table and spot Roman. If I can get to him, I can find out if she's here, or maybe he'll have some mercy and send her a message to meet me here one of these days. I stare at him, trying to get his attention; maybe he'll pick up on my desperate signal waves. Once I give myself a headache from staring so hard, I turn back to the bar and let out a loud groan in frustration.

"Rough day?"

I turn to my right and see a man holding a glass of amber liquid. His mouth is turned up into a grin.

"You could say that," I retort warily.

"Well then, the next one is on me." He smiles again, except this time it doesn't reach his eyes. He's handsome in a way, but not like Artyom. Artyom's features hit you like a ton of bricks and make you forget how to breathe in his presence. This guy has a more subtle handsomeness, still alluring but more playful. His sandy brown hair curls below his nape and around his forehead. He's wearing light-wash jeans and a white T-shirt, which makes him stick out like a sore thumb. Everyone here is either dressed for the red carpet or an orgy. If I weren't a little tipsy, I'd think he dressed this way on purpose, almost like he wants to stand out.

"Fine with me." I smile. "Actually, I'll be right back," I tell him, seeing Roman finally leave the VIP area and make his way toward the restrooms. If I'm fast enough, I can get to him before he goes in and ask about my dad and Andrea. I don't even look to see if the guy heard me, I just quickly leave my seat and walk toward the neon green restroom sign. In an instant, I bump into something hard.

"Shit, sorry!" I say, not even looking up, and move to the side, but the brick of a man moves with me.

"What are you doing here?" he growls.

I instantly know who it is, and something in me stirs. I pretend it's the alcohol. "I've been cooped up in the operating room all day. I just needed a drink," I tell him, hoping he'll buy it. I look around, but don't see Roman anymore.

"Tonight isn't a good night. I can't babysit you," he says through gritted teeth.

"Then don't." I push past him, walking toward the restroom. *Please, please, please don't follow me.* I glance back, and of course, he follows me.

He takes my hand and pushes me into the room, locking the door behind him. "Remember what I said, *kroshka*. Let anyone touch you, and you'll be responsible for what happens next."

I look up and see that his expression is laced with possessiveness and… danger? "Well, that's rich coming from you," I scoff. "You can have half-naked women all over you, and I can't be touched? I'm not your property," I spit out. Clearly, the alcohol is giving me more courage than I usually have.

His expression changes from possession to desire in a second flat. My breath catches in my throat when he stalks toward me and grabs the back of my neck, pulling my face to his, a mere inch away from his perfect mouth. He looks like sin tonight, and I'm sure he'll taste like it too. He's dressed in a black silk dress shirt with two buttons open at the top. His black slacks cling to him like they were made for his body, sewn and put together just for him.

I'm lost looking at his mouth when he goes to whisper in my ear, "If you want to be touched, all you need to do is ask. I can make you writhe against this door until you forget your own name."

I close my eyes and almost let out a moan. The way he talks feels like whiskey going down my throat, scorching everything in me. He bends down slightly and snakes his hand up my thigh. I bite my lip to keep from making any noises that'll give him the satisfaction he's seeking.

"Don't do that," he says, closing his eyes. He exhales slowly through his nose, and I release my lip while staring at him, growing obsessive over his reactions to me. His hand travels higher until his fingers graze my panties. I look up at him, lust dripping from my mouth, begging him to go further. My body is screaming for him to touch me. *Please*, it begs. His hand pauses at my entrance when a clear picture of a half-naked lady sitting in his lap, her hands around his neck, his hands on her thigh, the same hands that are on me right now, comes into view.

"Why don't you go feel up the blonde? I'm sure she'd love that." I push him away, going for the door.

He follows and puts his arm out to stop me. "Go back to your room, Petrovna. Or I will carry you back to that room myself if I have to," he threatens.

"But I'm not done with my drink, and didn't you promise me a pole?" I smirk at him and then open the door, leaving him there.

I look around for Roman, but I don't see him. I look out onto the first floor, scanning the sea of people, but I don't see anyone who could help me. The thought of just asking someone for their phone crosses my mind, but now that Artyom knows I'm here, I know he's watching me. I go back to the bar and order another shot, feeling hopeless. The guy I was talking to is gone. Figures. My eyes find Artyom once again, getting settled back in with his men. They all look so intense, dressed in suits. I wonder if they all work for him. I feel the alcohol fueling my anger, and I decide to show him exactly what I'm made of. I walk confidently toward the VIP area, not even stopping when I reach the guards.

"I'm with Art over there. I'm his special guest, if you know what I mean." I wink at them. The guys smirk like I definitely look the part. I continue walking toward the men sitting down, taking in the more intimate ambiance. As I approach them, my eyes dart to the guy I was talking to earlier. He's sitting across from Artyom, scowling at him, but when he sees me, his eyes light up. Five more guys are sitting there, none of whom I've seen before. All look terrifying and dangerous. The alcohol fades just a fraction, and unease settles in, which gives my conscience enough time to scream *get the hell out of here*.

My eyes meet Artyom's. He's sitting on an overwhelmingly large, whiskey-colored leather armchair, and somehow, he fills out the entire chair, making it disappear with his presence. He's looking at me like I've just come into the club with bombs strapped to my body. It almost makes me retreat completely. Almost.

The guy I talked to before grabs my hand to get my attention, and I'm immediately back to tipsy Lena. "Hey there," he says, smiling at me. I grin. He looks so out of place here, it's almost laughable. He's not as big in size compared to the other men, but his confidence makes up for it.

"I'm ready for that drink you promised," I say, feeling Artyom's gaze still on me.

He laughs and flags down the waitress, who brings us a tray of six shots. He hands me one, and I take it down without a second thought. He takes my hand and leads me to sit next to him, his arm coming around my shoulders, bringing me close to his chest. Great, now I have nowhere else to look except at Artyom. His expression is murderous, his words reverberating in my head. Would he actually break fingers just because they touch me a certain way? The way he's looking at me tells me he would, and he might even enjoy teaching me a lesson. I shift slightly away from this guy until I'm no longer leaning on his chest.

"I didn't catch your name, sweetheart," he says.

"Lena," I tell him, looking at Art. I can't seem to take my eyes off him. I wonder what he would do if I came over to him and sat on his lap like the blonde from earlier. *Get a grip, Lena.*

"I'm Nico. It's nice to meet you, Lena." He takes my hand and kisses it.

"Finally, a gentleman," I say to Nico. Art's gaze doesn't leave mine, shooting me daggers. I honestly didn't think he'd let me get this far. He cornered me in the elevator for just being nice to Alec. Why is he letting me flirt with Nico right in front of him? I'm fully aware of what I'm doing, but Nico doesn't seem to be afraid of Art whatsoever. He's not oblivious because I can tell Nico senses something between Art and me, the way

Art keeps looking at me.

"Don't worry about him, sweetheart. He's harmless, almost like a puppy," he says, the last part directed right at him, all humor dying. Suddenly, there's a sinking feeling in my chest. Something about this guy is wrong. My head starts spinning a bit, and I shift away from him.

"Well, it was nice to meet you, Nico. Thank you for the drink." I get up from the sofa, the leather groaning after me.

"Already?" He reaches for my hand to stop me from going further, his hold a little tighter than I'd like. Art shifts in his chair and downs whatever's in his glass.

"Uh, yeah, sorry. I'm supposed to meet a friend on the dance floor. She's probably looking for me." I give him a tight smile and pull away from him.

He stands up and leans in for a side hug, his hand a little too low on my back. "I'll see you again, sweetheart. Next time, you'll have to stay longer." As I turn to leave, his hand brushes my ass, and he keeps it there just a second too long. I stop and swallow hard, not because I feel any type of way about his touch, but because I fear the wrath that might be coming. I turn around at the same time Art stands up, and it takes him a total of two seconds to make his way over to us, grab Nico's throat with one hand, and bend Nico's fingers with the other. I hear a pop, and the next thing I know, Alec is hauling me away. The last thing I see is Nico's face contorting into agony.

"Alec! Wait! His… his … hand. I have to go see it, I can fix it!" I stumble over my words, too shocked to even make sense of what just happened.

"I think you've done enough, Ms. Petrovna. I'm sure he'll find a doctor that can fix his hand… if his fingers remain intact," he says, mumbling the last few words.

All the threats are real. I should've known not to mess with him. I should've minded my own business and kept as far away as possible. This is all my fault.

"Why did he do that? How could he do that to one of his own guys?" I ask, my heart sinking. "I am not his property, Alec. I might be working for him, but I am my own person."

Once we make it out of the club, the silence rings loudly in my ears.

"Those are not his men, Ms. Petrovna. His men would not have touched you."

"What? Then who are they?"

"They are… business associates, ones we want to make sure never come around again," he says, looking at me hard. "And now I think they might have a reason to."

We walk into the elevator, and I let his words sink in. Nico and the other men are also gang members, just not a part of this one. That's why Artyom wanted me to go back to the room. He didn't want me around any of them. The longer I think about it, the more nauseated I become. All my questionable decisions start to come right back up. Artyom didn't budge when Nico was rude to him, but he acted within seconds as soon as Nico touched me. Did he do it to teach me a lesson, or was he protecting me? I let out a groan because this is just too much to think about while in shock and absolutely shitfaced.

"Ugh, Alec, I think I might be sick."

Alec picks me up and walks faster to the apartment, opening it and setting me down carefully.

I run to the bathroom, stumble over my shoes, and throw up. I hear the door close and slump down, resting my head on the toilet. This right here is a new low for me. Actually, being locked up in a mafia house and forced to use my nursing license illegally is a new low. Oddly enough, my head in the toilet is the most normal thing that has happened to me in days. After throwing up a few more times, I lie down, still in my outfit, on the cold bathroom floor and let sleep take over.

14

Artyom

even years earlier
S I've seen men stabbed, shot, decapitated; the list goes on and on. My father made sure I had the stomach for this job. However, when your face is the last face a person sees before their life leaves their body, that realization never really goes away.

"He's gone," Alec tells me, like I don't already know. But I can't move. I can't even think about what to do next. I just stand there, staring at the boy lying on the cold floor of my basement, his eyes utterly empty. He died for the Brotherhood, and I don't even know his name. He has my mark on his arm. And I don't even know his fucking name.

The screaming next to me snaps me out of this spiral and turns my attention back to the other boy, still alive but barely holding on. Alec's eyes are trained on me, waiting for my command, but I have nothing. I can tell him to take the boy to the hospital, but that would put everyone in the Brotherhood at risk. The feds have been up my ass since my father died, and they thought it would be easy to get to me now that he's gone.

It's been hard to secure a physician since taking over. Our last one lasted thirty years with my father, and as soon as my father died, he told me about his cancer spreading and how he wanted to live out the rest of his life with his family. My father would've looked him in the eye and told him we were his family, and that was exactly what he was going to do. But I'm not my father. I'm just not sure that's a good thing because we would've had a doctor if I forced him to stay.

I look at the boy and instantly feel a pang in my gut. Why do people say doing the wrong thing is easier? Because what I'm about to do feels like utter shit. I pull out my phone and dial the one person who might not pick up the phone.

It rings twice, three times… I can see that Alec is nervous, but I can't let them see that I am too, that I'm in over my head, drowning. I need to have this under control, or the whole business goes down. He picks up on the fourth ring but doesn't say anything.

"Ivan…" I begin to say, "I need you to come to the building."

More silence. "I just got in, Artyom. I can come later this week." We haven't spoken since our father passed; even then, it was short. I have Alec keep tabs on him, where he is and what he's doing, which is how I know he got back today.

"I need you now," I say, through gritted teeth. I have never asked him for anything before, and I hate that I'm asking now. I'd rather keep him as far away as possible from me and all this shit, but right now, he's my last resort.

"What is it that can't wait until tomorrow at least?"

I will have two dead boys on my hands if I wait until tomorrow, but I can't tell him that over the phone in case anyone is listening. Fucking feds.

"Either you come now, or I will come get you myself. Which will it be, Ivan?"

Silence, then I hear him sigh. "I'm on my way."

As soon as we hang up, I feel like I can actually breathe. I look at Alec, and he nods.

"A doctor is on his way. Just hang on a little longer," he tells the boy. Fifteen minutes later, he arrives, looking harried and annoyed. His expression changes the second he sees the bloodied mess in front of me. The two men are sprawled on the floor, one dead and the other heaving, eyes wide and pleading for help.

"Shit, Artyom! I can't be here right now! I can have my license suspended and fucking go to jail. I won't do that for you." He begins to turn around, and I pounce on him, grabbing him by the collar and dragging him to the boy.

"You can pretend all you want that you're not a part of this family, but today you're going to save this boy's life, Ivan, because that's what you fucking do for a living." I push him toward the boy once more.

The boy sputters, "Please," as if on cue. Blood coats his entire body. His lips are turning blue, and he's not even screaming in pain anymore, which makes me angrier. Another brother dying under my watch.

"If this boy dies, you die," I lie. "Do you understand, Ivan?" My expression is murderous.

"Our father would be proud, Artyom. You even sound like him." His words turn my blood cold. He has no idea how much I hate being compared to our father. He hates me. That much is clear, but he's going to help this boy, not because he's afraid of me, but because he's a good doctor and an even better person.

Ivan quickly gets to work, pulling out instruments I've never seen before, different from the kind of tools the last doctor used in this makeshift operating room.

"Get me whatever drugs you have. I need him sedated. This is going to hurt like a bitch," he tells me.

I ransack every inch of this place and finally find little glass bottles of God knows what. When I hand them to him, he raises a brow.

"Was Doc running a dog shelter or something? Shit."

I look at the bottles, confused. "What are you talking about?"

"It's Benadryl for dogs," he mumbles as he takes a syringe and fills it to the brim. I never questioned Doc or even wondered where the hell he got his stuff from. I guess now I know.

"Will it work?" I ask.

"Two of these should do the trick." He fills another syringe and injects it into the boy's bloodstream.

I try not to look so dumbfounded at everything he does, but I'm entirely impressed with him. This son of a bitch is good at his job, and he actually likes doing it. When it comes to cauterizing the wound, he doesn't even flinch. His composure is like nothing I've ever seen. At this moment, I know what I have to do. Everything in me screams to let him go and be happy that he got away from all this. He'll get to live the normal life he always wanted. And yet, there's this other part of me. The part responsible for dozens of men in the Brotherhood, the ones who risk their lives every day for me. And that part refuses to let him go.

15

Lena

I wake up to my head pounding. I sit up, rubbing my eyes. I haven't had that much alcohol in years. I open my eyes and realize I'm in bed, naked. Panic rises in my chest as I try to remember last night's events. I remember Alec taking me back to the apartment, throwing up… multiple times, and then passing out on the cold floor. How the hell did I end up naked in bed?

I instantly remember I've been sharing a bed with the devil, and my eyes dart around the room warily. There's no way he'd pick me up and take me to bed, right? He was furious with me last night. Wait… Nico's face when I left… his fingers. Did Artyom break them? The fog in my brain starts to clear, and I begin to remember exactly what happened, down to the sound. I get up as soon as a metallic taste floods my tongue. I speed-walk to the bathroom, splashing cold water on my face. He did it. He said he would and he did. I completely and stupidly underestimated him. I turn on the shower and get in, not needing to undress. As I submerge under the water, I all but have an orgasm. The hot water instantly melts the last twenty-four hours away.

The glass shower door opens, and my heart catches in my throat when I see a very naked Art stepping into the shower with a very naked me. Instead of screaming, I stand there frozen; my eyes are the only things I can seem to move, which are shamelessly studying every part of him that has been haunting my dreams. My eyes track downward, following the trail of dark hair going from his muscled chest down to his…

"Are you done?" he asks, his tone laced with annoyance. Like I'm the one who invaded his space.

"What are you doing here?" I ask, coming to my senses. My hands trying to cover up whatever they can.

"Showering." He reaches for the body wash, his chest almost brushing mine. My nipples harden from the heat that radiates from him.

"Well, so am I! Can't you wait for me to get out?" I'm trying hard not to look down his body again. It's like he was sculpted out of clay, and my hands itch to touch him and see if he's real.

He moves closer to me, his eyes catching mine. Somehow, they become darker, desire written all over them. His large hands snake up my arms, so slowly that it makes me yearn for more. My eyes automatically close as he grips my shoulders. I feel him walk me back until I'm up against the shower wall and he's under the stream. I wait for him to do anything and everything, waiting until I hear the thud of the shower door close behind him.

Embarrassment creeps into my chest as I stand there exposed and alone. This feels like a punishment for bad behavior, which I'm starting to think I deserve. I let myself get drunk and parade around like I'm unafraid of him and this place. I unintentionally made things worse for all people involved, and I'm afraid what I saw yesterday is just a glimpse of what he could do. I sink to the floor and let the water hit me, trying to calm my breathing.

As I dry off and put on some clothes, I think of what Alec told me last night. I should explain myself to Artyom and tell him I didn't know that guy wasn't one of his men. I was clearly trying to get a reaction out of him. I was being a complete idiot. When I open the bathroom door, I step out quietly, trying to gauge where he is. When I don't see him, I go to the door and pull it; it doesn't budge. Right, I forgot it's a one-way lock, and I have no way of opening the door if it's locked from the outside. I knock with a little more force.

"Alec? Are you there?" No answer, so I pound harder. "Artyom! Open the door! You can't just keep me here all day!" I look at the table and see that he left food for me in takeout boxes. I guess my punishment is still ongoing. Now, this really does feel like a prison.

* * *

I spend the day reading the doctor's logs and studying surgical procedures. Thank God I brought them with me last night, or else I'd be staring at the walls, going crazy. Going through every nook and cranny in Art's room only takes me thirty minutes, and I don't find a single thing. I guess even mafia men are simple creatures when it comes down to it. His items consist of black everything, spearmint gum, and exactly one watch. It's worn and has a brown leather strap, but I'm having a hard time picturing him wearing something like this. Almost as if it isn't his. I eventually give up on sleuthing and end up eating all the takeout and reading everything there is to know about head injuries. Let's hope none of these guys get a subdural hematoma. Brain surgery is definitely not my thing.

When I look at the clock, it reads 11:00 p.m., and I've officially spent the entire day alone. It has been the most uneventful day since I got to New York, and I have actually started to miss the bustle of the city. With my stupidity last night, I didn't even get to really look for Andrea or a way to contact my family. I need to think of a way to get my phone back or maybe use someone's phone to tell my family I'm okay. Maybe, with good behavior, Art will let me... I gag at that thought. I have to be on my best behavior to maybe talk to my family members. What has my life turned into?

I finally get up from the couch and angrily walk toward the door, pounding on it out of frustration. "Open the door, you mother—" I turn the handle, and the door easily opens. I stare at it, dumbfounded, and wonder how long it's been open for. Maybe Alec took pity on me and opened it. I hold the cool brass knob and push the door out a bit more, peering out into the hall. Empty and quiet. It doesn't seem like the club is open tonight, so I put on my sneakers and see if I can make my way to and from the operating room on my own. I wander around aimlessly once I get down to the basement; it feels like a maze. As I pass all the apartment doors, I wonder if any of the other guys live here too. What could Artyom be hiding behind these walls? I stop in front of a door and reach out, turning the knob. Locked. I try the next door, locked as well. I go up and down the halls, trying each door, curiosity getting the best of me. The last door I try before giving up creaks open. I look around to see if anyone is here, watching me. I push it all the way open with my foot, afraid of what might be in there.

The apartment is dark except for one light in the middle

of the living room. I walk in, my head screaming to get the hell out of here, but my damn legs keep moving. The room is totally bare except for a wooden chair directly beneath the light. As I approach it, I see that the chair is covered in dried blood. Panic begins to rise within me. This place looks a lot like a torture chamber, which is the last place I should be in right now. I begin to turn around, but something catches my eye: a tray of different kinds of tools lay near the kitchen counter. I edge closer, close enough to see the tools: knives, pliers, and then two severed gray-white fingers in the sink. My throat locks. I clap a hand over my mouth and force the swallow.

I've seen a number of severed appendages and limbs while working in the trauma unit, but none have been because of me. I'm starting to think this was set up for me to stumble upon and see. To learn my lesson. I turn and run toward the door, but when I get to it, I see Artyom at the entrance, and my feet instantly stop. He slowly walks in and closes the door, locking us inside.

"How did you find me?" My voice is shaky. His eyes dart to the little red blinking dot in the upper left corner of the room. Of course, there's a camera in here.

I back up. "What is this place?" I ask, already knowing the answer.

He walks toward me slowly until I back up into something hard. "Sit," he commands, his voice low but demanding. My heart feels like it's going to explode out of my chest and onto his face, adding to all the blood that is already crusting the room.

"Is this because of last night? I, uh, didn't know that..." I stutter. I crossed the line yesterday, and now he's angry and

I'm in deep, deep shit. I feel my hands begin to tremble at my sides.

He walks toward me, and I lean back until I lose balance and fall into the blood-crusted chair.

"You let him touch you, *kroshka*," he says softly.

I blink away tears that are seconds away from spilling out. "Jealous?" I ask, my voice betraying me. I'm terrified. I look up at him, pleading. He looks like the Grim Reaper dressed in all black, here to take my soul.

He kneels until we're face-to-face. "Unless you want to be one of the dozens of girls who are drugged and locked in a cage to fuck, I'd stay far away from that piece of shit."

"And you're any different? How do I know there aren't women in cages here?" I spit back, my fingers going numb from squeezing the armchair, feeling the ragged nail marks on my fingertips.

He looks at me, and his eyes harden. "I don't deal in sex trafficking, Petrovna. I run two things, paper and protection. You should count yourself lucky."

"Oh, I definitely feel lucky," I reply, dripping with sarcasm.

"Was my dad held in this room too?" I narrow my eyes at him, anger seeping out of me like blood from a wound as I remember that my father was taken and held somewhere for at least a week until I found him. Was he beaten? Starved? Will I be?

He stands up slowly, his eyes still on mine. He brings his fingers to my chin and lifts it so I'm looking at him. "Yes," he says through gritted teeth. "People like you and your father need to remember that bad people exist."

"Oh, don't worry about that, being locked up in this place with you is reminder enough."

We stare at each other for a long time, his lips twitching with either amusement or anger; I'm not sure which.

He reaches down and takes my hand, pulling me up until I have to crane my neck to see him. "You need to thank whatever God you pray to that you're in my bed, *kroshka*, and not Nico's. If he touches you again, there will be nothing left of him when I'm through. Now go back up to our room and stay there until you're needed."

I want to be stronger; I want to tell him to go fuck himself, but his commanding voice reverberates through me, and I submit to him willingly. I don't want to be in this room a second longer.

I get back to the apartment and scrub my hands raw from all the crusted blood under my fingernails. His words keep going round in my head, and I try to make sense of them. I've underestimated everyone I've met here. Roman and Lev are gangsters through and through, no matter how normal a life they seem to have outside of this. They will do what they are told to do. Nico from the other night is also one of them, but apparently, he's worse. If what Artyom says is true, he deals in sex trafficking and hurts a lot of women. I shudder at the possibility of ever meeting him outside of this place. Somewhere I'm not protected. Is that what I am, though? Protected? In the home of a mafia man. I sit on the couch and curl up into a ball, thinking of all the people who have been locked in that room, strapped to that chair, and begging to be set free. I close my eyes, willing the images to leave my mind, wishing for sleep to take over, but it never does.

16

Artyom

She looked at me like I was some sort of monster, her eyes full of fear. I should want her to see me that way, my true self. But something starts to eat at me the second she walks out of this godforsaken room. I knew she'd try to wander, and after what happened last night, I wanted her to see what men like me are capable of, what could happen if she ended up in the wrong hands. Nico's hands. I slam my fist into the wall hard enough to split the skin. Blood trails down my arm, but I don't stop. I keep going until I can't see Nico's hands on her anymore. Until I can convince myself she's where she belongs. With me.

When I woke up this morning, I knew she'd become my weakness. Someone I can't control myself around. Someone I don't want to share. And that makes things really fucking difficult, because I need her here for my men, not slipping under my skin every time she looks at me.

I move to the sink and rinse the blood from my hand. The room around me is a wreck, but it's staged that way. I had one of my guys leave it messy on purpose. I'd never let a place like this stay exposed; it's too much of a liability. I pull out my phone and call Alec. He answers on the first ring, like always.

"Have the room wiped. I'm done here," I say.

"I'll call in the guys," he replies, then hangs up. Thank God for cleaners, because I can't stand the smell of bleach. I step out and hear the lock slide into place behind me. It's automatic and only I can shut it off. I glance at my watch and see that it's midnight. The club's closed tonight, so I head upstairs, hoping she's asleep because I don't think I can take that look in her eyes again.

I make my way upstairs, dragging it out. If she thinks this is easy for me, she's dead wrong. I don't even remember the last time I felt ashamed of what I've done or what I am. My whole life, I've been hard, controlling, and protective of what's mine. And she is mine.

I open the door quietly. The place is silent, the only sound coming from the wind outside. I sigh, exhausted. I lean against the door, take off my shoes, and set them down softly. I should get cleaned up. I fucking reek of metal and blood, but my body won't move in that direction until I've seen her, safe and in bed. I step into the moonlit bedroom and stop cold. The bed is perfectly made. Lena's nowhere in sight. My heart stutters. I turn and head straight for the bathroom, shoving the door open so hard it slams against the wall. It's empty. Panic crashes through me as I remember that I unlocked the door earlier, but didn't lock it again when she came back. She could be anywhere, somewhere in this building, or outside for all I know. I tear through the apartment, every nerve in my body on fire, until I hear her voice, low and annoyed, coming from the couch.

"I didn't run away, if that's what you're thinking," she says.

I close my eyes and let out a breath, my pulse starting to slow. I think about turning around, heading back to the bedroom, but my feet are already carrying me toward her. She's scowling when I reach her, and I almost laugh. A scowl is so much better than fear in those beautiful eyes. A second later, she's sitting up and grabbing my hand.

"What the hell happened?" she asks, staring at my still-bleeding knuckles.

I'd almost forgotten about that. Her fingers are silk against mine, soft and grounding. For a moment, I don't feel a single fucking thing. This is what she does: takes the pain away just by being near.

"Does it hurt?" she asks, her expression shifting from annoyance to worry. For me.

"No," I say. "I'm fine."

She studies the wound for another second, then gets up and jogs to the kitchen. I watch her go, fighting a smile. She comes back with a wet rag in her hand, reaching for me again. No hesitation. No flinching. She just takes my hand like she's done it a hundred times, like it's the easiest thing in the world, and presses the rag to my knuckles. I watch her like she's been sent from heaven to convert me, and I'm one breath away from falling to my knees.

"I don't think you need stitches," she says, focused. "But I should wrap it up and clean it properly with alcohol. Whatever wall you hit, left paint fragments in your wound."

"There's vodka in the fridge," I say.

She sighs and tugs me toward the kitchen. As she opens the fridge, she mutters, "Of course you have vodka."

Then, without warning, she pours it straight over my knuckles. I don't even flinch because she is just that distracting.

She looks up at me, eyes narrowing slightly, like maybe she wanted it to hurt.

"Maybe it's expired," she says dryly.

I laugh, and it surprises us both. Her lips twitch, and a smile slips out before she can stop it. A second later, she clears her throat.

"I'll get the bandages. I saw a first aid kit in the bathroom earlier."

I go sit on the couch, letting my body sag into the cushions for the first time all day. When she comes back, she sits beside me and holds out her hand, waiting. I place mine in hers without a second thought. She wraps it carefully, her fingers sure and gentle. When she's finished, she clears her throat but doesn't move. It takes me a second to realize what she's waiting for, then I look down. I'm still holding her hand, my thumb tracing her skin like I've done it a thousand times before. I let go slowly, dragging it out, my eyes locked on hers the entire time.

"Thank you," I finally say.

She doesn't respond, just gives a small nod and turns away, curling up on the couch. I reach for the remote and turn on the TV, trying to remember the last time I sat anywhere and watched a show or just existed in a room that wasn't soaked in blood or strategy. As the apartment fills with voices from the screen, I see her start to relax. Her shoulders loosen and her breathing slows. Eventually, her body shifts until she's lying beside me, feet almost touching my leg. Just a hair's distance away. It feels so normal it almost hurts. I lean into it anyway, trying to believe just for a second that this is real.

We sit there in silence for nearly an hour. No words. No tension. Just the soft flicker of the TV and her steady presence beside me. Her eyes finally flutter shut, too heavy to fight anymore, and she slips into sleep. The room grows still, almost peaceful, but of course, peace in my world never lasts too long.

My phone buzzes in my pocket. I pull it out and glance at the screen. It's Alec. I sigh and answer, my voice low, *"Da?"*

"You need to get down here. It's Mike. Bring the girl." Then he hangs up. A second later, a coded text comes through. I read it once, and that's all I need.

17

Lena

I feel warm fingers caressing my cheek. "Wake up, *kroshka*, your job starts now."

I get up abruptly, almost knocking our heads together. "What? What do you mean?" I ask frantically.

"We need to get you to the operating room. One of my men was shot," he tells me, his eyes unreadable. He offers his hand, and I take it. When I get up, he pulls me toward the door, and we're once again back in that elevator together.

"What happened? Who shot him?" I ask.

"It doesn't matter, Lena, just attend to him like you would someone who came into the hospital."

"I usually know a little bit more about my patient, Art." My tone comes out sharper than I intended.

He pauses for a moment, like he's surprised I called him that. I realize this is the first time I've called him Art to his face. I tell myself it's just easier this way. It's definitely not because we're friends or anything else for that matter.

"His name is Mikhail. He was shot in the shoulder with a nine-millimeter Glock. It looks like it went straight through.

That's all I can give you."

The elevator doors open, and we speed-walk to the operating room. Once I get in, I'm in my element. I approach the table and see a large man lying on it, his hand covering his shoulder. He's grimacing and looks like he's in a lot of pain.

"Hi, Mikhail, I'm Lena. Can you tell me what happened?" I ask him while looking at his wound.

He looks back at Artyom like he's looking for permission. "I was shot," he says, grimacing.

"Yep. I got that rundown. Anything else I should know?"

"It hurts like a bitch." He winces again.

Clearly, I'm not going to get much out of him. "Alright, I need someone to keep pressure on his wound while I get everything I need." I look at Artyom, and he comes over with a clean towel, holding it at the wound. The blood soaks the towel in seconds. *Shit.* "He's bleeding too much. I need you to put your finger in there. That might be the only way to stop the bleeding right now." I go straight to the cabinet full of street drugs and look for the blue pills I found the other day. I'm not sure how they got fentanyl, but it might be the only thing that will help this guy while I basically perform surgery on his shoulder. I look back and see Artyom just watching me.

"Now, Art! Before he bleeds out," I shout, and instantly hear Mikhail scream out in pain. I crush up the fentanyl and walk over to him. "Without any bags of fluid or morphine drip, this is the best I can do." I prop up his head with my arm. "Snort this. It'll hit you faster than swallowing it."

"Fuck it," he says and snorts the powder like he's done it before. A few seconds later, I see his eyes constrict, telling me it started working. This guy will be on cloud nine for the next couple of hours.

"Art, I'll need to get in there and feel around for the vessel to see if I can stitch it up. When you take your finger out, I'll take your place. Please keep an eye on his pulse. Put your fingers on his wrist, feel his pulse, and count." I look at him to see if he's overwhelmed, but all I see is calm, like he's been here before. We lock eyes for a second. He nods at me and then takes his finger out. Blood starts gushing, and I instantly take his place, putting my finger in and feeling for the vessel.

"I can feel it, but at this point, I don't think it would be safe to stitch it up. He's bleeding too much. I need you to get me a rounded knife and heat it with a lighter."

He moves to the set of knives on the tray beside me and takes out his lighter. He takes the dullest knife, heats it under the flame, and quickly gives it to me. I take out my finger and put the knife in, scorching his flesh. The smell of burnt skin fills the air, and I try not to gag. I could never get used to that smell. I've seen other doctors cauterize wounds before, but I've never done it myself. For him to trust me to do this on my own is insane. One wrong move and this guy can bleed out and die. I peer up at Art, and I can tell he's holding his breath just like I am. I let it out when I see the bleeding has finally stopped. I take the knife out and check his pulse.

"Are you doing okay?" I ask Mikhail.

"Mm," is all I hear.

I open his eyelids and check his pupils. They're still constricted. I look at the time and only thirty minutes have passed, so we still have time until the drugs start to wear off. I spend the next hour cleaning and sewing up the wound as best I can. When I'm done, I almost give myself a high five. I look up at Art and smile, feeling triumphant. My smile fades as soon as I see his eyes; it's like they're looking right through me, making me feel utterly exposed. No one in my inner circle has ever seen me in my element before. I'm not embarrassed or anything, it's just I sometimes feel like being in this setting brings out an alter ego, one that is just for me.

"Do you mind getting him a cold towel and putting it on his forehead? It'll help bring down his fever until I can get him antibiotics." Once I finish patching up his shoulder, I make sure I cover all my bases twice and then again. I feel as though this man's life is tied to mine, and I sure as hell want to live.

After checking his blood pressure, I give him antibiotics, which I noticed are prescribed for horses, but beggars can't be choosers, I guess.

"You're a champ, you know that?" I say.

"Thanks, Doc. I'm still high as a kite, though."

"Yeah, that'll pass soon. When it does, take one of these pills morning and night. You did great. I want to see you here tomorrow so I can check on you, okay?"

He smiles. "Sure, Doc."

Artyom comes over and puts his hand on my shoulder. "His brother will stay with him tonight. You should go and get some rest."

"Alright, there's not much I can do now. Have his brother call me immediately if his fever spikes, okay?" He nods and takes my hand, leading me out of the room.

I still feel the adrenaline pumping through me when we leave. I always get a high after working on something big. It feels like I can do anything. When we walk into the elevator, I feel Artyom's eyes on me, and I realize he hasn't said a word the entire time I was working on the wound. Two hours of him watching me and not saying anything.

"I'm sorry," I say, "for last night." I eye him warily.

"What exactly are you sorry for, Lena?" He raises an eyebrow.

I sigh, exasperated. He's definitely going to make me work for this. "I didn't know he wasn't one of your guys."

He stares at me for a moment and then comes closer. "One of my guys or not, what did I say I'd do if someone were to touch you?" He asks, his voice stern.

I hold his stare, too high to cower. "You'd break their fingers and send them to me."

He moves in even closer until I can almost hear his heartbeat. "Who is the only one allowed to touch you, *kroshka*?"

My eyes go wide, surprised at his question, while my body hums with need, with the truth that I've wanted him to touch me since the moment I saw him. "You," I whisper.

Whatever restraint he has left breaks the second I say it, and his lips come crashing down on mine. His warm hands press me to him, and I sigh against his mouth like I've been waiting for this exact moment my entire life. We kiss slowly at first, drawing them out, relishing the taste. The moment I take his lips between mine and suck, our kisses become heavy. I open my mouth and let his tongue in, dancing with mine. Our bodies become fused, and I feel every hard, muscular inch of him. His hands roam from my face to the small of my back, grinding into me. I let out a moan, needing more of him, needing to see exactly what I do to him underneath his clothes. We kiss desperately, grabbing onto each other. When the elevator dings, he picks me up, carries me to the apartment door, and kicks it open.

Once we're inside, he sets me down in the entryway, breathing heavily as he takes off his shoes and mine. As soon as the last one comes off, I bring his mouth back to mine, greed taking over. I fumble with his shirt, trying to undo the buttons quickly. His hands go to the top of my jeans and unbutton them.

"Take them off," I beg, my skin feeling as though it will burst into flames if my clothes stay on a second longer.

He breaks our kiss and sinks to the floor, taking my jeans with him. I run my fingers through his hair, liking him down there. He looks up at me and moves my panties to the side with his finger. "You're so wet for me, *kroshka*," he says. My hips impatiently sway forward, and he smiles in response, holding my hips steady and diving his tongue into my core.

"Fuck. Me," I moan in ecstasy.

He makes a noise of approval. A pure animalistic growl, a predator enjoying his meal.

My moans become louder as he devours me until I feel myself coming apart, holding his head between my legs, begging him not to stop. "I'm going to…" I pant. "Don't stop."

He growls against my skin, then I feel his fingers stretching me, filling me just the right amount. I ride out my orgasm panting and spasming around him. He doesn't stop devouring me until I tug on his hair, needing more.

"I need you to fuck me. Now," I demand.

He rises and kisses me hard, letting me taste myself on his tongue, then leads me to the bedroom. As soon as we get to the bed, my hands go to his waistband, sliding a hand inside, needing to feel him. When my fingers touch the tip, I feel its wetness and lick my lips. Looking up at him, I see his breathing pick up as he pins me to the bed with his body. My tongue darts out, licking up his neck, and when I get to his mouth, he takes my tongue and sucks on it. As soon as our lips part, a hint of clarity snakes its way into my mind. This is a bad idea. A really bad idea. I shouldn't want him the way I do; I shouldn't crave him so intensely that I forget all the red flags. Feeling his cock at my entrance, all the warning signs disappear, and all I see is him and me. Two people who crave each other, who want at least one semblance of normalcy. And what's more normal than this?

"No one touches you except for me, *kroshka,*" he says as he pushes into me. We both let out a moan, and he begins to pump faster. His muscles ripple with each thrust, and I cling to him, not wanting him to stop. "I will break more than just fingers next time. Do you understand?" he says against my lips.

I want to believe he's just saying that in the moment, but I know he means it. Everything in me knows he will do just that if anyone ever touches me in a way he or I don't like. In this moment right now, that thought doesn't frighten me; it excites me in every possible way.

"Yes," I breathe out as he pushes into me harder. "Yes, yes, yes," I say over and over again until the sight of him sliding into me drives me off the edge. I feel the orgasm coming at me like a wave until it crashes over me, tears rolling down my cheeks. He's close; I can feel him throbbing within me. "You're beautiful, kroshka. Too fucking beautiful to belong to anyone but me," he murmurs low and possessive. Before I can even register what he said, he slows down. Everything in me begins to protest.

"Don't you dare stop," I say, wrapping my legs around him tighter. I feel him smile against my neck, and a second later, he brings my legs to my chest, driving into me harder, until he throws his head back, and I feel his release all over me. We both stare at each other, panting, still coming down from the high, glistening in sweat. It takes everything in me not to pull him into me once more and do that all over again.

18

Artyom

Six days earlier

I feel numb. Like morphine is steadily dripping into my veins, numbing everything inside of me. Alec treads lightly around me these days like anything he says could set me off, but I can't explode if I'm numb. I hear a soft knock on the door, and then Alec pushes it open.

"The car is ready."

I stare at my computer screen, reading the same email for the thousandth time. "I don't remember calling for a car," I say without looking up.

He sighs softly, so softly I barely hear it. "You should be there."

"I have work to do, Alec, so if that's all, you can go." I take the papers scattered across my desk and shuffle through them again, hoping he will get the hint. He stands there for a moment longer, burning a hole in my head.

"I didn't mean as Boss. I meant to be there as his brother." With that, he turns and leaves.

Fucking Alec.

When I'm confident the building is empty, I go to my room. I shower and put on the black suit I wore to my mother and father's funeral. I need to remember to burn this suit. As I head out, I pass a mirror and stop, taking a good look. I also need to remember to break every single mirror in this place.

I knew the business cars would be taken since all the men in the Brotherhood were going to the funeral. I don't mind, though. I need to get out and walk, to think, and I can't do that with everyone watching me all the time. The closest train station is twenty minutes away, which will give me some time.

The closer I get to the cemetery, the less numb I feel. By the time I reach the train station, I feel as though I'd been cut open, bleeding out for everyone to see. It is a risk coming here alone, unarmed. They could get to me now; someone could see me right now, call up their guys, and they could finish the job because it was me they wanted to kill, not Ivan.

I look around the train station, not because I'm scared, but because I want to see it coming. I want to see who has the balls to try to kill Artyom Volkhov right after killing my brother. I'm not afraid of dying. God, I know I probably won't last into my fifties, but what I am afraid of is losing. Losing anything that's mine. But life already took the last thing I loved, so what's left to fear?

I look around frantically, slowly losing my mind, and then I see… *her*. I want to look away, but I can't. I should be worried that she's seen me or maybe recognizes me, but I'm not. Her eyes are like mine. They're heavy. Not tired, not dull, but weighted. Like she's carrying the same kind of storm I am. The kind you can't put into words. The kind that lives in your bones. And then I feel it: the absence of pain. The pain that's always there, clawing at the back of my ribs, is gone. Just like that. There's silence in my head for the first time in years.

I sit there, frozen, watching her like she already belongs to me. Her eyes rip away from mine, and it takes me a moment to realize her train is coming. A slow panic settles in as my body goes cold and rigid, as I realize she's about to leave. I hate it. I hate the way the distance grows between us with every second. Every part of me protests, and I nearly throw myself onto the tracks just to get to her. The train barrels in, fast and merciless, and instinct is the only thing that keeps me from moving. She doesn't even know what she's doing to me. I watch the train steal her from me, and that's exactly what it feels like. A theft. And I let it happen. As the last car disappears, I make a silent vow: you're mine, kroshka. You just don't know it yet. I'll see you again. And next time, I'm not letting you go.

19

Lena

When I wake up, I'm alone, spread out on the bed. I look for any sign he's still here, but I know in my gut he left a long time ago. I can't seem to picture him in the mornings, waking up in each other's arms and making breakfast. That life doesn't fit with his. *My* life doesn't fit with his, and he knows it. *Good,* I lie to myself. I wouldn't even know what to say after a night like that. A night where we connected in a way I've only dreamed about. A night of desperate sex minutes after working illegally on a gunshot wound. I shake my head, trying to get the images out of my mind. His words last night excited me, but now regret starts to creep in and settle in the pit of my stomach. What was I even thinking? I know men like him. They're possessive and domineering. They want what they can't have, and when they finally get it, they never let go. I can never be his. Not if I ever want a normal life after this.

With that thought in mind, I get dressed and go find my purse, shuffling through it until I find the circular pink pill dispenser. Thank you, Mother Nature, for giving me abnormal periods so I can be put on birth control. I am entirely in your debt right now. I take the pill and stride out of the bedroom, going into the living room where I see Alec standing awkwardly, looking at all the clothes scattered on the floor from last night.

"Uh, hey, Alec. What are you doing here?" I ask, quickly picking up my bra and chucking it into the bedroom.

"Ms. Petrovna." He nods. "I'm here to take you to the operating room."

Right, how could I forget about Mikhail? I guess I was expecting Art to take me there today. Or maybe even give me an update on him. I wait a minute to see if Alec has a message for me from Artyom, maybe some sort of explanation. But he says nothing.

"I'm ready," I say, putting on my shoes and ignoring the shame building in me.

By the time we get to the basement, I've decided it's best we see very little of each other. No attachments. Especially when it concerns the devil. As we enter the operating room, I hear male voices laughing.

"Oh shit, hey, Doc!" Mikhail says, lifting his chin to see me better from the couch at the far end of the room.

"Hey, how are you feeling?" I ask, picking up the antibiotic bottle to check he's taken his dose today.

"Not bad considering I had a hole in my shoulder less than twenty-four hours ago," he chuckles. "This is my brother, Rob." He points to the large man beside him.

"Hi, I'm Lena," I say, extending my arm.

"Rob," he says, making it a point not to shake my hand. I'm guessing this guy is not very happy about me being the new doctor. *As am I, dude.*

"Can you sit up for me? I want to check your wound and clean you up a bit," I say, putting on gloves.

"Sure, Doc. But can you call me Mike? It sounds like my mother is calling me home from the playground every time you say my name." He sits up, groaning.

I chuckle. "Sure, as long as you stop calling me doc." I go over to him and uncover his wound. I am relieved to see exactly what I wanted to see, some redness and swelling, which means it's healing and not dead and rotting.

"Artyom would have my balls if I called you anything other than Doc," he laughs.

Not only is no one allowed to touch me, but they're also not allowed to call me by my name? I feel like I'm in a bubble.

"Looks great. You've been taking the antibiotics, right?"

"Yeah, but what I really want are those blues," he says, pointing to the fentanyl on the counter.

Maybe I should've put that away, but then again, this isn't my practice, and anything in here is easily accessible to anyone.

"I'd stay away from those. If you can get your hands on some oxycodone, that would be fine; just ten milligrams every six hours. No more than that." I give him the same look I'd give my brother.

He laughs and agrees, fist bumping me. "Where you from, Doc? You don't seem like a native."

I pause, not sure if I should disclose where I live. However, keeping anything from these guys doesn't mean anything because Art already knows everything about me.

"Uh, born and raised here; currently living in Arizona."

"No shit? Rob and I visited there when we were younger. The palm trees are dope. Never seen any until that trip."

I smile. He weirdly reminds me of my brother. "Yeah, they

are pretty dope. Can't wait to go back," I add without thinking. I look up at Mike, and he looks at me with pity in his eyes. Here's this guy who lives a life of crime, and he's pitying *me*? I look at Rob, and he just stands there like I'm the one to fear. Like I'm unwelcome here in their world. I don't let it bother me, though. I won't be here long, and I let that thought soothe me as I finish up the conversation. "Well, you're all set, keep taking your antibiotics, and don't do anything crazy. I'll check on you again tomorrow."

"Thanks, Doc," Mike says just as Alec walks in and tells the men they are needed in Artyom's office. As they leave, I can't help but feel a little at peace. It was nice to have a normal conversation with someone and not feel every emotion all at once. A picture of Art between my legs fills my mind, and I groan out of frustration because this has been happening all day.

Alec eyes me, confused. "Sorry," I mutter. "Can I actually go back to the apartment alone this time? No surprises, I promise."

He hesitates, then tells me to go straight there and reminds me of the directions.

"Alec, I'll be fine. If I get lost, just find me on one of your stupid cameras, I know you guys have everywhere," I say, giving him a little bit of sass.

He gives me one of his famous tight smiles and heads out after the guys. I spend some time cleaning up and taking inventory of the place. Writing down everything I'd need if there were another emergency like the other night. I add an assistant at the top of the list and then cross it out, not really wanting to add anyone else into this mess. I put the list in my pocket to give to Alec when I see him, because I can't really think about talking to Art right now.

After closing the door and heading toward the elevator, a flash of someone going past the other side of the hall gets my attention. I know the club is open tonight, but no one is allowed to enter through this side of the building, not unless… I jog to the other side of the hall, rounding the corner, and see a familiar man walking, his back to me. Before I can chicken out, I shout his name. Lev turns around, and his face instantly pales. I almost look back to see if someone is standing behind me. It's like he's seen a ghost. I'm not entirely elated to see him either, but I'll take what I can get. I haven't seen Roman since the club, and I don't think Art will let me back in for a while. As I come closer, he moves toward me, still staring like I've stunned him somehow.

"Lena?" he asks, looking around warily.

"Hey, yeah. Um, I won't keep you long or anything, but I need a favor." I chew on my lower lip, feeling nervous. His eyebrows shoot up in surprise, but before he can say no, I just come out with it. "Could you send a message to Roman for me? I haven't been able to talk to him or Andrea in days," I say, hoping he will do this for me.

"Uh, Lena… I don't think I can do that," he says, rubbing his neck.

"Lev, you left me alone in the lion's den. You owe me this. Please?" I beg, trying the guilt trip route.

"I'm sorry, Lena, I'm new to the uh… group and didn't know what to say that night." He pauses. "Are you okay?" He scans my body like he's looking for bruises. And what if I had been hurt? Would he even do anything about it? Just how much of a monster is Artyom that his men think he would hurt a woman?

"I'm fine," I say, feeling a little on edge now. "But I really need you to deliver a message for me."

He looks around nervously. "Okay, I'll tell Roman, and whatever he does with the message is on him."

"Thank you," I sigh, feeling hopeful. "Please tell him to bring Andrea to the club. I really need to talk to her and tell her I'm okay. I won't say anything about what I'm doing here, I just need to see a friend."

He nods, and we stand there for a minute, both feeling awkward. "Well, I'll, uh… get going," I say, turning around to leave.

Once I return to the apartment, I'm greeted with takeout boxes on the kitchen counter, but I don't see Artyom anywhere. I settle in on the couch and turn on the TV. Hopefully, something on this thing can help take my mind off last night. I open the take-out boxes, inhaling the scent of all my favorite foods: pierogi with sour cream, puff pastry filled with potatoes, cabbage, and cheese, and two slices of pizza the size of my face. I dig in without giving it a second thought and stuff my stomach to the brim. This is my favorite thing about New York. The food tastes so authentic you'd think your mother made it. As I lie there on the couch with the TV on, I decide to sleep here because the thought of sleeping next to Artyom after what we did last night makes me feel really uneasy, especially since I haven't seen him all day. It's for the best, I think, as I close my eyes.

20

Artyom

I feel the tremors in my hands once again. I replay the recording on my screen once, twice, ten times over, trying to decode whatever Lena and Lev were saying. My cameras don't pick up sound very well, so I'm only able to see what's happening and use my imagination for the rest. And my imagination is sucking the life out of me. Last night's events have left me feeling things I never wanted to feel. The need to have her close but also as far away as possible is overwhelming. I ultimately chose the latter; I always do, always for the better of others. I need to drown myself in work rather than in her pussy. I can still smell her on my fingertips and feel her on my cock.

The image on my screen snaps me out of it and brings me back to where I'm supposed to be. I need to keep her away from me. I need to keep her happy but away. Whatever Lev said to her made her happy, and finding out what it was is consuming me. I pick up my phone and dial Alec, and he picks up in one ring, always one ring. I start talking before he can say anything, feeling impatient.

"Have Lev come in," I say without explaining.

"He'll be there." We hang up, and I stupidly continue staring at the computer screen, replaying the same moment when he made her smile. Did I misread their first interaction? No. After our night together, I know what her eyes look like when they're filled with desire, and when she looks at Lev, it's definitely not that. So, what *does* she want from him?

There's a knock on the door, and then it swings open, Alec coming in first and then Lev behind him. Just the sight of him makes me feel bad for bringing him in. He fears me, that's for sure. Lev waits for me to speak first, nervously looking around the room.

"What did you promise Lena?" I get to the point. I wouldn't put it past her to guilt-trip him into bringing her a phone or getting her out of here for a few hours.

His eyes widen. "Boss?"

"In the hall, she stopped you. What did she say?" I don't mean to sound possessive, but I do.

"She wanted me to get a message to Roman. She, uh… wants him to bring his girl here."

That's all? So she didn't try to leave? "And were you going to tell him?"

"Yes," he says, straightening.

Good. He's growing some balls. I sit back in my chair, pretending to think about what he said, letting him come to whatever conclusions he wants.

"Do whatever she wants," I finally say.

He hesitates for a beat, then clears his throat. "Yes, boss."

"You can go." He turns around and leaves faster than I've ever seen anyone leave this room. I sit here thinking about what he said, that she just wanted to see her friend. Not a phone, and not a way out. I sigh, feeling an enormous weight lift off my shoulders.

I glance at the clock and see it's now 2:00 a.m. She's probably asleep right now, in my bed. I can get my shit and get out without even waking her. I decide to head up and do just that.

When I open the door, I see the TV on and my angel curled into a ball on the couch. Everything in me stills for a moment. It would be sinful to disrupt peace like this. I should leave, shove my shit in my bag, and get the hell out of here, but my legs go the opposite direction, as always. The need inside of me grows bigger: the need to be close to her, to hold her, and have her take my pain away. The selfish fuck that I am, I pick her up without even thinking and carry my angel back to bed.

21

Lena

I'm woken up by Artyom lifting me from the couch and pressing me to his chest while he carries me to the bedroom. "What are you doing?" I ask, my voice groggy. "Taking you to bed, *kroshka*," he says, like he's done it a million times.

"I was already sleeping. You can just take the bed, it's fine." I try wriggling out of his arms. He keeps walking, not fazed by anything I'm doing or saying. As we get into the room, he sets me down gently and begins to undress. As if he senses the tension in my body, he moves to the other side of the bed and sits down, facing away from me.

"I didn't bring you here for sex, Lena. I just want to sleep next to you." He lies down with an exasperated sigh.

I hesitate for a minute and then reluctantly lie down next to him, closing my eyes from embarrassment. We lie there listening to each other breathing. I finally get up the courage to turn and face him. He's looking up at the ceiling, deep in thought, and I take this opportunity to really look at him. He looks solemn in his expression, dark circles cover his eyes, and for the first time, he's not clean-shaven. He looks like he's had a rough day, and I get a gnawing urge to touch and comfort him, but I know I can't. That's not my role in this. I'm not his lover or girlfriend. I'm nothing, and that's exactly what I want to stay as.

I focus on the tattoo on his chest, the V tattooed in Russian. It's bigger than the one on Roman's and Lev's forearms, and I also notice it has a quote underneath, which I can't really make out.

"You're staring," he says without looking at me.

"Yes," I breathe out. He stays silent. "What does your tattoo say?" I ask, desperate to fill the silence.

"It says duty above all else." His head turns to look at me.

"Did you get it when you took over?"

He hesitates. "No."

"When did you get it?" I ask, genuinely curious.

"When I turned thirteen."

"What? But you were just a kid." I say, horrified.

"It was important for my father that I knew what my future held," he says, turning onto his side, fully facing me.

"I'm sorry." And I mean it. I can't imagine what his childhood was like. What his parents were like, to make their thirteen-year-old get a tattoo.

"Don't be. With or without this tattoo, this was always going to be my future."

"You're probably right. I'm just sorry you didn't get to choose." I look at him.

He pauses and then says, "There's not much I've been able to choose in my life. Being in my position isn't a choice, it's a privilege."

I roll my eyes at the last part. "Close your eyes." I don't know why I decide to keep going, why I don't just turn around and go to sleep, but in this moment, it feels like we're in our very own bubble, one where we can be honest with each other.

He looks at me, confused, and then closes his eyes.

"If you could choose, what would your life look like?" I ask.

He sighs. "I don't even know where to begin."

"Well, where would you want to live?"

"Here." Not even a second of hesitation.

"Here? As in Brooklyn?" My voice hitches amusingly, and I immediately rein it back in.

"Yes."

"You can choose any place in the world, and you choose here?" I push up onto my elbow to see him better. I can't think of anyone who would stay here willingly if they could live anywhere. I find myself wondering why and if he's even been anywhere else.

"This is my home," he says matter-of-factly.

I sigh and lie back down. "It used to be mine, too. But lately, I just feel so lost here. It feels foreign somehow." It's so weird, actually. I spent my entire childhood here, but I can't wait to go back home, not just because I've been forced to work illegally and live with a mafia boss. Obviously, that doesn't help things, but even before that, the memories just tainted everything, and I couldn't wait to escape.

"But it feels like home in Arizona?" he asks.

"Yes, I think it does. For me, home is wherever my family is, where we're happy." The silence grows between us, and I begin to chew on my lip nervously.

"What made you hate it here so much?" he asks a minute later.

I shift my body, suddenly feeling on edge. I debate telling

him about Dima, going back and forth with myself about whether I even want to know. Maybe my hatred for this place stems from that incident and the fact that I never got closure. Maybe I need this. I sigh and turn my head to look at him. His face is soft. Somehow, the moonlight has lightened his features, making him look angelic, making me feel safe enough to tell him everything.

"When I was younger, a boy I knew went missing. His name was Dima," I say, my heart pounding in my chest. "It wasn't so much that he went missing that scarred me. It was the fact that everyone pretended like he didn't even exist in the first place. His mom went crazy looking for him, but no one helped her. It felt like they all knew but couldn't say anything."

His brows are drawn. "And the cops?" he asks, already knowing the answer.

"Did nothing," I say, closing my eyes and building up the courage to say this next part, no going back now. "He had your tattoo on his wrist." I search his eyes for answers.

Artyom sighs deeply and pauses before saying anything, almost as if giving me time to prepare.

"Dimitry Aronov was one of the boys my father hired before he passed. He was young, too young to work for us, but my father was worried I wouldn't be able to choose my own men once he was gone," he says, shifting uncomfortably.

I stare at him wide-eyed, waiting for him to keep going. When he doesn't, I reach out and touch his arm, pleading for him to tell me more. I can feel him tense, then his eyes meet mine.

"When my father passed, I misjudged the amount of work and pressure that was put upon me. I sent two boys, whom I never even spoke to once, and never got to ask their names, to do a collection. I didn't care who went; I didn't care that the people who owned the shop where we were providing our services had gone broke for months. They'd had extensions even my father didn't know about. When the boys got there, I guess the owners panicked and shot them both. They barely made it back to the club."

He pauses, and I see something soft but pained passing through him. "I'm sorry, Lena, but Dima didn't make it." When he sees my expression, he sits up, sliding his legs over the bed and away from me.

"I didn't know his name until one of my men told me a woman was making trouble at the club. They brought her to my office, and that's when it clicked. He looked so much like her. I gave her the place where we buried him and money so she wouldn't talk. I remember her looking at me like I was the one to be pitied, like she saw right through me. She set the money down on my table and left without a word. I never heard from her again."

Tears slide down my cheeks and onto the pillow. I should be angry with him for so many reasons. I should yell and scream and demand… what exactly? That he change? I cannot change him or his world, but I can keep mine far away.

"Thank you for telling me," I say softly, wiping away the tears. He sits there for a while longer, looking out the window where the sky is full of stars tonight.

"I'm not a good man, Lena. Don't start changing your mind about me now," he tells me, his back to me.

I don't know what to say to that. My heart constricts and pulls me in different directions. I need more time to figure out how I feel and how I should feel. Right now, however, even though I know deep down he's right, I want to live in this ceasefire a little longer. So for now, I stay silent and reach out my hand to him once again, placing it on his back. He looks back at me, and for a moment, our eyes meet, understanding the silence. He lies back down and raises his arm slowly, his fingers brushing my hair from my cheek.

"Goodnight, Petrovna."

"Goodnight," I whisper, closing my eyes and feeling the closure washing away years of hurt and confusion.

22

Lena

Over the next few days, I barely see Artyom. He stays in his office most of the day and then goes to the club in the evening. The only time I see him is when he comes to bed at around 3:30 a.m., and if I'm being completely honest with myself, that's when I'm at peace the most. It's like my body can sense when he's home, and my eyes instantly snap open, waiting to hear the door click shut. Tonight is no different, and once again, I'm wide awake predicting all his moves. He first removes his shoes and puts them away in the closet by the door. Another click rings through the place. He then goes into the bathroom and showers for approximately seven minutes. My heart hammers on like a stalker, memorizing his every move, but I can't help it. The anticipation of him falling asleep next to me is overwhelming.

Once he enters the room, I shamelessly close my eyes, pretending to be asleep. I can't see him, but I'm almost certain he's standing by the door looking at me. I feel the most exposed at that time. I wonder if he can hear my heart pounding in my chest. I hate that I can't see him, but I can't give myself away; I can't let him see this obsession. He silently moves toward his side of the bed. The bed dips for a fraction of a second, and his scent invades my space again. Only when I can hear his breathing even out do I open my eyes and look at him, studying his facial features, trying to piece together his day, mood, and everything in between.

Each night, we sleep a little closer to each other. Sometimes, I can feel his body heat so close that I curve into it. It's magnetic, the way my body migrates toward him. It usually starts with just our legs touching, crossing each other, and testing the waters. Then our arms find each other, a hand on his chest, an arm around my waist. I blame it on the stillness, on the quiet, the warmth, the safety.

Tonight, however, feels different because my body wants more of him, his scent, his rough hands on my body. I turn to face him. We're nose-to-nose, so close I can almost taste his lips on mine. His eyes are closed, but I can hear a change in his breathing. I bring my fingers to his mouth and trace his lips, going over his sharp Cupid's bow. He opens slightly and kisses my finger. I keep it there, entranced by his mouth. He opens a little more and snakes his tongue over it. My breath hitches, and I almost let out a moan in response. His eyes open, irises wide and full of need, his jaw twitches when he sees mine are the same. I take the finger that was just in his mouth and bring it to my own, licking it as I stare at him, tasting him any way I can.

"Lena…" he growls, leaning in until our foreheads touch. "Tell me what you want," he says, inhaling deeply.

"Touch me," I say, taking his hand and leading it down my body until I reach my shorts. I feel him pause for a moment, giving me time to back out. What he doesn't know is I'm too far gone to back out. I crave him in every way, and right now, I need his touch. *Just one more time*, I tell myself. *This is the last time.*

He slides his hand with mine into my panties, not wasting another moment. When he feels the wetness, his eyes dilate, and he crashes his mouth against mine, kissing me hard, his tongue devouring me. He leaves my hand on my clit, and I circle it, feeling a bolt of pleasure shoot through me. I feel his fingers make their way to my entrance.

"Yes," I moan, pleading. Art's mouth instantly covers mine.

"Your sounds will be my undoing," he says against my mouth and pushes two fingers inside me.

"Make them again, *kroshka*, moan for me," he demands, quickly finding the spot inside me that makes me lose my breath. I can't stop my voice from growing louder, giving him what he wants. His fingers go in and out faster.

"Yes," I breathe out, "please." I shift closer, feeling him go deeper. The curve of his fingers hits just right until I'm moaning his name over and over again, pressing myself closer to him. My hands grip his arms tighter, feeling every curve of his muscles. This man is built like a Greek god, which only adds to my pleasure. My moans grow more sporadic. "Oh my god, Art, yes… yes… yes," I keep saying over and over again until I'm coming apart, shaking in his arms. He holds me, kissing every inch of my face, capturing each sound that escapes my mouth. I feel my heart rate slow, my eyelids grow heavy, and my body starts to feel like it's levitating.

"Art…" I begin to say, but he pulls me closer and kisses my forehead.

"Go to sleep, *kroshka*."

So, I inhale him one more time and drift off.

* * *

The following day and every morning after that, I wake alone, and I thank the heavens for that because what would we even say if we woke up holding each other, not wanting to let go? Would we make breakfast together and pretend we're a couple? I can see everything more clearly when we're not in this bed. The less time I spend in this damned bed, thinking about the night before, the better off I will be.

I spend most of my time in the operating room, noting things I'd need and handing them to Alec to give to Artyom. Somehow, the things I write down always appear on my desk the next day. As I look around the room, I see it's stocked with gauze, sterile syringes and tools, and even PPE, wrapped and untouched. The place even looks cleaner since I got here. I've had a few men walk in with broken noses and dislocated shoulders, but nothing major since that night, which I'm grateful for. I try to keep it professional, but I can't help but get to know some of these guys on a more personal level. They're different from what I thought they'd be.

Most are young, still in college. Sometimes, when I talk to them, I forget where I am and who they are. It feels like I'm talking to one of my brother's friends, and oddly, it feels like home. I find myself itching to ask what the hell drove them to sign their souls over to the devil.

"You're all set, Peter," I say, throwing away the bloodied gauze.

"Thanks, Doc." I make a face at him. "You should be used to it by now," he says, trying not to laugh.

I've corrected him and every other man who calls me Doc that I am *not* a doctor and, therefore, should not be called that, but of course, they don't care.

"Maybe one day, when I finally get the courage to apply to medical school and become a doctor, then I will eventually get used to it."

"Even if you quit and become a rodeo star, we will still call you Doc." He laughs at his own joke.

"Yeah, yeah," I mumble, remembering I am whatever Art says I am to these guys. "Can I ask you a question?" I say, my back to him.

"Sure, Doc."

"Why… I mean, what made you…" I stumble over my words, not knowing where I'm going with this and how to even get it out. I turn around and see him smirking, his tattooed arms crossed over his chest.

"You're almost there, Doc, just get it out."

I roll my eyes, starting to feel more at ease. "What made you want to join the Brotherhood?"

"Ah, there it is." He sighs. "I used to live in Queens, where my brother was murdered by the Italians. I wanted to get revenge on the people who did it, so I joined the Brotherhood." He says it so plainly, I find myself thinking I'd do the same.

"And did you?" My voice is low.

"Yes," he says, looking me straight in the eyes. "I lost a brother then, but Boss made sure I got a piece of him back."

We're quiet for a moment, letting his words hover between us. When I feel the tension dissipate, I pull out a bottle of pills.

"Want one?"

His mouth widens into a grin. "Never said no to an oxy, and I'm not going to start now."

I roll my eyes and hand it to him, trying to hold back my smile. "One, Peter, as needed for pain, you hear me?"

"Thanks, Doc. Gotta run, have a date with my girl." He takes the pill and downs it without water, winking at me.

I chuckle, impressed he can juggle getting punched so hard in the face he needs stitches and going on a date all in one day. I catch myself smiling as he leaves. *This is temporary, Lena,* I tell myself over and over again.

As I get up to leave and return to the apartment, I notice something hanging on the back of my chair. Something that wasn't there before. I pick it up and see a white lab coat with my name in black stitching on the front. I stare at it for a second and feel panic rising in my chest. I grip the coat and head out of the room, my footsteps heavy. Alec is standing outside, waiting for me when I swing the door open.

"I need to see him," I say, trying to hide the panic in my voice.

He senses my urgency and leads me to the big metal doors on the other side of the basement. He knocks twice and then waits to be invited in.

"Jesus," I say, annoyed, and open the door before Alec can stop me. Art looks up from his desk with an eyebrow raised, looking at Alec for answers.

"We're fine, Alec. I'll be out in a minute." My voice comes out sharp.

Art nods at Alec, giving him the okay to leave us. Once the door closes, he looks at me and gestures to the chair in front of his desk, offering me a seat like we're in some meeting, which only fuels my anger.

"I'll just stand, thanks," I say, annoyance lacing every word.

"How can I help, Petrovna?" He leans back in his chair. He's so calm it's aggravating.

"I found this in the operating room. It's embroidered with my name, Art. Why?"

"It's a gift." He folds his arms. "For tending to my men the way you have."

"This feels like more than a gift," I spit out. "It feels like you're welcoming me to my new position, a more *permanent* one." My eyes narrow on him.

"That's why you're upset? Because you think I will keep you here forever?" he says, clearly bothered by what I said.

"Yes."

"I don't buy it." He stands up and walks around his desk to me. "I think you're upset that you actually like the gift."

"Wow," I say, my eyebrows shooting up. "Unbelievable. Thank you, but no thank you. I don't need anything from you," I snarl and turn toward the door.

He steps forward and grabs my hand, pulling me back to him. "Tell me why you're really upset, *kroshka*."

I push his hands away and roll my eyes. "What makes you think there's anything else? Don't pretend to know me, Art. We might share the same bed, but clearly, we are on different pages here." I walk toward the door again, ready to be done with this conversation.

He grabs my waist, bringing me in so close my chest is touching his. At this proximity, I can feel both of our hearts beating so hard that I feel as though they will explode.

"Oh, we're on the same page, Petrovna. When you moan my name, I'm there too. When we fall asleep panting and covered in each other's sweat, I'm also there. I don't pretend to know you, *kroshka*. I do know you. I know your favorite food is anything your mother makes. I know your worst fear is having someone die on you. And I know your pussy is dripping wet when you're angry with me."

I stare at him, mouth wide open, dumbfounded at what he

just told me. My brain says leave right now, but my heart and the pulsing between my legs say to give in right here, right now. I don't know how he knows those things about me, but right now I don't care. I stare at his lips, then his piercing green eyes, and I feel myself melting in his arms, ready to wave the white flag on only one condition.

"Promise me you'll let me go," I say, pleading with my eyes. As soon as he hears those words, he crashes his mouth with mine and brings my legs up around his waist. We kiss desperately, clawing at each other, needing more skin, more raw contact. I reach down for his belt buckle and undo it, reaching in and pulling out his cock. As soon as my hand squeezes his length, I hear a tearing sound and look down at the giant hole in my leggings. Before I can react, he slides my panties to the side and thrusts into me hard. Sparks fly in my mind as he pumps into me harder and harder. My body is molten lava, pooling all around him. I clutch him like he might get away, like he might stop at any moment, and this will end with me writhing against this door alone and wanting him even more. My moans become louder as his thrusts become deeper.

"Art," I moan, feeling myself coming undone in his arms.

"Not yet, baby," he says, almost pleading, like he doesn't want this to be over.

My mouth covers his entire neck, sucking and biting. "Artyom," I moan louder, not able to hold on any longer. He pumps into me hard, his hand on my breast, fingers rolling my nipple, sending me off the edge.

He groans, "Yes, baby, now." We cling to each other and come at the same time. Our mouths touch, feeling the orgasm ripple. In a moment, I feel myself go limp in his arms, and he carries me to the couch, setting me down gently and kissing me one last time. I sit there, trying to understand what just happened. I look over at him, waiting for him to say something.

"You don't have to worry, Petrovna. Once the debt is paid, I won't keep you here against your will.".

That's exactly what I wanted him to say, so why do I feel so empty when he does?

23

Lena

I lie awake waiting for him to get home, but when I hear the club music start to play, I officially give up because he's probably there tonight. My restless legs tell me I won't be getting much sleep, so I get up and decide to go back to the operating room to take inventory. I'm thinking he'll be back around three or four in the morning, and I am in desperate need of a distraction. I put on my shoes, still in my silk pajama shorts and shirt, and head out of the apartment. Thankfully, Art installed a two-way lock so I can go to the operating room anytime I want. I haven't asked him why he did that, but I'm afraid to say we've both grown to trust one another on a certain level now.

Once I get to the basement, I round the corner and bump into someone built like a tank.

"Ow," I say, rubbing my forehead. I look up and see Mike's brother, Rob, in front of me, unfazed by our collision. "Sorry, I didn't see you there. Is everything okay? Is Mike okay?" I ask.

"He's fine," he says, coldly, bumping my shoulder as he moves past me.

This broody act of his is really getting on my nerves. "Hey," I call out to him. "I know you're not happy I'm here, but neither am I. I didn't ask to fill in for the old doc. I didn't ask for any of this, so why don't you give me a freaking break?"

He looks at me and then smirks. "You think I care who the new Doc is? What I care about is you being the new distraction. I don't know what you think we do here, but we're not running a nunnery. We're not good people, *Doc*, and Artyom is the most ruthless of us all. That's why we respect him. If he even softens up a little, people will start questioning him. He's already not himself since his brother died, and now, you're here messing shit up further." He crosses his arms.

I look up at him. All kinds of questions float through my head, but only one makes it to the surface. "His brother died?"

"Whose place do you think you're taking in that room?" He nods toward the operating room. I look back and stare at the door. I try to make sense of everything he just said. When I turn to face him, he moves closer and bends down so I can hear him clearly. "Get out as fast as you can, Doc, because all of us will end up like Ivan, whether we want to or not." He straightens and then leaves without letting me respond.

I stand there trying to digest everything I just heard, most of which I already knew but kept ignoring. I walk to the operating room and look at it differently this time. His brother worked here before me; he's the one who wrote those logs. He was stuck here like I am, and now he's dead. I lie down on the couch at the far end of the operating room and begin to cry, hating myself for not being able to hate him, for knowing what he is and still trying to see some good. I lie there for hours until I can't keep my eyes open any longer.

* * *

I hear the door open and close, and then see Artyom stepping in front of me and crouching down. "Let's go home, *kroshka*," he says softly.

I close my eyes and take a deep breath. "Why didn't you tell me about your brother?" When I open my eyes to look at him, his face is rigid and cold. I sit up, face-to-face with him now. "He used to be the physician here, right?" I wait for him to answer, hysteria rising within me.

"I can't replace him, Art. I just can't," I tell him when he doesn't respond. I try to meet his gaze, but he stands up and turns away from me.

"Please, Art, tell me something real! I thought we'd built some kind of trust here, but maybe it's been one-sided." I stand and walk closer to him.

"You want to talk about trust? Why don't you tell me why you went to Lev the other day instead of coming to me? Because I'd love to know, Lena." He turns around to face me.

"Are you spying on me?" Anger creeping up my throat. "I only went to him because you were clearly avoiding me! And say I did come to you, would you have even listened to me? You made your position pretty clear the second I replaced my father."

We both stand there staring, arms crossed, not knowing what to do. I let out an exasperated sigh. "I have people who are worried about me, Artyom, and all I wanted was to tell them I'm alive and well."

He grabs my face and kisses me, and then pulls away. I stare, stunned, watching his facial features soften. "Ask me," he says, "ask me for anything, and I will give it to you. Ask me, and I will trust you." He reaches out to cup my cheek.

Tears start to well up in my eyes, blurring everything before me. I take his hands in mine. "Tell me about your brother," I say, looking into his eyes.

He stalls for a minute and then leads me back to the couch, pulling me down to sit next to him.

"Ivan was younger than me by eleven months. People would sometimes mix us up because of how much we looked alike. Since I was the older one, I was chosen to be the successor while he got to go to college and live his life away from the Brotherhood. He became a doctor while I became the Boss, taking my father's place. He told me many times he'd never want a life like mine, how he couldn't even stand to look at me sometimes." He pauses and looks down at the ground.

"One day, I sent out two of my men to pick up some money that was owed. It was supposed to be simple, in and out, but instead, they got attacked. It was the night that Dima died. The other boy that was with him had a bullet in his gut and was screaming in agony. So, I called the only person I knew who could fix him under the table. After that, I kept sending my men to him. It was easy. I knew I could trust him. Year after year, he threatened to leave, but I held on to him anyway I could. One day, a rival gang saw him leaving my place and thought it was me; they put a bullet in his head." He exhales like he's been holding his breath the entire time.

I wipe away my tears and squeeze his hand. "I'm sorry," I say. "I can't imagine losing my brother."

He looks at me and then kisses my hand. "Don't cry for me, *kroshka*. I've made this mess of a life myself."

As soon as I try to say something else, he takes my hand and leads me out of the room and back up to the apartment. Once we get inside, I have the overwhelming urge to take care of him, to show him he'll be okay. I approach him as he walks into the bedroom and take his hand, leading him to the bed.

"Do you trust me?" I ask. He caresses my cheek, his eyes glossy, and he nods. I start by taking his shirt off, unbuttoning and sliding it off his broad shoulders. I kiss his forehead, cheeks, and mouth and work my way to his chest. I kneel and take his shoes off for him, removing each sock, and then unfasten his trousers. I slide them down his legs, kissing up his abdomen lightly. He closes his eyes and inhales the scent of my hair. Once I reach his mouth, I kiss him tenderly, running my hands through his hair. I lay him down and hold him close, spreading light kisses over his chest. I look up and see him close his eyes.

"You are the only thing that scares me now, Petrovna."

I smile, thinking about how a big, bad mafia boss confessed that I scare him. We lie there holding each other until we both fall asleep in each other's arms. If only it could stay this way forever.

24

Artyom

Every night, she takes the pain away, even if she doesn't know it. Somehow, she even manages to keep the nightmares at bay, the ones where I see Ivan die over and over again, his wide eyes staring right at me. On nights like tonight, with her scent sprawled all around me, I can only dream of one thing. My angel. When we're in this bed, it almost feels like I can be a new person, the kind Ivan would be proud of. The kind of man who could give her everything she wants.

I've never thought of settling down. My father talked about the importance of having a family and even mentioned an arranged marriage once or twice, but he passed away before I could even start thinking of ways to get out of it. I couldn't imagine the kind of life where I come home from a long day at work, open the door, and have my kid run up into my arms, calling me papa, and my wife waiting for me to have dinner. Like one big happy family. The family I grew up with was just for show. My mother was a trophy wife, I was his successor, and Ivan was backup, just in case his successor failed. I wasn't made to love and care for a family of my own. I was made to take over for my father and ensure a successor so the name would be passed down for generations.

Lena deserves more than what I can offer, but damn, am I a greedy bastard because I want her like I've never wanted anything before. I can't imagine not waking up to her for the rest of my life. Even thinking about giving her up to some asshole makes me want to bury my cock inside her and make sure she knows she's mine. Just as I squeeze her closer to me, I see the screen of my phone light up, and I turn to check it. It's Alec. It better be fucking good because leaving this bed before she wakes up isn't in my plans today. I want to see her when the sun rises, to smell her skin freshly out of the shower, and hear her make those noises that drive me absolutely insane. I want to play pretend a little longer.

I slide out of bed as quietly as possible. She shifts a little when the bed dips, and my heart stills when I see her hand searching for me on my side of the bed. I make my way out and shut the door.

"*Da*," I say, picking up the phone.

"You're not in your office," he says flatly. "Are you ill?"

"No. I'll be late today. Hold my calls."

Since I took over the business, I've always been the first person up and in my office, ready to go. I've never been without work. I eat, sleep, and live for the business. It's all I've ever known, so Alec's confusion is to be expected.

"I can do that, of course, but I'd advise against it. There have been some problems lately with the collections."

Shit. "We've had that before. I'll deal with it later," I say, pinching the bridge of my nose, already feeling a headache coming on.

"It's been all the collections, Artyom. I suggest you sort it out now, before people start talking."

I look back at the door, feeling a pang in my gut, knowing I have to leave her again. "Bring the boys in. I'll be down in ten." I get dressed, putting on my suit of armor once again, and leave all notions of playing house at the door.

25

Artyom

Approaching the office, I see the boys I sent to collect on protection and outstanding loans. When they spot me, they look like dogs with their tails tucked, eyes anywhere but mine. I meet both their stares long enough to let them know I see through them, and I'll know who fucked up.

I go in first and sit behind the same desk my father sat behind. It does most of the work for me. When Alec walks in, I get straight to it. "How many?"

He spreads the sheets on the desk. "Three missed stops. Same faces at the doors."

"Bring them in."

Arkadiy and Peter walk in and stop a foot from the desk. They know not to sit. From the bruises, I already know it's bad.

Arkadiy speaks first. "They had someone there each time with a Glock. They knew we were coming."

Viktor. No one else would test the treaty this way.

"Did you recognize them?"

"Viktor's men. And they play dirty. We could've lit up the street, but there were civilians."

"Good. We don't need heat." I need a plan that lands clean.

"He's testing for soft spots," I say. "We show him there are none."

I point at Alec. "Two men on every door, he thinks he owns. Plates. Faces. Times."

I turn to Arkadiy. "Any shop that flipped last week gets a pause this week. No new paper. They want order back, they come home."

"On it."

"Peter," I say. "Any place paying him goes dark. Give owners a clean way back. Tell them how fast things turn on when they do."

"Yes, Boss."

"We wait forty-eight hours," I say. "He'll celebrate somewhere he shouldn't. We take that, and burn his businesses to the ground."

Peter grins. "And the son?"

"He can smile for the cameras while his father's pockets turn to ash."

Silence settles. We all know the stakes. It's not just my business; it's what puts money in our pockets and food on our tables.

"Get everyone ready," I say, and they instantly know it's game on.

Once they're gone, it's just Alec, and I let the frustration leak out in one breath. He's the only one who sees it.

"You worked with my father, Alec. What would he do?"

"Go straight for the throat," he says. "But you're not your father, Artyom. You readied the men; now retaliate."

My father liked war. I like endings. Brooklyn is mine, and I don't need a war to keep it. I need Viktor hungry, blind, and embarrassed. Then I take what matters, and he learns to keep his hands off my streets.

Alec clears his throat. "You've been a little distracted lately... It'll be good for the men to see you're still focused on business."

I know he's right. I know I've been distracted by Lena being under the same roof and in the same bed as me, but it still makes me angry to hear it from him. That means the others might be feeling the same. *Shit.* I've never been distracted by something other than business. Some people work a nine-to-five job, go home to their families, and shut off their work minds, but mine is always on. I work twenty-four-seven; it comes with the job. I know Alec is just reminding me of that. Fucking Alec. I sigh through my nose, releasing some pent-up frustration and hating myself for what I'm about to do.

"Have Lena moved to another room, the one closest to the operating room." He stares at me for a moment and then nods once and leaves. I know what that'll do to whatever trust we've built between us. I know she'll be confused and hurt, but once again, I am reminded she is too good for what my life is, and I don't get to have "good."

The rest of the day goes by painfully slow, and I resist the urge to check the cameras and find her. Alec's words replay in my head. A damn distraction. That's what she is. I need to get her out of my head and off my skin. I can still smell her all around me. My scent mixed with hers makes my cock hard, and my hands itch for her. I shake my head, needing this madness to stop. I decide to go back up to the room and take a cold shower, but when I open the door, I'm greeted with hard brown eyes, the same eyes that smiled at me just this morning when I held her close.

"Why?" she asks sternly. I know exactly what she's asking, but I play dumb. What am I supposed to say? You're all I think about, and that's bad for business?

"You're going to need to be a little more specific, Petrovna," I say instead.

Her eyes narrow on me, shooting daggers. "Why am I in a different room, Art?" Her arms are crossed over her chest, and her face is hard, but there's that little tell in her brows that shows exactly how she feels. She's disappointed.

"I need you to be closer to the operating room; my room is too far. It took us too long to get down there when Mike was shot," I lie. It only took us three minutes to get there. She searches my face for a minute longer, looking for the truth, but my poker face gives her nothing. I've had years to perfect it. Emotion is a sign of weakness, as my father always said.

Disappointment and a hint of embarrassment cloud her face. I ball up my hands and squeeze. It's the only thing I can do to resist bringing her in close and reassuring her that I would like nothing more than to sleep next to her tonight and every night, for that matter, but I can't. I just can't. So, I don't say anything, not even when she takes a step back from me and turns to leave, the opposite way of our home and the bed we've shared.

I go back to my office and slam my fist into the door until it hurts more than her leaving. I keep going until I hear a faint buzzing sound, then I instantly stop and close my eyes. This night just keeps getting worse. I stride behind my desk and remove the picture of Brooklyn in the 1950s, a city full of factory smoke, opportunity, and, of course, gangsters. Once I take it down, I stare at the iron safe my father installed when he took over. I input the numbers, feeling the cold digits beneath my fingers.

There's something so satisfying about having a place that keeps all your secrets, a place only you know about. When I open it, I take the pager out and look at it. It only ever goes off when there's been a meeting called, a meeting with the borough council; the bosses of the New York underworld. You don't skip it, and you don't come unready. I've only been a part of two since I was thirteen. I slam my already bloody hands on the desk out of frustration and welcome the sting. I dial Alec, and he comes into the office before the second ring even begins. Once he walks in, his eyes go to my bloody hands.

"I'm fine. I got a page. Get things ready," I rasp.

"It's about time," he says, like it's a fucking good thing.

I look up at him, jaw clenched. He's doing a great job at pissing me off today.

"It's been too long as it is, and I fear our alliances are hanging by a thread. They need a bit of reminding of who sits behind this desk."

He's right. My father passed down alliances with all five boroughs to me, and I haven't made any attempt to keep them in check. We've always had a code: You don't mess with mine, and I don't mess with yours, but clearly, Viktor needs some reminding.

"Call Eddie and set it up. I have a feeling the meeting place hasn't changed. Make sure our guys know not to bring their piece into the casino. Have five situated outside, ten inside, and you, Rob, and Nik come in with me."

"And the girl?" Alec asks.

My eyebrows rise in question. "What about her? She's

staying as far as possible from this shit," I say, a little too defensively.

"The club won't be as protected. She'll be alone, Artyom." He lets that last part sink in. I can't bring the new members with me to something like this, so they'll stay here, but I also can't trust the club won't be attacked while we're gone, especially since all my businesses have been hit recently.

"Then I'll leave two men here to watch her. I can't fucking take her, Alec. Trouble follows her like a damn stray dog. I won't be able to focus on anything except for her." I sound like an overprotective boyfriend, entirely out of character for me.

"Then you'll have less protection," he says, matter-of-factly.

I know he's right, but I can't bring her into the fire with me. "If I leave her here, she's in danger. If I take her with me, she's in even more danger. What the hell do I do then?" How can I protect Lena and be the boss my men need me to be?

26

Lena

He's avoiding me. He put me in another room, and now he's *clearly* avoiding me. I want to say this is for the best. I want to say I sleep better and feel safer, but I can't. I can't sleep at all in this bed. I miss his warmth and touch. I'm so confused because I thought I knew where we stood. I know he wants me, and I think I made it pretty clear I want him, but the way his eyes looked when I went to see him, just empty and emotionless, tells me something else.

I pace around my new room, thinking of possible reasons why he put me here and why the hell he couldn't tell me himself. He sent Alec to do what he should've done. The anger and embarrassment of picturing Alec moving my things to another room takes over, and I grab the pillow off the couch, screaming into it until I have nothing left in me. I settle on he's a coward and try to collect myself, breathing in and out slowly. I spy the stack of medical textbooks on the table and go over to them. Thankfully, Alec thought to bring these here, too. I pick one up and open it to the page I left off on. Some of these surgeries are so intricate that I wouldn't be able to do them here alone. Let's just hope no one needs open-heart surgery any time soon.

I hear a knock on the door, and instantly, my heart starts to beat out of my chest. Every noise around me, every knock on the door, has me jumping out of my skin, thinking it could be him on the other side. In one fell swoop, my heart sinks as I see Alec standing in the entryway.

"Ms. Petrovna." He gives me a polite nod, and I can tell he's trying not to look at all my scattered stuff that he put here. The last time my stuff was moved, it was folded neatly and put away for me; however, this time, it was set down on the entryway floor like he was rushed. I feel my face getting red again and take another deep breath, steadying my hammering pulse, and wait for him to get on with it because, no offense to Alec, he's been the bearer of bad news lately, and I don't know how much more I can take.

"Artyom has some business to attend to in Atlantic City, and he asks that you accompany him there," he says, not giving me any other details.

"What for?" I scoff.

"As a precaution, in case your services are needed," he adds.

"Tell him I politely decline. I will not be going anywhere, further risking my career and life for him." I emphasize the last part so he understands I want nothing to do with Art after he basically kicked me out of his room. The audacity of that man.

"If safety is your concern, you will be protected at all costs. He would not be taking you if he felt you were not truly needed."

"I said no, Alec. Please tell him he'll have to take me kicking and screaming because I will not go willingly." I'm seething at this point. A part of me feels terrible for Alec. He got the short end of the stick here, being Art's errand boy. The truth is, if Art had asked me himself, I would've considered going. It would've made a difference in how I feel about leaving this building and being taken to a place where I could be seen helping him.

I sigh, softening my tone. "I'm sorry, Alec, but my answer is no."

His face drops, looking slightly defeated. "I will let him know." With that, he turns toward the door and leaves.

I sit here huffing and puffing, cursing Art's name until I exhaust myself mentally and physically. I go to bed angry, hungry, and just overall mentally exhausted. Just as I begin to drift off, I suddenly feel my body being ripped away from my bed and hauled over something massive and hard. My eyes tear open, and it takes me a minute to realize I've been thrown over Art's shoulder, and he's carrying me out of the apartment.

"What are you doing?" I yell, thrashing against him.

"You brought this upon yourself, *kroshka*. When I say you're coming with me, it's an order, not an invitation."

"Are you out of your damn mind, Art? Let me go!" I pound on his back. The man doesn't even flinch, but my hands are already aching. This man's back is built like stone. An image of him naked invades my mind, showing me every hard muscle that covers him.

"You promised me kicking and screaming, so let's hear it, baby." His voice is teasing, very different from the last time I spoke to him.

"You're insane, do you know that?" I wriggle against him one last time and then start to sag, feeling winded.

Once we get outside, I'm greeted by a few other men, one of whom is Mike.

"Hey, Doc," he says with a low chuckle.

I give him a tight smile, mortification spreading over my face. I'm suddenly aware I'm still wearing my pajamas, the ones with Strawberry Shortcake all over them. These shouldn't be seen by anyone other than me. I let out a groan, and Art pats my ass.

"I thought you'd give me more of a show, *kroshka*. I'm a little disappointed," he says, humor in his voice.

"Put me down, Art," I grit out, the blood already rushing to my head.

He sighs and puts me down next to his car. "Get in, you're riding with me."

I let myself regain my composure and cross my arms, trying to decide whether I could still win this one.

Art looks at me, his eyebrows rising in amusement. "You can try running," he dares me.

My eyes narrow on him, and I reluctantly slide into the passenger seat, feeling the cold leather beneath my bare legs. I really hope Art packed something else for me to wear before he practically kidnapped me from my bed. I cross my arms and pout like a child. The door opens on the driver's side, and Art gets in, adjusting the mirrors and seat.

Once we get on the road, he looks at me, smirking. "I've never seen those pajamas on you."

"I didn't see them in the closet before," I lie, embarrassed. I've been sleeping in the nightgowns Art kindly got for me when I moved in. The silk nightgowns that leave little to the imagination.

"I should thank Alec for finding them for me when he packed

up my clothes without me knowing. It really was the best surprise," I say sarcastically.

He grips the steering wheel tighter, not saying a word. I let a few minutes pass, allowing him to gain the courage to explain himself. When he doesn't, I let it go. I don't know if I can handle the truth right now anyway.

"Where are we going?" I ask instead, looking out the window. I almost forgot what the city looked like at night. In the daytime, the buildings are a depressing rust color; they hide the sky and all its beauty. But at night, the sky is on full display, the stars illuminating the city. The skyline is a star on its own, filled with shimmering lights that are almost blinding. I can't help but smile at the view, feeling like a tourist seeing the big city for the first time.

"Atlantic City. There's a casino where we meet sometimes."

I gape at him. "You dragged me out of bed to go to a casino?"

"More or less," he says, not taking his eyes off the road.

"Well, which one is it, more or less?" I press.

He exhales, exasperated. "There's a mandatory meeting happening at one of the casinos. The less you know, the better, Lena."

"What do you mean by the less I know, the better? How am I supposed to help or be of service if I don't know what's going on?" He's quiet for a moment, so I reach for his hand resting on the clutch. "Just tell me what you need from me. Tell me what's happening, I need to know, Art." My voice softens a bit.

His eyes go to my hand on top of his, and his expression becomes pained and conflicted, so I do us both a favor and remove it, immediately missing his warmth.

"Lena, all I need you to do is stay in the hotel room and not leave until I return. If you are needed, I will contact you. Like I said, the less you know, the better."

I can't help but feel hurt that he doesn't trust me enough to tell me what's really going on. We ride the rest of the way in almost complete silence. The humming from the A/C is the only thing keeping me from going crazy. As if he senses the tension, his hand moves to turn the radio on, and Cyndi Lauper's "Girls Just Want to Have Fun" starts playing on full blast, my insides vibrating from the bass. My eyes widen in surprise as I peer over at him questioningly.

"Cyndi Lauper, huh?" I smirk.

"Remind me to strangle Mike when I see him. He does this shit all the time." His voice comes out rough and annoyed, but his face looks slightly embarrassed. He meets my eyes, a smile dancing on both our lips, and we let out a bubbling laugh, slowly relieving some of the tension. "You should do that more," he tells me.

"What?"

"Laugh."

I smile. "You too. I actually didn't know you knew how to laugh. You've got the broody, terrifying thing going on most days," I tease.

He looks at me briefly, his eyes smiling. "I think I forgot how to before you showed up."

I hold his gaze and then turn away, looking out the window again, thoroughly confused by his intentions. He kicks me out of his room and then says things like that, things that make my heart melt and my body grow with need.

We end up arriving an hour earlier than what the GPS predicted. I'm surprised we didn't get here sooner because of how this man drives. I'm starting to think the speed limit is just a suggestion for him.

Once he parks the car in front of the hotel, I go to pull the door open, but it doesn't budge. I look over at Art as he reaches over to the back seat and retrieves a black grocery bag.

"Before we head inside, I need you to get dressed," he says, handing me the bag. Great, he's embarrassed to be seen with me looking like this. I peer into the bag and pull out fishnet stockings, a black strapless mini dress, and four-inch stilettos. I stare at him questioningly because there is no way I am dressing like a hooker.

"It's just a precaution, Petrovna."

"Let me guess, the less I know the better?" I roll my eyes and begin taking my shirt off.

He clears his throat. "Come out when you're ready." He opens the car door and comes over to my side, blocking the window with his body. *Now* he's being a gentleman.

I tug on the tights and dress as fast as I can, hearing other cars pull up around us. Once I strap on the sky-high stilettos, which will probably be the reason I fall and break my neck today, I open the car door and step out. Art's eyes meet mine, and I swear they darken in a way that has me clenching my thighs together.

"Hey, baby," Mike says as he wraps his arm around me and kisses the top of my head. "Just go with it, Doc," he mumbles into my hair.

I freeze instantly, looking at Art for answers when it all dawns on me. The dress, heels, and Mike… Art wants it to look like I'm *with* Mike. I'm *supposed* to look like a hooker.

Art looks at us for a second longer, his face hardening as he looks at Mike's arm around me. He nods once and walks past us, going to the entrance of the casino.

I look up at the massive building before me. It's tall, with fourteen floors going up the front and sides of it. The exterior is painted a gold color that almost gives off a mirrored effect. I've never been to Atlantic City, but I always envisioned it to be somewhat like Vegas. I wasn't wrong, the bright lights of the casino are blinding, and everything about this stretch of casinos screams Vegas. I wouldn't be surprised if there was a chapel around here with an Elvis impersonator.

"Let's get you to your room," Mike says, pulling me closer to him, making walking in these heels even more difficult.

Once we're in the casino, my eyes go wide with awe at the hundreds of slot machines in front of me.

"I'm guessing you've never been gambling, huh, Doc?"

I turn to see Mike towering over me and smiling. "Not really my thing. As you may know, I'm already in enough debt," I say dryly.

He releases a boisterous laugh that has me laughing along with him; it's the type of laugh that makes you forget you've been kidnapped and forced to go to a casino full of mafia men. All laughter disappears when Art looks back, giving us a chilling stare.

"And that's our cue to get the hell out of here." He takes my hand urgently, weaving us through the aisles of slot machines until we get to an elevator.

"So, are you going to tell me what we're doing here?" I ask as soon as the door closes.

"You know I can't, Doc." He sighs. "I don't even know much myself, never even been to one of these. Everyone is tense as hell."

If he hasn't been to one of these meetings before, then how rare are they? And how dangerous is it that he needs all of his men here, including me?

Reaching the top floor, we swiftly tread over a deep red carpet until we arrive at room 807 at the end of the hall. He slides the room keycard in and ushers me inside, looking both ways down the hall before shutting the door. The hotel room is incredibly spacious, with ample room in the large living room, a king-size bed in the main suite, and a dining table that could easily seat sixteen people.

"This is my room?" I ask in disbelief.

"Yeah, crazy, right? I heard the vice president once stayed here."

I chuckle because I really can't picture the Vice President of the United States coming here for any reason.

"Why here, though?"

He ticks it off on his fingers. "Top floor, single hallway," he says. "Two exits, plus a freight that's ours. We own the cameras up here. Elevator's keyed. Pit boss comps the room so there's no paper trail." I breathe out; I didn't know this much went into keeping us safe here.

Mike's phone rings, and we both go still, looking at each other.

He picks up the phone and starts talking to whoever it is. "Yeah, I did. She's fine… Yeah, I know, Easy's crew is all over the fucking place. I'll be down in a minute."

The whole time he's talking, it feels like I'm holding my breath. I'm trying to make sense of anything he's saying, but I just don't have enough information. I need someone, anyone, to trust me enough to tell me something.

He stops talking and reaches out to me, handing me the phone. "He wants to talk to you," is all he says.

When I take the phone, Mike walks into the bathroom,

giving me privacy.

"How are you?" Art's voice comes through the phone.

"Fine," I say, so totally not fine.

"Lena, I need you to promise me you'll stay in your room until I personally come get you." His voice is almost a plea.

"What's going on, Art? Who's Easy?" I ask, hoping he'll let me in just a little. He pauses for a second, chewing on what I just asked.

"Promise me."

I sigh, a part of me knowing he wouldn't tell me. "I promise," I say, feeling defeated. He hangs up without another word, and Mike emerges at just the right time. I hand him the phone, feeling my anxiety build until I want to scream.

"Doc," I hear him say. "You'll be okay. He won't let anything happen to you." He looks into my eyes and then adds, "*We* won't let anything happen to you."

At this moment, I begin to realize he didn't bring me here to take care of his men. I was brought here to be protected.

27

Artyom

It took everything in me to walk away and leave her with Mike. To leave her with anyone who isn't me makes my blood boil. It's not that I don't trust my guys to keep her safe; I just want to be the one doing it. I want it to be my arm around her, to hold her close and make it known she is mine. But I can't do that, I know I can't, especially not here, where the wolves are lurking in every corner. They watch my every move, trying to carve out any weakness of mine and use it to their advantage. My mind shows me flashes of Ivan dead on the concrete, his lifeless eyes looking up at the sky. I ball up my hands and keep walking to the back of the casino to a room no one would find unless you're one of the council members. The door itself is part of the wall, with no handle, and no indication of anything behind it. The only way to lock it is from the inside. I see Alec standing outside the door, along with a few other men who work for the other members. He gives me a nod when he sees me approaching, a silent wish of good luck. I don't need luck, I just need to remember why Ivan died, why I have to hide away every good thing in my life, and that is what helps me put on my suit of armor and go into that room with my head held high.

The door seals behind me. This isn't Bratva business or Cosa Nostra business, it's both. The old men call it a borough council that seats whoever runs the streets: Easy from the Bronx, Rico out of Staten Island, John Jay in Manhattan, Viktor running Queens, and me for Brooklyn. We don't share blood. We share rules and break them carefully.

The vast, dark room grows quiet when I step in, all eyes on me. A part of me loves that feeling, controlling a room that way. I make my way over to the end of the large rectangular table. The black gloss reflects the artificial amber glow from the overhead chandelier. I sit down at the head and take out a cigarette, lighting it particularly slowly. Easy lets out a low chuckle, knowing I just took Viktor's spot.

I take a long drag of my cigarette and let it out. Smoke lingers in the air around us, adding to the heavy presence in the room. Each man sitting at this table radiates power and control; anyone outside of this room would shit a brick just making eye contact with one of them.

"If we're done sizing up our dicks, can we start this shit?" John Jay says.

I look him over, remembering he took over for his uncle a few years back, though we've never met until now. He's a little older than me, but his short stature gives him a boyish look. Still, there's something about him, frat-boy energy, the kind that fits his market. In Manhattan, rich college kids are always hungry for a hit. He could pass for one of them if not for the sharpness in his eyes, a mirror of his uncle's. Every word, every movement was deliberate, and I doubt his nephew is any different.

The door swings open, and Viktor strides in, slow and lazy, scanning the room until his eyes land on me. I take another deep pull and let it out, the smoke obstructing my view of his inflated face. He reluctantly moves toward the seat next to Rico, making it a point to grunt in disapproval when sitting down.

"So, what the fuck we here for?" Rico asks in a heavy Hispanic accent. He's not one for patience, but you'd think running Staten Island's suburbia would make him a more peaceful, easygoing guy. Especially since no one ever suspects arms dealing between soccer practices. Fucking genius.

We're all silent until Easy's booming voice fills the room. "Y'all know what that page means. It means one of y'all fucked up. So, who was it?" Easy isn't always a straight shooter; he likes to play around a bit before getting to the point, but not today. There's no humor in his eyes as he scans the room, looking for something I'm not really sure of yet.

"I don't know what you're talking about, old man," Rico says.

I take another pull. I haven't had time to send my men to do any damage to Viktor's businesses, so it can't be about that. Plus, how I handle business is of no concern to the circle. However, Easy has never called a meeting before. He's the oldest member at this table. He was running the Bronx when most of us were still having our asses wiped, so no one dares mess with his shit. Unless… my little problem is also connected to his. I look over at Viktor, his smirk tells me he's loving seeing Easy this way.

"Let me spell it out for you, boy. We got lines for a reason, so if you wanna cross into mine, then we crossin'."

"All these damn riddles," Rico puffs out, and I guess he's not one to read between the lines.

"Watch your fucking mouth, *ese,*" John Jay spits out. "What's going on, Easy?" His attention turns to the man on the other end of the table. "Someone stepping on your turf?"

"Oh, it's more than that, boy," he drawls. From the menacing look on his face, I'm guessing he's lost some of his men to this, and if I don't strike back, my men will be next.

"Your boys getting cozy with a Glock?" I ask him, remembering what my men told me just days ago. The room grows quiet, all eyes trained on me.

"Is there any reason you know that, boy?" Easy asks, the tension in the room is suffocating, each man sitting perfectly still.

I take another drag, then put it out on the ashtray in front of me, taking my time before answering. "I've been having the same issue."

Easy holds my stare, trying to read me. "You have any idea who, kid?" Easy asks me, a slight warning in his tone, a warning that if I hide anything from him, it'll be me he'll be coming for. I contemplate whether I should hand Viktor over to him on a silver platter, but if I'm being honest, I want him all to myself. I want to see him go up in flames, for Ivan.

"We used to have boundaries and respect!" Viktor bellows, his fist slamming into the table. "These kids coming in here thinking they can take what's ours."

I almost laugh. This fat bastard thinks he's untouchable because he's fucking old. If I were to guess, I'd say he knows Easy is on his way out, and he wants to take over before he appoints a replacement. This asshole is biting off more than he can chew.

"You on something, old man? If you're saying it's me, then you must be high," Rico snaps back.

"Calm down; no one is saying it's you, and it sure as shit not me. You think it's Jersey? I hear they have a new boss, might be wanting to expand," John Jay chimes in, and that would be an interesting theory if my men weren't positive it was Vik's men who were at my pickup spots.

"Jersey don't know our lines; could be them. Who's going to handle that?" Viktor asks, his voice steady now, pleased the heat isn't on him anymore.

"Oh, I'm going to handle my own. Don't you worry. I just wanted to give y'all a heads up," Easy retorts, knowing nothing else will come out of this. "We gonna handle our business." He looks at me when he says that.

I nod once, feeling a bit more at ease since arriving here. The rest of the meeting goes by smoothly, mostly bickering between John Jay and Rico, more speculation about the newly appointed New Jersey boss, and new territory lines no one agrees with. We know the meeting is over when we hear a knock on the door. We're allotted a specific amount of time here; having all council members in one place anywhere for too long can be bad for everyone, just in case one of us is being tracked.

We take turns exiting the room. Rico goes first, then John Jay, then Viktor, who makes a point to drag out his departure, eyeing me and Easy warily. He knows it'll just be me and Easy once he leaves, which is the last thing he wants.

"It was nice to see you, Vik. Give your family my regards, would ya?" Easy says. To anyone, it would've sounded friendly, but to us, it was a full-blown threat.

Viktor finally gets up and strolls toward the door. Then, as the dramatic asshole that he is, he turns to face Easy once more. "I heard your nephew Marcus passed. My condolences.

It must be hard when your second dies, and you're so close to the end."

"Oh, I've got a few years left. I might even outlive you, Vik."

Viktor's mouth pulls up into a smirk, and he throws the door open and strides out without saying another word.

"I had a feeling it was that motherfucker," Easy tells me. "How many has he hit of yours?"

"Enough," I say, too prideful to give him an actual answer.

He nods, studying me. "I heard about your brother. My condolences."

I nod once, letting him know I'm not about to talk about Ivan with him. I haven't talked to anyone about Ivan, except for Lena.

"If I can give you a piece of advice, kid, grief is a weakness that will destroy you. Your brother was destroying you, and that pretty little piece up in your suite will put you in your grave."

My heart stills for a moment, and I feel my body grow cold, my mind unraveling. How would he have known about Lena? My mind races with thoughts of her being taken by his men while I was in this room.

"Easy…" I start to say, my voice deadly, threatening. I know I should play it off like he's got it wrong, but everything in me is on fire. I can't think straight when it comes to her.

"Just some friendly advice from an old friend," he says, grinning.

I want to grab him by the throat and squeeze until he forgets about Lena. Until he forgets I have a weakness. Before I can do anything, he chuckles and walks away from me, his men behind him. Nothing is ever friendly between any of us. We didn't get to be in a position of power by being friendly.

"Boss?" I hear a muffled voice beside me. I turn to him, my senses coming back to me.

"Lena," I finally say, but I don't have time to ask questions; it could already be too late. I turn and run toward the stairs and sprint up eight floors, not feeling a single thing with the adrenaline rushing through me. All I know is I need to get to her. I need to make sure she's safe. I'm a fucking idiot for bringing her here. I should've left my men with her at the club. I should've left *all* my men with her. I'm a coward. My heart is pounding out of my chest when I finally reach her floor. I look around and see one of my guys standing outside the door. Peter. He's pacing back and forth, looking at the ground. When he sees me, he straightens.

"Boss, everything okay?" he asks, but I push past him and let the door slam behind me.

"Lena!" I shout, going from room to room. "Lena!" I shout again, then I see her small frame standing by the bedroom window, and I sigh in relief.

When she sees me, her full lips frown. She immediately rushes to me. "Are you okay?" Her worried expression tears through me. I stare at her, my eyes roaming over her body, making sure she's not hurt. When I'm satisfied, I pull her into me and inhale her scent, letting it wash away my panic. She begins to pull away, questions dancing on her tongue. Without a second thought, I crash my lips against hers and wait for my angel to, once again, take the pain away.

28

Lena

My mind is reeling, going a mile a minute. Something must be wrong. He's hurt, or someone is injured. The pained expression on his face, the relief in his eyes when he saw me, I know in my gut something went down he wasn't expecting. I was utterly taken aback when he kissed me, but it didn't stop my lips from kissing him back. His lips are demanding and passionate; his emotions spilling into me, filling me up. I moan, my treacherous body opening up to him greedily. I want more of him, to feel, taste, and explore all of him. But my mind won't turn off. It won't let me have this moment. Pictures of his pained face flash before me. There's something he's not telling me. He doesn't trust me. I tear away from him abruptly, panting, desire still coating my mouth.

"Tell me what happened," I demand.

He takes a deep breath, steadying himself. I know that kiss affected him as it did me. He wants more. I know it, but I won't give in until I get some answers.

"Lena, you know I can't," he breathes out.

"You can. You don't trust me, I get it, but I've had no choice but to trust you with my life, Art. If you want to drown out the pain of your life by fucking me, fine. But I will never be yours this way. I deserve better," I say, my voice shaking, but my stance is firm despite my knees wanting to buckle.

His expression darkens at that last bit: *I'll never be yours.* "It's not you I don't trust, Lena. It's everyone else." He edges closer to me. "You have all our lives in the palm of your hand, especially mine, and I give it to you willingly. Only you. You think I'd have you in that operating room if I didn't trust you?"

My heart is beating so hard I can feel it in my throat. He's so close I can smell him, the aroma of smoke and mint invading my nostrils.

He grabs my jaw with one hand and tilts it up so I'm looking at him, eyes flaring, bursting with need. "You have been mine from the moment I first saw you, Petrovna, whether you like it or not. Tell yourself whatever you want to help you face reality, but we both know your mind, this body, and your wet pussy are mine." With that, he lets out a growl, devouring my mouth, leaving no crumbs. I let him have all of me. He lets me go for a minute, looking at me in a way that has me stripping eagerly. His nostrils flare when he sees me naked. I rise on my toes, and he lifts me, carrying me to the table where he sprawls me out on my back, like a four-course meal only for him.

"This is how I want you every day, *kroshka*, spread out on the table like a feast for me to enjoy." He kneels, his breath hitting my clit.

I arch my back and stifle a moan. "Art, I need you," I say, already feeling dizzy.

"Tell me you're mine, and I'll eat every last drop." He swipes his tongue over my already-drenched core. Another lick, and I'm on fire.

"Please," I beg.

"Say it," he demands, his voice possessive and deep. The kind of voice you play on repeat, like your favorite song. My favorite song. I can tell he's losing his restraint just as much as I am, but fuck if I don't love him like this. I want more.

"No," I breathe out.

His breath halts, and I feel his lips turn up into a sadistic smile against my thigh. A smile that can convince people to join his cult and pray only to him. I'm in this cult now, praying for him to touch me. To fill me. To make me feel everything. In an instant, he flips me over onto my stomach, face down on the table.

"No?" he muses. "You'll be screaming yes once I'm done with you, *kroshka*," he vows, giving my ass a hard spank.

Yes, I want to scream. But I can't. I'm moaning the second his hand touches me.

"This ass is mine." Another smack, and I want to scream. I'm writhing in pleasure laced with pain. His rough hands prop me up so my ass is in the air, face still pressed against the smooth wood of the table. "You're a masterpiece, baby, with my handprint on your ass." At the feel of his stubble on my bare skin, I shudder, goosebumps trailing my body. He spreads me open and blows lightly on that little ring of muscle, the place no man has ever gone.

"Would you let me fuck you here, Lena? I'll make you come on my fingers while I'm fucking your ass."

"Please, Art," I beg, my body screaming to release the orgasm already building within me.

I lose all sense of control when I feel his tongue slick against me. He drags it up slowly, relishing in the response my body is having to him. I feel his fingers at my entrance while he licks, and I begin to move into him, needing him inside, anyway I can get him.

"Yes," I moan. "Fuck, yes, Art."

"Say you're mine," he demands, driving a finger in; I gasp. More. "Say it, baby." Adding another finger, he begins fucking me, going in and out slowly while he consumes me.

"Make me," I rasp between moans. I look over at him, and a devilish grin spreads across his face. He knows he won this one.

He begins to unzip his pants, and my core clenches in anticipation. He repositions me again, my legs on the floor, stomach pressed to the table. I look back, and a moan escapes my mouth as soon as I see his cock spring free, my voice desperate and needy. He slips into me without a single word, taking my sanity and breath away with each thrust.

He leans over me, grabbing my jaw once again and turning my face to see him. "Say it," he growls, thrusting deeper. I let out a cry, and he takes my lips with his, capturing my whimpers. I feel myself letting go, completely unraveling under him. I tense, squeezing him inside me.

"Lena," he groans into my ear. He keeps up the pace, letting me ride out my orgasm until tears spill down my face.

"I'm yours," I whisper.

I feel him slowing down, his breath hard, panting on my skin. A second later, he spins me around to face him, spreads my legs, and sinks into me once again.

"Again," he commands.

"I'm yours, Art," I moan, toes curling from the sensation on my swollen clit.

His movements become ragged, and his head drops back in ecstasy. "Again," he rasps, his neck muscles constricting.

When I feel another orgasm reaching its peak, I say, "Only yours." I repeat the words over and over again until we're both panting into each other's mouths, coming apart together, feeling the trust building between us once again.

We spend the next twenty minutes exploring each other in the shower. The things that man can do with a loofah have me curling my toes again.

"You're my angel," he murmurs in my ear.

I giggle, remembering the first time I saw him, and how I thought he looked like one too. How drastically that changed. "I used to think you were the devil," I say against his lips.

"Used to?" His hand travels to the small of my back, pressing me closer to him.

"Still do." I kiss him, parting my lips when I feel his tongue lick my lower lip.

"I will be whatever you want me to be, *kroshka*," he says between kisses, our breath becoming heavier under the stream of the shower. All the blood drains from my face when I hear a sound coming from outside the bathroom. I know Art hears it too when he puts a finger to my lips, signaling me to stay quiet. He slides the glass shower door open slowly and picks up a towel, wrapping it over his lower half. I stand under the hot stream, trembling, my mind racing. We're in danger, my mind screams. The front door automatically locks, so who would have the key to open it besides Artyom and me? My eyes beg him not to go out there, but he looks at me, motioning me to stay here. His expression is firm but gentle. When he opens the door, I hold my breath, and then he's gone, shutting the door behind him. I wait and listen for anything that would signal distress. I get out of the shower and wrap a towel around myself, locking the door as quietly as I can. Everything in me tells me he will handle it, whatever it is; he will take care of it. Take care of me. So, I wait. The handle begins to move, and my heart skips a beat. *No, no, no, please.*

"Lena, it's me. It was only Alec," I hear Artyom say. I let out the breath I was holding and feel the blood return to my face. Before opening the door, I grab the hairdryer from one of the drawers and hold it above my head. Do I actually think it will do much to save me? Probably not, but it could do just enough to let Art do his part if he were forced to have me open the door by some asshole holding him at gunpoint. I reluctantly open the door and stand back.

As soon as Artyom sees me, he smirks. "That's my girl." I lower the hairdryer, and a smile spreads over my face.

"At least forty-five different scenarios played out in my head when you left. I was not about to just open the door without a fight," I say.

"I don't have a single doubt about that, Petrovna." He comes closer and kisses my forehead. "But I want you to know I would die before being forced to have you open this door."

My heart melts when I hear him say that, and I bring him in closer and kiss him deeply. He would rather die than see me get hurt.

"As much as I want to take you right here in the bathroom for the second time, it's time for us to leave."

While getting dressed, Artyom hands me a bag he had Alec pack for me before we left. There's something so normal about having sex, showering together, and getting dressed. Like a normal couple doing normal things. I steal a glance at him, and I have to press my lips together hard to keep myself from smiling like an idiot. Right now, he doesn't look like a mafia boss. He just looks like Artyom. *My* Artyom. My boyfriend? I shake my head at that thought and continue to get dressed. Thank you, Alec, for packing sweats.

When I walk into the living room, I see Alec and two other guys sitting on the couch, looking very awkward. I then notice all the scattered clothes everywhere, and I feel my face redden. Artyom strolls in after me like he hasn't got a single care in the world, not noticing our clothes sprawled out, or maybe not caring. I go over to the kitchen and grab a complimentary water bottle from the mini-fridge.

"We're fine, Alec," Art says, annoyance creeping into his voice.

"Peter said he saw you running into the room, and when you didn't come out…" His voice trails off, looking between Art and me, now understanding why he didn't come out. My cheeks flush again. "Next time, answer your damn phone," Alec says, standing and walking over to the door. I've never heard him speak that way before, worry coating every word. I wonder how long he's been working for Art and if he worked for his father as well.

Once he and the other men leave the room, we pack up our things and head out hand in hand. We leave the hotel through the basement, which looks like it shouldn't exist. The basement leads to a shady back door with about a billion locks. I can't help but wonder what happened while he was gone and if what we're doing now is a direct result of that. Outside, the cars are ready for us, and the door is already open. I feel like the president, the way he's covering me, the way they all are. He's silent at first. He knows what all of this must look like, right?

He reaches for my hand and squeezes. "You're not going to let this go, are you?" He sighs, not really asking me. I look at him and squeeze back.

Once we're on the road, he finally starts talking. "A meeting was called between all the bosses from all the boroughs. Not going is not an option, and with the nature of my work, I need to have most of my men with me. I also couldn't leave you unprotected at the club. I didn't tell you because knowing any of this risks your safety. People around me die, Lena, for knowing far less than you know now." He pauses, not looking at me, almost like he's afraid to look at me, to see my expression.

"When I saw you in the hotel room... you looked terrified, Art. And the relief on your face when you held me... I need to know what happened."

His hand tightens around the wheel, and his voice shifts from worry to anger. Not at me for asking the question, but at himself as memories of the past few hours start flooding his head again.

"One of them found out about you and knew exactly where you were. I should've known better and kept you away from this." He's beating himself up now, and I see the gears turning in his head, all of the "what ifs" spinning round and round. I know I should feel afraid by what he's saying, but all I want to do is reassure him it'll be okay, that I will be okay as long as I'm with him. I want to believe that.

"Art," I say, trying to snap him out of it.

"I'm okay. I'm with you." He looks at me, and even through the stark light of the cars passing by, I instantly see his anger melt out of his emerald-green eyes into a puddle at our feet. He gives my hand another squeeze. My stupid heart aches for him, and I can't help but acknowledge to myself that everything feels different now. Before, we were in a bubble, playing pretend. But now, it doesn't feel as easy. I'm less afraid for myself and more for him. I want to ease his worry and pain. I want to hold him and be held by him. I want… more. The question is, is Artyom Volkhov capable of giving me more?

"I don't know what this thing between us is, and there's still so much I don't know about you. I mean, you could have a Russian bride you've been promised to waiting for you back home, but what I do know is that things need to be different. I need to know what's happening and my role in everything. In your life. I know you can't tell me certain things, and I'm still not sure I want to know everything, but I do need to know when my life is in danger. Or yours. Because as much as it scared you to lose me in that hotel room, it scared me too." My voice is low and vulnerable. He has seen almost every side of me except for this one. The one where I pour my heart out and wait like a puppy dog for his response, for anything.

"I don't," he says simply. Like I should know what he's talking about.

"Don't?" I repeat.

"I don't have anyone but you. That's all I need. All I want. You're right, though. It's become clear that not knowing also puts you at risk. I won't keep anything from you that can harm you. You have my word." His calloused hand warms my thigh, making small, soothing circles on my skin. I resist the urge to smile like an idiot, which is what I want to do so badly.

"When I was younger, I had a dog named Scooby. He looked nothing like Scooby-Doo. I don't have a favorite color because I've never thought about it before, and I don't have time now. I've never had peanut butter because the thought of it sticking to the roof of my mouth is aggravating."

The man is losing his mind, and I am loving it. My schoolgirl smile is plastered on my face, and I can't contain the giggles bubbling up to the surface. "Why are you telling me this?" *And please don't stop.*

"I'm telling you more about me." He smirks. "I can stop if this is too much."

"No, no, please continue," I say, turning to get a better look at him. He's smiling, this hard-ass mafia boss is smiling, and it's absolutely glorious. I want to take a picture of him and stash it away so I can see it whenever I want, whenever I need evidence that Artyom is, in fact, human.

"What would you like to know, *kroshka?*"

"Who was your first crush?" I ask, feeling giddy, like I'm at a sleepover playing twenty-one questions. I know I should take this opportunity to ask more serious questions, but I can't help but want to know things that make him more human. Things that make my heart leap out of my chest. Good things.

"Never had one."

"You're kidding. How did you ever get a girlfriend then?"

"I didn't," he says. "I've never had time for a girlfriend, and there are other ways to get what you need without the commitment."

I roll my eyes. "You're a walking red flag, you know that?"

He chuckles, bringing my hand to his lips and pressing a soft kiss between my knuckles. He keeps it there for a while, and I welcome the warmth of his breath.

"Do you have a best friend?"

"No."

"Not even Alec?"

He sighs, not in an exasperated way but in a thinking way.

Like he's mulling the question over in his head. "Alec is more of a right-hand man. Having him any closer would mean I have another weakness, which I can't afford to have."

"Another weakness?"

He looks over at me, his eyes pained. It hits me then that *I* am now his weakness. It scares him.

"Can I ask you a serious question?" I ask, my tone losing its humor.

"Anything."

I pause. "How much money do I still owe you?"

His eyebrows shoot up questioningly, and we stare at each other for a moment, letting the question sink in.

"Are you asking because you want to leave?"

"Eventually, yes. But I also want to make sure my father's debt is paid. He was wrong for taking a loan he knew he couldn't pay back."

He sighs and removes his hand. "I haven't been keeping track of the money. It wasn't about that for me. I needed to be close to you. I'm not a good man, Lena. I've done worse to keep people from leaving."

I wonder if he ever let go for long enough to see if they would come back on their own. It must be hard thinking no one would ever choose to stay. If he were to let me go, would I come back?

"I'm here, Art, and I'm yours," is all I can say. Locking away all the red flags and caution signs in the back of my mind.

29

Lena

I wake up to the warmth of Artyom's body, gently tucking me into him. His arm around me, his face in my hair. I want to capture this moment forever. How the sunlight streams into the room, highlighting everything in golden hues. The stillness and quiet of it all make it feel like time has stopped for a while. I feel him inhale a second later, and he pulls me closer, so close I can feel his heartbeat against my back. I smile because this is the first time we have woken up in each other's arms, and it feels so right. When I feel him lightly kiss my head, I turn to see him. His dark hair tousled perfectly, like it was styled to look that good. His eyelids open, and I see his emerald irises expand as soon as he sees me. We just stare for a while, like we're seeing each other for the first time. I trace his features with my finger, committing them to memory. I start at his eyebrows, noting every dark curve of his eyelashes, down to his nose, chiseled and defined. I dip my eyes to his lips and linger there, scanning the outline of his Cupid's bow, taking in his fuller bottom lip. There's nothing delicate to his mouth; it's strong and captivating to the point of not wanting to object to anything he says. I feel his warm breath on my finger as he kisses me, sending shivers down my spine.

"You're beautiful," I say, mostly to myself, and then feel his rumbling laughter against my finger.

"That's a first," he says, and leans in to kiss me. It's quick, but it makes my heart swell.

"What? The guys don't tell you you're beautiful?" I tease.

He pins me to the mattress a second later, and the way he looks at me sends hot liquid between my thighs. "You are the one who is beautiful, *kroshka*. I thought having you say you're mine would give me a little bit of peace, but now I just want to possess every part of you." His forehead touches mine, and he closes his eyes. "Like you have possessed every part of me." When I don't say anything, he pulls away and searches my face for something, but I'm just speechless. It feels like he's just confessed something big. Something I can't think about right now. His face softens, and as soon as I think he'll say something, my stomach releases a low grumbling sound that can probably be heard from the first floor. His face turns up into a grin, and we both chuckle, the tension melting away.

"I'll get us some breakfast," he says, leaning down and kissing me lightly.

I watch him walk away, still naked. It's like I've dreamed him up in one of my fantasies.

When we got home last night, Art picked me up, carried me back into our room, and then he had Alec move all my things back into *our* closet. After giving him a lot of shit about kicking me out before, he made it up to me in more ways than one, and I pretended to be reluctant to forgive him.

When the aroma of something buttery and sweet fills the apartment, I get out of bed and put on one of Art's shirts, the hem hitting my knees. I laugh, thinking how ridiculous I must look.

In the kitchen, I see at least five takeout boxes on the table, all smelling heavenly.

"It smells like my mother's cooking." I inhale again, and my stomach growls once more.

"I had Alec pick something up for us. Eat, *kroshka*." He pulls out my chair. I open the takeout boxes, and my eyes go wide at all my favorite foods. Russian crepes filled with jam and cottage cheese. I close my eyes, letting the scent bring me back to my childhood. I know this must be a favorite for most Russians, but this and the other food he ordered don't seem like a coincidence anymore.

"Are you just good at guessing what I like, or have you been in contact with my mom?" I chuckle.

"It's my job to know everything about everyone," he says plainly.

"So, what's Alec's favorite food?" I know I should ask how he gets this information, but I'm not sure I want to know the answer just yet.

"Grechka," he says.

I smile because, of course, Alec's favorite food is buckwheat. "I'll have to ask him and see if you're right," I tease.

He smirks, and once again, my heart fills with warmth. We sit at the table, sharing our food and moaning at how good it tastes. Food is definitely my love language, and Artyom knows precisely what he's doing. As soon as we're done, I insist on clearing the table while he gets dressed. His phone has been vibrating for about an hour now, but he hasn't even glanced at it. When he comes out of the room, I have to press my lips together, stopping myself from smiling like a schoolgirl. He's dressed in a black textured polo shirt, the sleeves hugging his biceps, showing off just how much work he's put in at the gym. My eyes trail down to his black trousers, pressed and tailored to him.

"You're staring," he says, knocking me out of my daze.

"I can't help it," I say, moving closer to him and wrapping my arms around his neck. He leans down and picks me up, our noses touching.

"Kiss me," I whisper. A second later, his mouth slams against mine, and I let out a moan of pure need. My legs wrap around his torso, and he presses me into the door. We kiss desperately, like we haven't just had a whole night together. Like we won't have another night. I feel his leg vibrate, and I almost whine.

"I think if you don't go now, Alec will break down the door," I say, panting.

"I'll see you tonight, *kroshka*. Wait up for me?"

"Okay," I whisper against his mouth.

He sets me down, and I watch him as he puts on his shoes, already missing his touch. *Get a hold of yourself, Lena, you're acting like a lovesick puppy.*

As soon as he leaves, I sag against the door, feeling my face warm. I must be coming down with something, right? There's a light knock on the door, and a smile spreads over my face as I hurl the door open.

"Forget something?" I ask, only it's not Art's face that stares back at me. It's Lev. I'm suddenly aware that I'm still wearing Art's shirt and nothing else. "Lev?"

"Uh, yeah, I won't be long. I just had to tell you I delivered your message, and um, she said she would be at the club tonight and wants you to meet her there." He turns around to leave.

"Wait," I say. "Thank you. I know it must've been uncomfortable to do that for me."

"At first it was, but then the boss gave me the green light."

"What?" I ask, dumbfounded.

"He told me to do whatever you asked."

My mind is racing. "He said that?"

"Yeah." He looks uncomfortable. "Anyway, I should get going."

"Um, yeah, okay. Thank you again." I close the door, feeling more confused than ever. I spoke to Lev forever ago. Way before Art and I… I can't seem to finish that thought. Before we developed feelings for each other?

I get dressed, trying hard not to overthink, but I can't stop my brain from spiraling. He told Lev to deliver my message to Andrea. He is okay with me seeing her. He *trusts* me. That word sticks with me all the way to the operating room. He trusted me then. He was going to let me see her even after the mess I made the last time I went to the club. I spend the entire day obsessing over what Lev said.

"Something on your mind?" a deep voice grumbles, and I spin around to see Roman standing by the door. I don't know why, but a full-on smile spreads over my face when I see him. I think it's because he's my only connection to the outside, as sad as that sounds.

"How'd you know?" I ask.

"I've been standing here for a good five minutes." He looks at his watch.

"Sorry, I've been distracted today."

He finally walks over and stands by the operating table, across from me, and nods. "I wanted to check up on you. I should've come around sooner. I'm sorry," he says, his eyes meeting mine.

My mind flashes to the night he drove me here, how he waited until I nodded that I was okay. "It's okay. I'm okay now," I say, and actually mean it.

He nods again, and I can tell he's contemplating telling me something, but it's almost as if he's not sure if he should.

"Lena…" I can tell he's struggling to say whatever it is, but I wait him out. "I've been thinking a lot about what you said to me in the car, about telling Andrea. I used to think my two lives would never work together, that I'd have to keep this part of me a secret forever, and I made myself believe I was fine with that." He pauses. I'm holding my breath because I think if I ask any questions now, he will stop talking, and whatever realization he's coming to will be lost. So, I just stay quiet and watch this giant man come to terms with his life.

"I think I'm going to tell her," he finally says. "She deserves to know all of me, and I need to pray to God she accepts this part of me because the Brotherhood is my life. It's intertwined in everything I do."

My heart feels light and heavy at the same time. Andrea does deserve to know. I'm happy he's going to finally tell her, but there's fear in his eyes. He's so afraid he'll lose her. Right when I think he's got everything off his chest, he looks up at me and asks me the one question I wasn't prepared for.

"Do you think you can love Artyom, knowing what he is and does?"

My heart beats so loudly I wonder if he can hear it. He waits for me to answer, but I can't even begin to think about that right now.

"I see the way he is with you. It's the way I am with Andrea. Maybe even more intense. I've never seen him this way. I've seen the way you look at him, too, it's one of the reasons I've decided to tell her. Because if you can still look at Artyom like that after knowing all of him, then maybe I have a shot."

I don't know why he's telling me this; I didn't think anyone knew about me and Art. I thought we were our in own quiet, private world

When the silence has stretched so far that it's reached an awkward level, I finally speak.

"I'm glad you're going to tell her. She does deserve to know. I can't tell you how she'll react, but what I do know is she's crazy about you. She has been with you for much longer than I've been trapped here. If I can see the good in all of you guys in this short amount of time, then she will too. But it's her decision."

He stares at me for a moment longer and then clears his throat. "Thank you." I give him a small smile.

"I should get going." He turns around and leaves.

I stand there completely confused about myself and my feelings for Art. I know I want more of him, of whatever this is, but can this turn into love? Is Artyom capable of loving me and letting me go? Can we mesh our two lives together? I think back to this morning, finding out Art trusted me enough to let me have contact with Andrea. He's trying. He's been trying, and that thought alone propels my feet out of the operating room and straight into his office.

30

Lena

As I approach the metal door to Art's office, I push aside any nerves building inside me. All I know is that I need to see him. I knock twice and wait. A second later, Alec opens the door, his eyebrows shooting up in surprise when he sees me.

"Is everything all right, Ms. Petrovna?" he asks.

"Uh, yes. Is this a bad time to see him?" I ask, very quickly losing my nerve.

He looks back for a second and then opens the door for me to come in. Artyom is at his desk, which is covered in papers. When I enter, he looks tense and deep in thought, which almost makes me turn around and leave. Whatever he's working on is really weighing on him; I can see it in his eyes.

"I can come back when you're free," I offer, standing by the door.

He motions for Alec to leave us and then stands up. "Are you okay?"

"Yes, I'm fine." His worry makes me smile. "I just wanted to see you." As soon as that sentence leaves my mouth, I regret it. It sounds juvenile, and clearly, he's busy with something probably important.

He sits back down in his large leather office chair and holds out his hand, gesturing for me to come over. The closer I get, the more embarrassed I feel about coming here. I round the desk, and he takes my hand, pulling me into his lap. "Say it again," he whispers into my neck.

"I just wanted to see you," I say, breathing him in. He sighs deeply and then pulls back to look into my eyes, his expression soft and gentle.

"What's on your mind, *kroshka?*"

I pause for a second, not knowing how to bring up what Lev told me. "I saw Lev this morning. He came to tell me Andrea is going to the club tonight." I pause again, giving him time to react.

"Good," he finally says, and I bite my cheek to keep from smiling.

"He said he had gotten your blessing a long time ago."

"Did he?" he muses.

"I guess I just want to say thank you." I wrap my arms around his neck and lean in to kiss his neck. He sucks in a breath as I nip at him. "Will you let me thank you?" I ask, grinding my hips forward and back.

"Lena." He sighs, his eyes closing. I pull back and kiss his lips. Deep and lingering. I pull back and sink to my knees, looking up at him. "Petrovna…" he begins. I can tell he wants this by how his chest rises and falls rapidly, cupping my cheek softly, almost pleading for me to keep going.

"Thank you," I say, kissing the outline of his cock. I feel it jerking and begin to salivate, wanting him more than anything right now. I unzip his pants, still looking at him, and take out his cock. It's hard and fucking glorious. In all our sexual encounters, I have yet to actually see him, feel him, and taste him the way I want, the way he deserves to be savored.

"Show me how you like it," I whisper before taking him in my mouth. I slowly go up and down his shaft, moaning as I do. I go faster when I feel his hand on my head, taking him deeper. I hear him let out a sigh, and I look up he's watching me with hooded eyes dripping with lust. "Fuck, Lena," he hisses, and I know he's close. He pushes my head faster, and I moan in approval. When I begin to taste his release, I go deep and hold him there until he moans in satisfaction. Until I feel him shudder around me. I lick him clean, and then he pulls me into his lap again.

"Be ready at ten."

31

Lena

I'm wearing all black tonight. I tell myself it isn't for him, but who am I kidding? I want to get his attention. I want to be the only one he sees in the club. I tug on my corset top, making sure it stays up, and give myself one last check. Once I put on my black stiletto heels, I'm ready to go. I open the door to leave and am greeted by Alec, who is waiting for me. Of course, he sent a babysitter.

"Hey, Alec. Are you my date for tonight?" I ask, teasingly. I knew I wouldn't be going with Art because he hasn't been back since I saw him in his office. Since I got to taste him and feel him come undone.

"I'll be accompanying you tonight, Ms. Petrovna," he says with a polite smile.

"Lead the way!" I'm giddy tonight. I'm practically prancing my way to the elevator. Alec eyes me warily, as if he's seeing a different person. Maybe I'm hallucinating, but I think I see the corner of his mouth twitch up into a smile, just for a split second.

Once we enter the club, I scan the first floor for Andrea.

"Do you see her, Alec?" I shout over the music.

"Red dress," he says, leaning down and pointing to the dance floor. Even with my four-inch stilettos, I still have to stand on my toes to see over the sea of dancing people. As soon as I see a glimmer of a red sparkly dress, I bolt. "Bye, Alec!" I shout over my shoulder, hoping he won't follow.

Once I reach her, I put a hand on her shoulder, and she spins around, facing me. "Lena! You're alive!" She brings me in for a hug and then quickly pushes me away. "Wait, I'm mad at you! Why didn't you say goodbye or anything?" she yells over the music.

"I'm sorry!" I shout back. "It's a long story!"

She folds her arms over her chest and narrows her eyes. I don't know what I can tell her right now. I'm pretty sure Roman hasn't told her anything yet, and I'm not about to be the one to tell her Roman is in the mafia and that I've been kept here working for them to pay off my father's debt.

"I met a guy," I say, which says it all and nothing at the same time.

She eyes me warily and then laughs. "Of course you have! Baby, when I met Roman, I went off the grid for a month. In my bedroom." She winks. I sigh, relieved, then the song changes, and she pulls me to her again. "Dance with me," she says, pulling me by the waist and swaying me.

I throw my head back, laughing, feeling the weight slide off my shoulders. We dance hand in hand like teenage girls, laughing and doing embarrassing old-school moves. Once Roman shows up, he grabs Andrea by the waist and twists her around, kissing her. I smile. I think they will be okay. I have to believe that.

I sway to the music, my hands snaking up and down my

body until I feel his arms on my shoulders, going down my arms and interlocking his fingers with mine. I lean into his body, getting high off his cologne. I tip my head up and kiss his jaw, not caring who sees anymore.

"You're distracting," he says in my ear.

I turn around and smile up at him. "Good," I say, then I kiss him. He's reserved at first, his hands rigid. I just want to make his worry melt away. I lick his lips, begging him to let my tongue in. When he does, he moans in my mouth, our kiss growing heavy, needy, and messy, just like whatever this is between us. I feel him grow hard through his pants, and I press into him.

"Not here, *kroshka*," he says as we break the kiss, my lips begging for more. He looks around. "Let's go home. I'm done sharing you."

I laugh. "But I just got here! You don't have to share me. Not here, not in bed… or in the upstairs restroom when you're fucking me." I wink at him.

His eyebrows pull up, surprised. "Let's go." He smirks, pulling me toward the stairs. I giggle and look at Andrea, her mouth is open in complete shock, and I mouth sorry the best I can. When we get upstairs, I can see Art hesitate for a moment, as if something else caught his attention.

"Let me take care of something really quickly, and I'll be back in a minute, okay?"

"Hurry or I might just change my mind," I tell him, giving him a quick peck on the lips.

He smiles. "Not a chance, Petrovna." He walks away, going to the VIP area at the back of the room.

I stand there, looking around at the people dancing, feeling genuinely happy. Maybe it could be like this all the time, and we can figure out the rest later. I feel a hand on my lower back and turn around, smiling. "Just in time, I was just about to…" I stop, my smile fades, and I lose my voice entirely.

"It's good to see you again, Lena," Nico says, his hand slipping around my waist.

"Uh, hey," I say, looking around for Artyom.

"I've been wanting to see you." He pulls me closer.

"Um, Nico, I'm here with someone." I begin to push him away.

His face suddenly changes. "See, I heard you might've been with him, but had to find out for myself. But the thing is, I had you first, and I don't share well with others." His smile fades, and his hold on me tightens.

"I was never yours, Nico. I'm sorry if I led you on. Please let me go." I try turning around to leave, but he holds on tighter, squeezing me hard. I begin to panic, thinking of all the ways this can end. I open my mouth to tell him Art will be here any moment, but it's too late.

Artyom yanks me away from him and steps between us. "Get your fucking hands off her," he says, anger seeping out of him.

"Damn, Artyom, I didn't peg you for someone who enjoys sloppy seconds." He laughs, looking at me. "I would've given you the ride of your life, sweetheart." He winks, and my eyes go straight to Art. The thread holding him together snaps, and he lunges at Nico, grabbing him by his throat and slamming him against the wall.

"There are two hundred people in this club, and every single one of them will see you die if you fucking open your mouth again," he snarls.

I inch toward him, wanting all of this to end, wanting to take back the last five minutes. I approach him and put a shaky hand on his back. He turns his head and sees my eyes pleading for him to let Nico go and leave with me. *Please, please, please stop*, I chant in my head.

He finally lets Nico go, stepping back slowly, still looking at him. I grab his hand, pulling him to me. I look back at Nico and see him practically foaming at the mouth. I pray he doesn't say another word.

"I guess she turned you into a pussy. Just like your brother." His laugh is cold and jagged, slicing through the air like a warning. "You know, I heard he saw it coming and just stood there waiting for it to end, like a *pussy*."

I close my eyes, knowing what's coming next. Artyom lets go of my hand and turns around, swinging at Nico with everything he's got. He takes him down to the ground fast, putting his weight on him. Whatever control I had over him fades into nothing. All I see is red in his eyes. I scream for Alec, who comes running, but he doesn't try to stop him. He just stands there. Everyone is just watching, waiting to see if this man is going to die. I scream at him because, at this point, I'm afraid there's no going back from here. I scream until my sobs take over, until the shock of what Nico's face looks like now makes me numb. I can't watch him die. I can't. I turn around and run like a coward. I run from him, this place, and all the memories I've created.

I follow a group of people out the door, the guards shouting something at me, but I can't hear; I can't understand anything right now. I run out in the cold, barefoot, tears running down my face, wishing I could forget him. I run to the only place I can.

I run home.

32

Artyom

Blind rage, that's all I feel. I see nothing and no one. I feel fury for my father, my brother, and my fucking life. In this moment, I have to protect, I have to avenge, and I have to destroy. When Alec pulls me off, I almost tear into him, too.

"Artyom!" he shouts, using all his weight to keep me from murdering this piece of shit in front of me. "This is not for your brother, not for Ivan! It will not bring him back, but it will bring a shitload of problems if you kill this man." He squeezes me one more time before letting me go.

I look down at Nico, and I can't even tell that's him anymore. People are screaming as his men pull out their guns and aim at us. They should know better since I have this entire place surrounded. It would be an unfair fight for them, and I dare them to try. Everything inside me is screaming: *do it*.

"Take this as your warning," I spit out. "Take your corpse and get the fuck out of here, and if I hear that any of you are anywhere near my territory again, this will be you tenfold."

They slowly lower their guns, pick up the body, and peel out of here. I can see from my men's faces that they feel conflicted about what they just saw. If it were anyone else, it'd be fine, but I can tell they're worried because it's Viktor's son. There will be retaliation, and we have to be ready. I know it in my bones, it was his gang that killed Ivan, and when I heard Ivan's name leave his mouth, I lost it. I feel the pain again, the loss, the despair creeping back in, and that's when I remember her. I look around frantically.

"Where is she?" I growl.

"She ran, and for good reason, Artyom. You were out of control." Only Alec can talk to me like this, like I'm still a kid following my father around, still learning the ropes. I run to the apartment, screaming her name. I turn over every piece of furniture that doesn't have her in it. She's gone. I get my phone out and dial Alec; he picks up in one ring. "Bring the car around."

"I don't think that's a good idea, Artyom. She was scared; she needs some time away from you, and you need some time to calm down."

"If you value your fucking life, Alec, you will bring the car around now," I say, and drive my phone into the wall, shattering it into a million pieces. I need to know she's safe. Word is going to get back to Viktor about what happened, and Lena will be in danger. Anyone I have ever gotten close to has been taken away from me. I will not let Lena be one of them.

The first place I drive to is her father's house, and I pull up just as she reaches the door. She drops to her knees, sobbing, pounding her fists against the wood like it might crack open and save her. The sight of her guts me. She looks so small, so broken, and it's because of me. My hand grips the door handle, ready to open it, to run to her, to take it all back. I shift forward in my seat, but I force myself to stop, my fingers white-knuckling the wheel instead. My hands start to shake. I did this to her. She's afraid because of me. She's afraid *of* me. I want to pull her into my arms and tell her how stupid I was. How broken I am. I've been carrying so much loss that I wouldn't have recognized love if it stared me in the face, and when it did, I destroyed it. I wanted her to fix me, to take away the pain, but all I did was give her more of it. I won't do to her what I did to Ivan. She needs to be far away from me. As far as possible. Even if it tears me apart.

33

Lena

I pound on my father's door, crying hysterically. "Dad! Dad! Open the door! Dad!" I yell over and over again. I hear the door unlock, and I fall to my knees, overcome with relief.

My father opens the door, eyes going wide when he sees me. "Lena! What are you doing here? What happened?" He kneels and pulls me to him, hugging me. I cry into his shoulder, not wanting to let go. "What did they do to you? Did he hurt you?" He leads me inside, setting me down on the couch carefully, as if I could shatter into a million pieces at any moment. The couch sags when I sit, it's the same rust color as I remember, but it doesn't feel familiar anymore. Nothing about this house feels familiar anymore. My dad brings me a glass of water and a wet towel, wiping the blood and dirt off my feet.

"Tell me something, Lena, I'm going crazy here!" he says.

"I think he killed him, Dad." Tears roll down my cheeks. "I couldn't watch, I just couldn't."

"Those men are monsters, Lena, and he's the worst of them. I told you he was dangerous! I should have stayed, not you!"

He looks up at me, shaking with anger, or maybe fear, for me. We sit in silence for a few moments. "So you ran. He didn't let you go?" he asks. I shake my head. "Then we need to get out of New York as soon as possible. Because he will find you, Lena. He might already be looking." He goes to the window and looks out, checking to see if anyone is out there, then turns off the lights.

"We won't have much time, but I think we're okay for now. Get cleaned up and rest. We'll fly out tomorrow morning. I'm getting the flight now." He gets his phone and starts looking for flights.

Once the stinging in my feet subsides and my breath evens out, I go upstairs to shower. I look in the mirror and don't even recognize my own reflection. Who am I right now? I was sleeping with a man whom I knew was dangerous. What did I think would happen? He would change? My mind conjures an image of what Nico looked like when I last saw him, and I double over, gagging at the thought. He was unrecognizable. I throw up whatever I have left in my stomach and sit in the shower for a long time, scrubbing my skin raw, trying to get his smell and touch off me.

When I leave, I go to my old room and I am surprised to see it's as I left it. Two twin beds sit in opposite corners of the room, my desk sits by the window, and some of my old clothes are still hanging in the closet. I grab my sister's old grey sweatshirt and pants and put them on. I slide into my bed, and it creaks in protest. My gaze fixes on the glow-in-the-dark stars above me, and I fall asleep to a time when I felt safe, loved, and sure of what my future would bring.

* * *

"Lenachka, get up, sweetheart, we need to go." I open my eyes and see my dad standing by the door. I groan and get out of bed, rubbing my swollen eyes. Yesterday's events come flooding back, giving me a rush of energy to get the hell out of this place.

Once we are ready, my dad calls a cab, and we get in and head to the airport. I sit there, letting the wind from the open window hit my face. I tell myself I won't miss it here: I won't miss the people I've met, I won't miss the food, and I won't miss *him*.

At the airport, my dad gives the driver a fifty and whispers something to him.

"What did you say to him?" I ask.

"To keep his mouth shut. He's Russian. I just had to make sure," he says while getting the bags. Inside, I tell my dad to get the tickets while I go to use the restroom.

"Our flight leaves soon; don't be long," he says, checking his watch as the PA blares a final-boarding call for someone who isn't me.

I rush into the restroom and lock myself in the stall. I sit there, breathing in and out slowly, trying to calm myself. I'm finally going home. I should feel more at ease now that I'm minutes away from leaving this place. So why does my heart ache so much? Why does it feel like I'm leaving a part of me behind? I sit there with my face in my hands, breathing in and out until I hear someone enter the restroom and decide to head out. As I open the door, my heart drops. I actually thought he'd let me go. I thought he cared about me enough to let me go. How stupid of me. I stand there facing a man in a leather jacket, blocking the entrance.

"Oh, he's good!" I say, hysteria crawling up my throat.

"Honestly, I thought he would've found me sooner. You guys are kind of behind." I wash and dry my hands, not looking at the man standing before me.

He comes closer to me, and in a hushed tone, he says, "You're going to walk out slowly with me, and we're going to get into the black SUV parked right outside. Do you understand?" I laugh again. "Look, if he wants me, he can get me himself." I push past him, but he grabs me by my hair and slams my face against the wall, holding me there.

"You have one chance to do what I say. No one said I needed to bring you alive. I have no problem bringing you to him in pieces," he tells me, a little too close to my face. He smells of cheap cologne and leather.

Whatever heartache I was feeling disappears and is replaced with terror. I don't say anything to him. I don't even know how my legs started moving; it all becomes a blur. The cold press of his gun digs into my spine beneath my sweatshirt, each shove forcing me forward. I see my dad at the kiosk and pray he turns around. I pray he sees me before it's too late. But, of course, life never works out that way. Tears stream down my face as we approach the door I just came in through. We exit and get into the car. After that, everything goes dark. The last thing I feel is a sting at the back of my head, and I hear the man say, "Take us to Viktor."

34

Lena

I wake up in what looks like a hospital room, a heart monitor beeping steadily. I sit up abruptly and feel the room spinning.

"Lena, is that right?" a deep voice with a heavy Italian accent asks.

Holding on to the chair, I turn and face the voice. "Do I know you?" I ask, my voice groggy, feeling the bruise at the back of my head swell to the size of a golf ball. His eyes go to the bed in the corner of the room, and I follow. I see a person lying there, hooked up to different monitors, his face bandaged. My eyes go wide. It can't be him, can it?

"Is that… Nico?" I ask, suppressing the urge to vomit.

"So you do know my son."

I look at him, not understanding. "Uh, we met briefly," I say, my voice shaking.

"I heard it was because of a whore that my son is barely breathing. Are you that whore?" His voice comes out harsh.

"I didn't do this to him," I say, trying to be careful of what I say.

He chuckles. "Well, of course you didn't! Your boyfriend Volkhov did."

"Then what do you want from me?"

"Oh, I just want to give you back to him, sweetheart, the way he gave me back my son. I need to teach the little fucker a lesson. I guess he didn't learn it the first time when we put a bullet through his brother's skull."

My thoughts are racing so fast I can't keep up. Art was right to suspect them. They did kill his brother. I feel myself sweating. How do I get out of this alive? He must want something else, right? Every gang wants to be top dog, and I'm willing to bet this guy is pissed he's not.

"I can negotiate with him. He'll listen to me. Whatever you want, he'll give it to you as long as I ask him," I say, hoping he'll go for it.

He laughs. "What I want, even you can't give me, sweetheart."

"You can get everything you want, I promise you. He'll do anything to get me back safe," I lie. At this point, I don't know what I am to Art. All I know is he's unpredictable and dangerous.

"Did you know it was my family that claimed Brooklyn as our territory before those fuckers took it? Thirty years ago, it was ours! Not the Volkhov! What I want is to slice their tattoo off their skin, one by one, and feed it to my dogs," he snarls at me.

"So you want this territory? You want Brighton?" I ask, guessing at our location.

"This is my home! We've been operating from here for years under the radar." My eyes scan the room as he answers, looking for anything that will tell me where I am.

"So, you want Brooklyn, I can get him to agree to that," I say, hopeful.

He laughs. "You think that's all? I need him to kneel before his men and declare his fealty to me." He laughs again. "Can you do that, sweetheart? Does he love you that much?" His tone is mocking.

I truly don't know the answer to this question. I just know I can't love him. I can't let myself. But what I do know is I have a greater chance of keeping my face intact by going about it this way.

"If you let me talk to him, I will get you what you're asking for. I just need to talk to him." I try not to sound desperate. I try to keep my tears at bay, to keep my body from trembling. Just a little longer.

He pulls out his phone and dials a number. I hear him talking in Russian to someone, asking them to bring a burner phone and the number to the Volkhov. The man who kidnapped me comes into the room a few moments later and hands him a phone.

"You only say what we discussed, nothing more, nothing less. Do you understand? Or you'll not only be missing your face but also your tongue."

I shudder at the thought and hold in the tears stinging my eyes. I hold the phone to my ear and wait for someone to pick up.

I hear his voice: "*Da?*"

My hand shakes as I hold the phone, and I get up and pace a few steps. Looking back, I see something on the chair I've been sitting on, a logo of some sort. "Art?" I say, not knowing how he will react or if he'll even care.

"Lena? Where are you? Whose car did you get into?" His

voice is raspy and strained.

The man reaches for the phone, and I give it to him. "Your whore has limited time, so shut the fuck up and listen to what she has to say." He gives me the phone back.

I glance again at the logo on the chair: it's shaped like a dagger, the hilt curling like a question mark. I don't know what it means, but I hope *he* will. I hold the phone to my ear again and draw a breath, preparing to give the performance of a lifetime.

"Art," I say, keeping my voice calm but urgent, "if I mean anything to you, you'll listen closely". I pause just enough to make him lean in to what I'm saying. "He wants Brooklyn." I let the weight of that sit, "Queens isn't enough anymore. He wants to take back his home." I pace more and take a few steps toward Nico's bed and angle the phone slightly, letting the monitor's soft beeping filter through. One beat. Two. Regular. Alive. Medical. I hope Art hears it. I hope he *knows* what it means. He doesn't say a word, so I continue. "He wants you to pledge your fealty to him in front of your men. I know this must feel like a *dagger* to your heart, but… if you love me, you'll do this." There's more silence. "Art, I feel so lost here; I need you." I give him the last clue: I emphasize *lost*, just enough to echo what I told Art weeks ago, that Brooklyn doesn't feel like home anymore. I don't know if he picked up on anything I said, I don't know if it's enough, if I could've done better. I'm out of time.

"Give him the phone, *kroshka*," he says at last, his voice so soft it caresses me, telling me everything will be all right. I hesitate for a moment, wanting to say more, wanting to say be careful, and these people murdered his brother, but I know I can't. I hand the man the phone and pray I get out of here soon.

* * *

The next hour passes slowly. Viktor left me as soon as he hung up the phone, so now it's just me and whatever is left of his son. With each beep of the monitor, I grow even more uneasy and shrink into myself, unsure whether Artyom understood any of my clues.

The door opens, and the man who took me from the airport comes in. "Get up," he tells me.

I start to panic. I can't leave here; I won't have another opportunity to tell Art where to find me.

"Where are we going?" I ask.

"Get the fuck up, bitch," he spits.

I realize then that there will be no talking to this man. Nothing I say or do will stall him in any way. What if Art failed? What if they caught on to my messages, and now he's here to kill me? Adrenaline kicks in, and my heart begins to pound.

"Fuck you," I tell him, shaking with fear or anger, I'm not sure anymore.

His eyes narrow, and he stalks toward me, squeezing my throat. "Let me show you what we do with whores with dirty mouths around here," he says, his breath hitting the inside of my ear. I feel the hair on the back of my neck stand up, and goosebumps begin to spread all over my skin like wildfire. He throws me hard to the floor and stomps on my stomach with his muddy boot. I can't breathe; I can't see; I'm gasping for air. I feel his palm on my face, blocking my view of him like, as if he can't stand to look at me. He starts to tear my pants down, bruising my skin while he does it. I'm still gasping from the blow to my stomach. I'm praying he'll hit me again, this time harder, so that I pass out and don't have to feel anything. When I feel his fingers ripping my underwear, tears start to run down my face, and I scream with everything I have in me. I scream like I've just been cut up, like I've lost a limb and am dying. The kind of scream that's laced with agony, one I didn't know I had in me.

He pushes my face down to the floor harder, trying to shut me up, but the screams keep coming. I can't hear anything over my screams and sobs, so when a bullet shoots through this guy's head, I don't even hear it. I see him lying limp beside me, blood pooling all around us. I stare into his hollow, unblinking eyes, and relief spreads over me. Familiar hands pick me up and cradle me. I close my eyes, taking in his scent, and it doesn't surprise me how much it feels like home.

I can't make out what he says next, but I'm being carried out of what looks like a clinic and put into a car. Volkhov men swarm the place, covering every inch of it like shadows waiting for orders.

When I look at Artyom, he stands by the door with Alec. His shoulders are tight, his jaw clenched so hard I think it might shatter. There is blood on his hands, and I don't know if it is his or someone else's. He doesn't even notice.

Then his eyes find mine, and the world stops. They are not just angry, they are feral, wild, a storm that nothing can contain. My breath hitches because I have never seen him like this. This is different from when he was ripping into Nico back at the club. He looks like he is one second away from tearing the world apart with his bare hands.

His voice is low, almost calm, but it's the calm that comes

before something catastrophic. "Kill them all."

A shiver runs down my spine. I don't know who he means, everyone or anyone, but I know he won't stop until there's nothing left.

35

Lena

The entire ride, Art keeps looking at me. I feel his eyes scanning my body. I turn from him, looking out the window. I don't want him to see me like this. Bruised and broken, I don't need his pity either. A mafia man pitying me feels like a sick joke. We stop in front of the hospital, and I look at him, confused.

"What are we doing here?" I ask.

"You need to be seen, Lena," he says, opening the door and getting out.

When he comes over to my side, I stay put. "How am I going to explain what happened?"

"I'll take responsibility, but you need a doctor." He holds his hand out for me to take.

"Nothing is broken, Art. I just have a few bruises," I tell him.

"When I came in… I saw him…" He looks away, shaking with the kind of anger that got us into this mess.

"He didn't get a chance, Art. You came just in time." I can't imagine what he saw and what I look like now. I know what will happen if I go in there and see a doctor. I've tended to many women who were brought into the hospital looking like I do now. I'm not ready for that. I'm not ready to be poked and interrogated. He hesitates for a moment, still scanning my face and body. "Art, just take me home. I need to get out of these clothes." He nods reluctantly and closes the door.

We drive in silence, and I welcome it. I wouldn't know what to say to him. Thank you for saving me? Or screw you for putting me in this situation? When we arrive at his apartment building, I let him carry me in, mostly because my legs feel like bricks and partly because I need to be held. That small part makes me feel pathetic, like I'm some stupid lamb wanting the comfort of a lion.

Once inside, I head straight to the bathroom and close the door, leaving him on the other side. I stop at the mirror, putting my head down, not quite ready to see my face. Not ready to relive the day I just had. Bloodstained tears roll down my cheeks and land on the vanity. I look up and slowly realize it's not my blood but the blood of the man who was shot on top of me. I can still picture his wide, still eyes looking past me as he lay mere inches from my face. I feel the burn of his fingers on my body, and I try to fight the urge to slice my skin off. I turn the shower on, strip off my clothes, and get in. The water needles my skin, making my bruises bloom from pink to violet. I scrub every inch of my face and body vigorously. I watch the water turn red and fight to close my eyes; I don't want to look, but I need to see him wash away into the drain.

The shower door slides open, and I don't have to look back to know it's him. He steps in and wraps his arms around me, holding me close. He's gentle and cautious. Tears stream down my face because I don't know who he is, maybe I've never known, not fully. What I saw the other day is not this. I saw a monster wanting to destroy, to hurt, to kill. His touch feels all wrong now. I don't need him to be loving. I don't need his pity. What I do need is to forget. I turn around, anger in my eyes, and push him off me and into the shower wall. His eyes are soft, understanding, and just all wrong. He's still staring at me, worry in his eyes. Screw that. I come at him, wrap my arms around his neck, and pull him to me. I kiss him hard; he kisses me back, but not with the same intensity, which only makes me angrier. I bite his lip, drawing blood.

He grabs my face and looks into my eyes, a silent apology written all over them. Except I don't want an apology right now, I just want him to make me forget. To fuck me into forgetting. I know what almost happened to me, and I am not running from it. I am in control, and I am choosing this anyway. I sink to my knees and take his cock in my hand.

"Lena…" he starts, then sinks, taking me by the shoulders and pressing me to his chest.

I pull his hands off. "What? Now that I'm bruised and broken, you don't want to fuck me anymore?" I push him off and stalk out of the shower, fully aware of the damage on my body now. The pink and blue patches, my swollen face, and raw skin are a reminder of the day's events. He comes after me, letting the door hit the wall. *Good,* anger is an emotion other than pity.

"Let me take care of you, Lena," he says softly.

I turn to face him. "I don't need you to take care of me. I just want to fuck. That's what we've been doing, right? Just fucking?" I'm a good few feet away from him, but I can feel the heat radiating off his body.

"I love you," he says, holding nothing back. His eyes are sullen, and I can tell he hasn't been sleeping.

Rage builds in my chest. "Screw your love! Did you decide you love me before or after you rearranged Nico's face? Was it before or after you saw me beaten up and almost raped? This isn't love, Art, it's pity! And I don't need it from you!" I turn around and grab my clothes, stuffing them into my bag. I need to get the hell out of this place.

"What are you doing?" he asks.

"If we're not going to fuck, then I'm leaving," I say, walking toward the door, still naked.

"The hell you are!" He grabs my elbow and takes my bag, throwing it across the room.

"Let me go!" I scream.

"Listen to me, *kroshka*, you are out of your damn mind if you think I'm ever going to let you go again."

I wriggle against him. "You said you'd let me go!" I bark at him.

"Look at me, Lena. I am never making that mistake again. I will never forgive myself for what happened to you, and I will spend my entire life protecting you. I will spend my entire life loving you. You are mine, do you understand?" he says while backing me up into the room. "You were mine from the moment I saw you at the train station, and you'll be mine until they put me in the ground."

I stare at him, eyes wide. I want to claw at him, to hit him until he takes those words back, but I just stand there speechless.

He grabs my jaw and makes me look up at him. "I love you, Petrovna, whether you like it or not. It's not pity in my eyes. It's love."

I look up at him, his heart open to me. "I don't love you," I lie to both of us.

"I don't care. Love me or hate me, just… have me, Lena, have all of me or part of me." He puts his hands on either side of my face and whispers, "just have me any way you want."

I close my eyes, not able to look at him. "I don't want you," I say, tears streaming down my face.

"Look at me, *kroshka*, and say that."

I open my eyes and look at him. My mouth opens, but the words won't come out.

He trails soft kisses around my face. "Tell me you don't want me like I want you," he says, then kisses my lips. Our kisses are slow, wet, and full of warmth. I feel his cock harden, and I take him in my hand, stroking up and down.

"I want you," I whisper. We fall onto the bed together, and our kisses become deeper.

"You have me, baby. You have all of me," he says.

I roll on top of him and straddle him. "Show me," I say.

He lifts me, then lowers me onto his cock. I let out a moan full of need and begin to ride him slowly, feeling every inch of him. I look down at this breathtaking man, memorizing his chest, his face, and his lips. I bring his finger up to my mouth and suck, wanting to taste him. He lets out a groan and then switches us, pinning me against the mattress, driving into me harder.

"Yes," I moan as he pumps harder, looking at me the whole time, kissing me, caressing me, and showing me his love. I want to cry, I want to scream that I love him too, but I'm scared. I'm afraid to love him, to lose him, to be in his world. We make love and come apart together, holding each other desperately, not wanting to let go.

As we lie there, I see Art looking at my bruises, his eyes growing somber. "Hey, my bruises will heal. I'll be okay," I tell him, kissing his chin. The truth is, the bruises will heal and fade. Not a trace will be left of that horrible day on my body. But I know that's not what he's worried about. He's worried about the scars I've developed on the inside.

"It's not okay. I will never forgive myself for what happened to you, Lena. I know why you ran. You were afraid of what you saw, and I don't blame you. All I wanted to do at that moment was rip him apart to defend Ivan. But even I know Ivan would be horrified with what I've done. When I didn't find you in the apartment, I looked for you. I found you at your father's house and was prepared to let you go. I didn't deserve you, and I still don't." He looks up at the ceiling. "I spent the night outside your house, making sure no one came for you. I followed you to the airport and silently said my goodbyes. When I saw you come back out of the airport and get into that car, my heart dropped. I knew my life had caught up to you, that it was about to swallow up another person I loved."

"When you called, I understood all the messages you gave me, but a piece of me wanted to give everything up. To give up the territory and my leadership, it's what I deserve. The only thing that stopped me was you. I wanted to make sure you got home safe because I know men like Viktor, no matter what I would've done, he wouldn't have given you back to me whole. When I saw you on the floor with one of his men on top of you…" He pauses and looks at me. "Killing him doesn't feel like enough."

I nestle closer to him, breathing in his scent and feeling his warmth. "It's over, Art. He's gone. It's just you and me now." We lie in silence, feeling the room grow lighter. "So… you did see me at the train station!" I say, propping myself up on my elbow to look at him.

He chuckles. "Yes, *kroshka*."

"I knew it! Why did you make it seem like you weren't there?" I prop my chin on his chest.

"It was my brother's funeral that day. I told the men I couldn't go. That I had business. So, once they left, I went to the train station. I just wanted to be alone. When I sat down, I saw you and couldn't stop looking. It felt like you were taking some of my pain away somehow. If the train hadn't shown up at that exact time, my legs would've kept walking across those tracks and into your arms."

My smile widens. "I felt the same way."

He looks down at me and brings me in for a kiss. We kiss each other slowly, not wanting to leave and face reality just yet.

36

Lena

I wake up to soft kisses and the warmth of his breath on my neck. We've been playing this game of who wakes who first with sex all night. So far, it's three points for Art and one for me. The man does not sleep.

"Mmm, not fair," I moan.

I feel his smile on my neck. "It's noon, *kroshka*." He trails kisses down my neck. "My phone has been blowing up since 5:00 a.m. I'm afraid I'll need to go do some damage control."

"Let's stay here a while longer. I'm not ready to leave this bed." I turn around, smiling wide as I see his face, the light illuminating his facial features. I trail a finger over his strong jaw, feeling his stubble on my fingertips.

He takes my fingers and kisses them. "You should call your parents, Lena. Your dad must be really worried. I had Alec contact him after I found out where you were. He's waiting for your call."

I sigh. "You're right. I need to do some damage control myself."

We get ready together, dressing and undressing each other.

With each moment, I want to tell him how I truly feel. The words are on the tip of my tongue, but each time I try, they just won't come out. My heart keeps telling me to shout it out, grab him, and scream *I love you*. I love everything you are, the bad, the ugly, the scary, and all the heart-swelling good. At the same time, my mind is screaming, I'll be signing my death warrant by telling him how I feel. The questions in my mind keep clawing at the surface, trying to get out. Questions of the future and what it would look like with him. A mafia man who breaks people, takes people like my dad, and tears families apart. Do I want a future so uncertain and dangerous? Can I close my eyes to what he is and what he does behind the doors of our home? It feels as though there is a war inside of me, and I don't know what to do.

Artyom walks over to the closet, reaches up to the top shelf, and pulls something out. He throws it on the bed, and my mouth falls open in surprise.

"You've got to be kidding me! My phone has been in this room the whole time?" I gape.

Artyom takes both my cheeks in his hands and plants a kiss on my lips. "Call your dad."

I turn my phone on and almost kiss it. God, you don't know what you have until it's gone. Art goes out to the living room and makes a phone call while I mentally prepare to call my dad. I don't know what to tell him about what happened. The phone rings, and dread settles in the pit of my stomach.

"Lena?" I hear my dad's voice shaking.

"Yes, Dad, it's me." A tear rolls down my cheek.

"What's going on? What happened? Are you okay?"

"I'm okay." I sniffle and draw out a sigh. "A lot happened."

"Lenachka, let me come get you. Where are you?"

"I'm with Artyom, at his place."

"He's still keeping you there? Tell him I have his money. I can give him whatever he wants, tell him to let you go!"

God, hearing the fear in his voice makes me feel physically sick. My father genuinely fears the man I'm sharing a bed with.

"Dad, it's not like that anymore. He's not keeping me here." How do I tell him I'm here because I want to be here? I can hear his heart breaking already. My feelings for Artyom will never be understood by my family members. It'll be either him or my family, and I'm not sure I'm ready to choose yet.

"I will come pick you up then. We can talk when I see you."

"Okay," is all I can say; no other words enter my brain.

"I'm getting dressed and heading over. This nightmare is almost over."

I hang up the phone, feeling the hole in my heart grow bigger, and all I want to do is crawl under this blanket and never come out.

Art walks in, leaning against the door, our eyes saying everything for us. I can tell he's tense. Whatever conversation he just had was not a good one.

"I need to go out for a while. I'm not sure when I'll be back today, but I'll leave one of my guys with you just in case."

I stare at him, wondering if he thinks I'll run away again or if he's worried for my safety. Either way, I need to be able to leave this place when I need to. I can't be a prisoner anymore.

"Art, my dad is picking me up. I need to go with him and explain what happened. I can't do it here, a place where we were both held captive." I see something change in his face, panic rising in his eyes. "Am I still your prisoner, Art?" My words come out as a whisper.

His stance softens, and he comes over to me, kneeling before resting his head on my lap. Instinctively, my fingers go to his head, and I run them through his silky hair, feeling the warmth from his breath on my thighs.

"If I say yes, will you stay?" he asks, knowing the answer.

"I want to stay here because I want to, Art, not because I have to. I need some time with my family to explain things."

He looks up at me. "Let me send one of my men with you then." He's scared for me. I'm also afraid, but I can't live like this; always watched and followed.

I trace his brows, trying to smooth them over. "I'll come home, Art. I'll come back to you," I say, and I mean it. I can't shut off all the questions circling in my mind, but I also can't keep denying my heart.

He takes my face and brings it to his, kissing me. "You already know how I feel, Lena. I will always find you. I will always know where you are. You are mine, *kroshka*, and I am yours."

Those words alone send warmth to my core, heat crawling through my skin. Am I a fool for reacting this way? I've learned there is no stopping the way I feel for him. I am his. As I open my mouth to tell him my true feelings, his phone vibrates, and once again, our bubble of bliss breaks. He picks up the phone and agrees to something I can't make out.

Once he hangs up the phone, he looks at me and holds his hand for me to take. "I need to head out. I'm sending Alec with you, but you won't even see him. It's not because I don't trust you to come back; it's for your safety. I won't be able to focus on anything if I know you're out there without any protection."

I sigh, knowing he has already made up his mind about this.

"Okay. But this isn't going to be a thing, Art. I refuse to have a babysitter for the rest of my life."

His lips curve into a smile. "But I thought you liked Alec?"

I push him playfully. "Yes, but he's going to start hating me if babysitting becomes his new job."

"It's not forever, *kroshka*. It's just for now." I watch him as he puts on his black loafers and unlocks the door. With each movement, I want to grab him by the waist and not let go. I want to look him in the eyes and tell him I love him, but my legs stay glued to the floor, and my mouth becomes dry as sand. He glances back again and winks at me before closing the door. My heart aches. *What's wrong with you, Lena? You know you love this man. Why is it so hard to open your mouth and tell him that?* His love is messy, dangerous, and ugly sometimes, but it's also the truest I've ever felt.

When I've finally decided, I fling open the door and run after him, practically tripping on the stairs. I run, smiling, and I run wholeheartedly to the man I love. When I see the metal doors, adrenaline kicks in, and I practically use my whole body to push them open. The light blinds my view of anything, but I hear familiar voices. I hear the car door close and then open a second later.

"Lena? What's wrong?" His tone is full of worry.

I raise a hand to shield the light and run to meet him halfway. My heart swells from the sight of him again, from the words reverberating through my chest. I love you, it screams over and over again. I throw myself into his arms and weep, smiling. "I love you. I love you, Art. I can't let you go without you knowing that," I say with my eyes closed and tears streaming down my face.

"Look at me, *kroshka*," he says in my ear. I open my eyes,

blinking away happy tears, and he stares at me with an intensity that makes me putty in his arms. We stare at each other like no one is there, like we're the only ones on this planet. I see words forming on his lips, but a second later, his face morphs into complete terror as he wraps himself around me, taking us both down to the ground.

My ears are ringing, and I feel like I've gone deaf for a moment. I want to ask Art what just happened, but I can't open my mouth; he's crushing my entire body under his. Someone tears Art from me, and I see the man's mouth moving, but I still can't hear him. I don't know what he's saying. He's kneeling and yelling at Art, so I look over at him, and in an instant, my heart drops. Art is looking up at the sky, not moving, blood pooling all around him. Everything seems like it's happening in slow motion. All the men are huddled over, yelling something to me, to Art, but I can't understand any of it. My brain isn't processing what just happened.

"Lena! Lena! Can you fix him? I need you to snap out of it! He's dying, can you help him or not?" Roman is yelling at me, and I look down at Art, seeing two bullet wounds in his abdomen. I start to snap out of it slowly, slowly realizing what the universe has done. What it's taking from me.

"Art? Art!" I move his face to look at me. I still see light in his eyes, but it's quickly fading. "He needs a hospital! Call an ambulance!"

Mike starts pacing. "Fuck! He can't go to the hospital, you know that, Lena! The feds will never let him go after this shit; it's what they need to take us all down!"

"Then he's going to die!" I scream, feeling all the blood leave my body until I'm numb. "There's too much blood, and I don't know whether any vital organs were hit," I say, tears spilling down my face. I feel useless. Utterly useless when it counts the most.

An older man comes into view and bends down next to us. "I know a guy. It won't be cheap, but he will help. We need to go now, though."

"What guy? Where is he?" I ask desperately.

Two men come over, lift Art, and carry him to an SUV.

"Where are you taking him? He needs a hospital! Alec! Tell them!" I look for Alec, but he is already in the car. They're moving while I'm sitting here paralyzed.

"We'll take care of him, Lena. As soon as we know anything, we'll let you know too. Just be careful. Get somewhere safe and stay there." That's all Roman says as he walks away from me and gets in the car, driving away with my entire heart in the backseat.

37

Artyom

The SUV swallows me whole, the car a dark contrast to the light of her face. I wait to hear her voice again, to feel her beside me, but it doesn't come. The car starts moving, and she's not in here. I try to move, but my body feels anchored to the seat. Leather sticking to my back. I can see Roman on my left, his hands buried in my gut.

"Packing's holding for now," he says, optimistic. "Pressure's good."

It's not. The world goes quiet at the edges.

"Stay with me, boss," Roman says.

I'm trying. The ceiling begins to blur. The ringing lifts and falls like a tide. My body feels so far away.

"Look at me."

I look at Roman, but it is not his face staring back. It's Ivan's. Ivan is dead, but he's sitting where Roman should be.

"You ready to join me?" he asks.

I stare at him. The crooked smile. The scar I gave him above his brow when we were little. It's him.

"I have no intention of dying," I say, shocked that I am seeing him again. A cold wave moves over my legs, and I feel a hand slap my cheek.

"Stay awake, boss."

"I am awake," I tell him, but Roman's mouth does not match the words I hear.

"It is only a matter of time. Today, next week, next year. They will get you, too. But if you give up now, you can spare her, Artyom."

Her. He means Lena, whom I left on the floor back at my building. Unprotected.

"I can protect her," I say, not sure who I'm trying to convince.

"Like you protected me?" He laughs bitterly. For once, he looks older than me.

"Boss. Who are you talking to?" Roman barks, palm back in my gut. Tires screech, the SUV takes a turn too fast, and I go weightless for a moment.

"I'm sorry," I say, realizing it's the first time I have ever apologized to him.

"Like I said. It's inevitable for us, but it doesn't have to be for her. Let go, Artyom."

"I can't, Ivan. I need to get the ones who got you. I need to keep her safe," I choke out.

He laughs again. "You want to avenge me? Let go. It was supposed to be you." His eyes are solemn. He's right. It should have been me. Ivan was meant for a long life, stitching people back together, growing old with a family. He should be alive, not me.

The SUV jerks hard right, and Ivan blinks out. Roman is back, sweaty and real, shouting something I cannot catch. The edges go dark. Her name slips out of me. "Lena." The ringing swells, and the voices fade to nothing.

38

Lena

The next few days go by in a blur. I sit in my old room, glued to my phone, waiting for a phone call that doesn't come. I know what I must look like to my dad. He thinks this is Stockholm syndrome, a fucked-up love for my captor. My dad hovers around me, blaming himself and aging before my eyes. His voice changes from soft to scolding when I don't listen to reason. He wants me to go back to Arizona and my life there, but I can't go when my heart is here. I can't go because I promised to come back to him, and that's what I intend to do.

My dad tells me Art is dead. In fact, he assures me he's gone. He's been by the apartment building and says it's abandoned and locked, with no one going in or out. He shakes me, trying to make me understand that I'm no longer a prisoner and can move on. He tells me this is the perfect scenario, and it couldn't have turned out better for me. Whenever Danny calls, he joins in on the fun, too.

"Lena, he kidnapped Dad and probably would've killed him if you hadn't gotten there in time. You have to know how crazy that is, right?" Danny asks, like I've been brainwashed not to remember the facts.

"I know how it all sounds, Danny, I know. But you weren't there with me."

He sighs, exasperated. "We're worried about you, and we want you to come home. I can fly out and come get you if you want. You don't have to be alone."

I'm tired of defending myself. I'm tired of everyone thinking something is wrong with me.

"I'm staying here, Danny."

"Fine. Take however long you need to put this behind you. But whatever you might feel for him, just remember that he kept you and Dad as prisoners. You're both free now."

I'm free. The words invade my brain like a virus, circling until that's all I can think of. I'm free. Free of his warmth, his scent, his love. If that's what free is, then I want to be his prisoner again. I miss everything about him, his touch, what he does to my body, and how much it hurts to love him. He is what makes me feel alive, and right now, I am just surviving. It's not healthy, I know. It's irrational and weak to hold on like this. I'm confused about how I should feel and how I actually feel.

Even though I know she won't understand, I call my mother anyway. Something about feeling this vulnerable makes me ache for her.

Except, telling her that I'm staying in New York to find my missing boyfriend doesn't go as planned. "Lena, you're breaking my heart," she sobs. I stay quiet, because what could I possibly say? Nothing I tell her will make her understand what happened to me, or how I feel about Artyom. How do I explain that I feel chained to him and I don't want to be set free?

"It's all your father's fault," she sniffs, and here comes the blame game.

"But it's mine too. I never should have let you go," she says, as if I'm not a fully functioning adult who can make my own decisions.

"Mom, please stop. I knew what I was doing when I came here. I knew the risks. I just fell in love…" The last words catch in my throat.

"You fell in love with a dangerous man, Lena. I'm worried for you. You've never been good at guarding your heart, and I don't know how it will survive this." Her tone softens.

"I didn't fall in love because I was weak. I fell in love because he made me feel seen, cherished, and loved."

"You're in shock. That's what happens to people who've been through trauma. Come home, and I promise you'll start to feel better. You just need a change of environment," she says.

But all I want is to be in his environment. Anywhere he is, is where I want to be. Of course, I can't tell her that, can't shatter her hope that this is temporary and I'll get better once I'm home. Shock is something I moved past a long time ago. The second I met Artyom at the club, it took me over like smoke. The night Viktor's guy held a gun to my head, it wrapped around my throat again. After what happened with Art, it isn't shock I'm drowning in. It's heartbreak.

I end the call. My hands still shake when the screen goes dark, but before I can even breathe, my phone lights up again. My heart lurches and I lunge for it, pulse hammering in my chest.

"Hello?" I croak into the phone, my throat dry and tired.

This is how I've been answering lately, like my life depends on it.

"Hey, honey, I got your texts and voicemail." Andrea's voice fills the line, and my heart plummets. It's not him. She sounds confused, and I don't blame her. I know how I must sound to her, like I've gone crazy.

I've left her six messages in the last few days asking if she's heard from Roman. I've even contemplated telling her everything, not caring that it might ruin her relationship. But before I do, I need to know what she already knows.

"Hi, Andrea," I say, my voice heavy with disappointment. "Thank you for calling me back. Sorry, I left so many messages, it was just really important..." My words trail off.

"Uh, yeah, girl, don't worry about it. Roman had to leave suddenly for a family emergency. I guess something happened to one of his brothers. He didn't say much about where he's going or when he'll be back... Lena, are you okay?"

I pause at her question, going back and forth about telling her the truth or keeping her out of it entirely. "I'm not. I've been seeing one of Roman's friends, and he disappeared on me... I just wanted to know if Roman had heard from him," I say, choosing my words carefully.

"Oh God, Lena, I should've told you sooner, and I'm a shit friend for not saying anything when I saw you two together." She pauses and sighs. "The people he works for are..."

Shit. She knows, she most definitely knows what he does. Probably always knew.

"Can we meet up? It'll be easier to tell you this in person."

I don't know if my silence is due to relief or shock that she knows. "Yes, of course, when are you free?"

"Tonight? I'll try to contact Roman and see if I can get some answers for you."

"Thank you. I'll be there," I say.

"Of course, Lena, I'll see you soon."

As soon as she hangs up, a sob breaks through me, feeling the tiniest amount of hope creeping back into the hole where my heart used to be.

* * *

Later that night, I tell my dad I'm meeting a friend, and that's when the interrogation begins.

"Which friend?" he asks.

"Andrea, you haven't met her."

"Where did you meet her?"

"At the hotel, Dad, when I first got here."

"Is that where you're going?"

"Yes." I put on my shoes and walk toward the door.

"Are you sure it's a good idea to be going out at night?"

I stop and look over at him. "Dad, I need to go. You've been wanting me to get some fresh air for days. I thought you'd be happy I'm getting out." I see the wheels turning in his head, weighing the pros and cons.

"You're right. You have the pepper spray I gave you, and the pocketknife?"

I nod. It was the first thing I packed in my bag before even getting dressed.

"Call me when you get there."

"I'll text you," I say, giving him a tight smile. He's not exaggerating; I know he's not. I would feel the same way if it were my child. The only thing that keeps me from staying in is what Art said when he found me at that small clinic, "kill them all." I'm ashamed it brings me a sense of peace. I often think of the other men who worked for Viktor; maybe they had families. I just can't seem to feel anything for them after what happened to me. After finding out from Art what they do to make their money.

While I walk, I think about what happened that night for about the millionth time. Clearly, it was Viktor who sent out a hit on Artyom after what went down at the clinic. I wonder what he thought would happen next. Did he think he would run Brooklyn? With what crew? Art annihilated his men, and all of the Volkhov are loyal to him; they wouldn't go with Viktor.

When I get to the hotel, I see Roman's car and stop dead in my tracks, looking at it like it's my saving grace. "He's here," I breathe out. I run to the lobby door and throw it open, sprinting up the stairs, not having enough patience to wait for the elevator. Once I reach Andrea's door, I'm panting and breathless. Before knocking, I take a second to regain my composure and try not to look like a complete mess. Once I feel like I've caught my breath, I knock on the door twice and step back. I hear hushed voices on the other side of the door, one person speaking harshly to the other. Oh God, they're fighting because of me. The door opens, and Andrea's scowl at Roman turns into a sincere smile when she sees me.

"Hey, Lena," she says, bringing me into a too-tight hug. I let her hug me for a long time. I just realized I hadn't seen her since that night at the club before all hell rained down on my life. We let go of each other only when Roman clears his throat.

"It's good to see you, Lena," he says, and I can't help but stare at him. Why does it feel like it's also been a lifetime since I've seen him? It honestly feels like I've been away from civilization for such a long time.

"You too," I finally choke out. I'm trying to organize my thoughts so I don't attack him with everything that has been on my mind for the past few days. I close my eyes and ask the most important question, the only one that truly matters: "Is he alive?" My heart is beating so loudly I almost miss what comes out of his mouth, almost. It's not hard to make out that one word: "no." Treacherous tears stream down my face, tears of sadness when they should be tears of anger. I should be feeling angry that he's lying to me. He has to be lying. There's no way he's gone. My body is reacting to his words, but my mind isn't there yet.

"You're lying," I whisper. Roman looks like he's going to take a step forward and hug me, but I can't handle that right now. I hold up my hand to him. His comfort would make this feel too real.

"Lena, I'm sorry," he begins to say.

"Sorry for what?" I ask. Sorry for leaving me and letting me drive myself and everyone around me crazy? Sorry for not updating me, letting me see him, or even letting me help him in any way? "When did he…" I trail off, unable to finish that sentence. My mind is going a mile a minute, and there's so much I need to get out, but I can't say them all out loud yet. The words are stuck in my throat, choking me, and I can't seem to get them out, no matter how hard I try.

"He died in the car, Lena. There's nothing you or anyone could've done to help him," Roman says softly.

Andrea grabs my hand and squeezes it. "Roman should've called you days ago. He should've kept you informed. I would feel exactly like you if I were in your position. He knows he screwed up, Lena. Sorry will never excuse what you went through." Another squeeze of my hand. Her eyes soften, and I immediately know what she's going to say next, so I beat her to it.

"But he's gone, and I need to let go?" I ask, tears streaming down my face. They both remain quiet. "It was nice seeing both of you, but I have to go." I turn and leave before either one can say or do anything to keep me here longer.

I need to get my thoughts in order to try to understand what happened in that car. Roman says Artyom died in the car on the way to see someone who could help him. As I walk, I replay the worst ten minutes of my life for the thousandth time. He was shot in the abdomen. If the bullet went through the intestines, he'd die a slow and painful death if not treated.

My phone buzzes in my pocket. I almost don't look, because what could possibly matter now? But I look anyway because I'm now programmed to feel a twinge of hope with every call. I take out my phone, it's Stella.

Stella: *I'm texting you because I know you won't pick up my call, and I need you to see this. I'm worried about you. Not because you fell in love with the wrong guy, but because he's gone and you're grieving alone. Say the word and I'll be on a plane tomorrow. Let me carry some of this with you.*

The words burn against my screen, blurring as fresh tears sting my eyes. Without thinking, I dial my sister.

"Uh, maybe you would've picked up my call after all," she says when she answers.

"I'm outside, and I need to talk through my thoughts without sounding like a crazy person. No opinions, no judgment," I warn her.

"Go for it," she says.

I swallow hard before laying it all out. "I keep thinking about where he was shot, and it just doesn't make sense to me. If the bullet had hit his intestines, they'd have had time to get somewhere and treat him. Roman says he died in the car, which tells me he was shot elsewhere. But I remember where he was shot; it was two bullets in the abdomen. That would give him at least thirty minutes. A shot that kills instantly would be if it hit the descending aorta, but then he would've died in my arms, not later in the car."

"Shit."

"What?" I ask, hopeful she's about to connect the dots.

"You do sound crazy."

"I'm hanging up," I say, and she laughs.

"I'm kidding. Sort of. Please keep going. I'm actually trying to follow, but my internet's slow and I had to Google descending aorta."

I roll my eyes, but a smile tugs at my lips anyway. She's the first person who hasn't gone straight into *you need therapy* or *you're in shock.*

"Anyway," I clear my throat, "when Art was shot, he was completely overcome by shock. His face was motionless." I can still see his pained eyes staring at the sky. "If his body was going into shock, things would've started shutting down, but that wouldn't kill him in the car. They knew time wasn't on our side, so they couldn't have gone far. Right?" I ask, mostly to myself.

"Do you actually want me to answer?" she asks.

I think about it, then say, "Yes."

"You're the medical professional, Lena. What you're saying sounds crazy to everyone else, but they don't see things the way you do."

"You're a genius, Stella! What I need is to talk to someone who's in the field. Thank you!" I say, and hang up before she can reply.

I scroll through my contacts and dial someone who sees bullet wounds in his sleep.

"Hello?" Riddick's deep voice comes through the phone, steady and sure, like maybe he has the answers I've been praying for.

"Hey, it's Lena," I croak. I've never actually called him before, just a few texts here and there about work. This kind of counts as work, right?

"Yeah, I know. That's why I picked up," he laughs. I glance at my watch and curse; he's at work right now.

"Sorry, Riddick, I just have a question. Well, sort of a scenario that I need your opinion on." The hospital loudspeaker blares in the background, and I wait to see if it's a code.

"Go ahead, kid," he says, no questions. This is why he's the best.

"Okay. Two bullet wounds to the abdomen. The victim is conscious, in shock, but still alert. He dies less than thirty minutes later, supposedly in the car before reaching help. Does that add up to you?"

There's a pause on the other end, and for a second, my heart stops.

"Okay," Riddick says after a beat, his tone shifting into the calm authority he uses when teaching interns. "Two shots to the abdomen don't usually mean death in thirty minutes. If it's intestines, he'd be in pain, sure, bleeding, maybe even septic later, but he'd have time. Hours sometimes. Definitely not dying in the car that quick."

I squeeze the phone tighter. "So what would kill him that

fast?"

"The only way thirty minutes makes sense is if the bullet hit something major. The liver, spleen, maybe the kidney, they can bleed out fast if the right artery's torn. But the aorta?" He pauses, and the weight of it presses through the line. "If the aorta was hit, he wouldn't have lasted long enough for anyone to put him in a car. He would've gone down right there."

His words slam into me, but under the crushing weight, a flicker of hope sparks to life.

"Thanks, Riddick. That's all I needed," I murmur, though my heart's beating out of my chest.

"Kid, you just gave me a trauma surgery oral exam over the phone. Next time, at least buy me coffee first."

I chuckle and promise to thank him somehow. When we hang up, I clutch the phone like he has just handed me a lifeline. If it does not add up, then maybe, just maybe, Artyom is not gone.

I keep walking, lost in my thoughts, and another reason he cannot be gone pushes its way in. If he died that same day, then why has there not been a funeral? He is not just some street soldier who could disappear without notice. He is a big-time mafia boss in Brooklyn. Men like him do not vanish quietly. There would have been a wake, a service, candles lit, people standing on corners whispering his name. The whole city would have felt it. That kind of power demands a spectacle, and yet there has been nothing. Silence.

My father says I am stuck in the denial stage of grief, but denial implies I am ignoring the facts, which I'm not. I am examining them the same way I would in a hospital room. Gunshot wounds to the abdomen do not equal instant death. Absence of a body does not equal burial. And silence from the people who swore loyalty to him does not equal mourning. The facts themselves do not line up.

Until I see him in a casket, I will never let him go.

When I finally stop to catch my breath, I realize that even when I am drowning in my head, my feet know where to take me. I am standing in front of the apartment building where I was once a prisoner, and now it looks different. It looks like home. The windows are dark, the halls silent, the air heavy with emptiness.

"Go home, kroshka," I hear his voice echo in my head.

"I can't. I promised I would wait for you."

I sigh and tear my heart away from the building, each step heavier than the last. I head back to my own place, more confused than I have been since this nightmare began. I tell myself tomorrow I will try again, ask more questions, chase down any scrap of truth. Because if the story does not add up, then somewhere out there, he is still breathing, still waiting for me the way I am waiting for him.

The city hums around me, distant and indifferent, but I move through it with purpose. Every step feels like a vow that I will not stop until I know the truth.

39

Lena

I chew on my lip vigorously as I stare at my computer screen. Whenever I think I'm getting somewhere with my search, I hit a dead end. I've been Googling Art and his family ever since Roman told me he was… gone. I just keep wondering what will happen to the Volkhov if he is… gone? It looks like he's the only one left besides a cousin who lives in Colorado. Shouldn't he be taking over if he's the last Volkhov? So many questions swirl around in my head. There's a knock on my door, and my heart skips a beat for a moment.

"Lenachka, dinner is ready." My dad pops his head into my room, scanning my face.

"I'll be down in a minute." I look from him to my computer screen and exit quickly, hoping he doesn't see me looking up Artyom's family again. He sighs, and I hear his heavy footsteps going down the stairs. I rub my eyes and close my laptop. I'm not even sure how many hours I've been doing this for.

When I get downstairs, I see my dad at the table with my uncle.

"Lena! It's so good to see you!" My uncle gets up and wraps

his arms around me, hugging me tight.

"Hi, Uncle," I say, smiling awkwardly. My uneasiness comes from my dad bringing someone new almost weekly to convince me to move on. I've heard everything from "you're better off without him" to "you're a victim of abuse," and I even got "you're traumatized, Lena. Therapy will help you." I don't agree with any of that. I'm not better without him; I'm miserable. I wasn't abused, I was loved. And no amount of therapy can get me to move on without the man I love.

"Lena, sit down with us. I have something to tell you." I roll my eyes internally and take a seat next to my dad. I look at my uncle, already checking out. My eyes grow hollow, and my expression indifferent.

My dad clears his throat. "Lena, we want you to move on with your life, and maybe what you hear now will help you with that." I look at my uncle and see him shift his weight in his seat. Whatever he's about to tell me makes him uncomfortable. "His funeral was today. He was buried with his other family members. He's at peace now, and you deserve the same."

They both look at me for a response to what he just said, but I can't seem to form any words. I can't even comprehend how he would have even found out about this when I've been digging around all day, every day, and found nothing. The only thing I can do is start laughing. I laugh until tears roll down my cheeks.

"Lenachka, I know this isn't what you want to—"

"Hear?" I interrupt mid-laugh. I swipe at my tears, still laughing. "No, this is the best one yet, guys. Truly, you have outdone yourselves this time." I get up to leave, but my dad reaches out and grabs my hand, squeezing it.

"Lena, please. Sit down. You need to hear this, damn it!"

I see the light in his tired old eyes fading, so I stop and sit down, letting him tear me down one more time. "I'm tired of watching you waste your time, health, and energy on a ghost. That's what he is. He's just a ghost now. It's time you let him go. *It's time.*" He looks at my uncle and nods.

"We are not doing this to hurt you, but to give you peace." My uncle chimes in and slides an envelope over.

I open the envelope, hands shaking, tears filling my eyes. I pull out three funeral photos. The first is of the casket. It's closed. Lilies drape over the mahogany wood. I can see Roman and Mike. Their faces are hard like stone, hands clasped like they're barely holding themselves together. In the second photo, a priest in black lifts a brass cross, breath fogging the air. A wreath stands near him with the Volkhov crest tucked inside it. When I see the third photo, my hope completely crumbles. The photo shows the last of the Volkhov, the cousin from Colorado with Artyom's jaw and that stubborn mouth, his palm flat on the lid. Behind him are the men whom I've gotten to know and treated; they're all bowing their heads. My heart hurts, and all types of emotions pass through me: grief for Artyom and his men, anguish for the love we'll never get to explore, and pure anger for not being there.

"How did you get these?" I ask while looking at the photos. "A man named Roman dropped them off at the house. He had the tattoo." He pauses. "He wants you to be at peace, Lena. We all do."

I start to nod, tears rolling down my face. "I love him, Dad. I don't want to let go," I sob. "It was real, everything I felt and went through was real. How am I supposed to be at peace when I couldn't save him? When I couldn't be with him when he took his last breaths? Why couldn't I be at the funeral? I didn't get to say goodbye!" I'm shattering into a million pieces, my heart feeling heavier in my chest. I tear away from my dad and grab my jacket, heading toward the only place I want to be.

* * *

I'm standing in front of his building. The place where my whole world was built up and then crumbled into nothing. It looks like a shell now, holding nothing, no fear or warmth, just nothing without him.

"I hate you," I whisper. "I fucking hate you!" I scream and run up to the door, pounding with whatever strength I have left. I sink to the floor, crying again, or maybe I never stopped. I'm not sure at this point. "But don't worry, I hate myself too. I hate that I couldn't save you. I hate that I didn't say I love you before that day. I hate that everything in me screams not to let you go." I stay there crying, feeling the night grow colder, and the silence around me. I wipe away my tears and walk away from the building, leaving my heart at the door.

40

Lena

F*ive months later*
I stare at the newspaper in utter amusement. My dad sees me staring and looks over my shoulder.

"Finally, someone put a stop to this man. All of Queens will be celebrating," he tells me, patting my shoulder.

A smile dances on my lips. It feels like a huge weight has been lifted from my chest, and I can finally breathe again. Viktor was murdered last night in his home. They describe it as a bloodbath between "gangs." I think Art would've been proud of his cousin. He's done well, as far as I can tell. I feel a pang in my heart, but I push it away. This is great news; this means peace. I can finally be at peace. I sigh and head out of my dad's apartment for the last time.

"I'm going to miss having you here," my dad says solemnly.

I chuckle. "You're saying you're going to miss all the moping and crying?"

He smiles. "Yes, even those moments I will miss because I got to be your crying shoulder."

I lunge at him, hugging him tight. "Thank you, Papa, for

everything. I forgot how much I needed you." We both cling to each other, crying.

"Are you sure you don't want me to take you to the airport? Because I will in a heartbeat, you know that."

"I know, Dad. I want to say goodbye to Brooklyn one last time. I'll be okay, I promise. I'll call you when I get on the plane."

He nods. Not quite understanding but accepting my reasons. As I walk toward the train station, I take in the smells, the culture, the laughter of children, and all the familiarity. This place gave me family, friendship, and love, and for that, I will always consider it my home.

At the train station, I take the stairs down to the southbound platform for the airport. The tiles shine unevenly; a fluorescent strip flickers in time with the far-off rattle of rails. A warm, metallic draft rolls through and lifts a curl at my neck. I sit and play the same game. Two teenagers lean shoulder to shoulder, sharing one set of earbuds, laughing at something on a cracked phone; her chipped black polish draws lazy circles on his knee. Across from them, a mom sways with a baby tucked under her chin, rocking on tired knees. A spit cloth hooks over her finger, a half-moon of dried milk on her shoulder. She looks wrecked and radiant, eyes full in a way that makes mine sting. She has her reason to keep going right there. The thought makes me smile.

While I watch them, I see a flash of black across the tracks leading to the northbound train. My eyes scan the area, looking for that shadow, and what I see in front of me tells me my sanity is going out the window. I see *him*. I see my angel. All in black, eyes boring into mine, leaving me breathless. I fight the urge to blink because what if it all goes away? So,

I stare back, letting my mind trick me, letting the universe laugh at me. I'm okay with all of it if it means I get to see him one more time. He begins to walk toward me, and my breath hitches in my throat. I lean forward, desperate, on the edge of my seat. My knuckles are turning white from clutching the seat so hard. He stops at the edge of the platform and slowly turns toward the stairs leading up, his head still turned, still looking at me. My eyes follow him. "No," I whisper. *No*, my mind screams. I'm not ready. Stay a little longer. I run toward the stairs on my side, needing to see him one last time. Once I reach the top of the stairs, I see him again, clear as day.

"Don't go," I plead. "Not yet." He steps forward and stands right in front of me. My eyes go wide because he looks so real. I can smell his aftershave, the clean scent of him threaded with smoke. Up close, I see the fine lines of his forehead, the shadows under his eyes, and the rough stubble on his jaw. I see *him*.

"Forgive me, Lena," he begins. I close my eyes, taking in his voice. I don't care what he says. I just want him to speak. "Open your eyes, *kroshka*," I hear him say. I feel his palm on my cheek, and I gasp, taking a step back. This feels so real, it's almost too much. I don't know what to do except stare. I stare at him like I've just seen a God, or maybe the devil, because how can he be in front of me right now? How can he look just as glorious as he did the day I lost him? He's standing in front of me, wearing that damned black suit I first saw him in months ago. The pale face that engraved itself into my memory the last time I saw him is now pink. He's healthy, alive, and he's right in front of me. I notice his hands twitching at his sides, and then he takes a step closer.

"Lena, I can explain everything, but before I do, I need to

hold you." He comes closer, his arms stretching out and pulling me into him. I'm stunned by the contact. *He's real, he's real,* I chant in my head over and over again. I feel him bury his face in my neck, and it all just feels like a dream. I stand there in utter disbelief, in shock, and let him embrace me. I let him breathe me back to life.

I feel him breathe in the scent of my hair, pulling me tighter against him. His voice is a low murmur, repeating "I'm sorry" again and again.

"How?" I whisper, clinging to him like he might vanish. "How are you alive?" The last few months come rushing back to me, and I move back and look into his eyes. "Roman said you were dead. I saw pictures of your funeral."

"I know. I know you're confused and hurt," he says, his brows bunching together.

"Hurt?" I cut him off. "You've completely destroyed me," I say, tears spilling down my face and into my mouth. "You let me drive myself crazy," I say. My mind is screaming, reeling into hysteria; it tells me to bolt away from him, but my legs won't let me because the sheer thought of moving even an inch away from this man makes my heart ache.

I see something shift in his eyes, and his stance hardens into an expression of anguish. "I was right there with you, Lena. I followed you into the madness, the despair, and the agony. Being away from you felt like having the wind knocked out of me repeatedly. Desperate and unhinged. I would have crawled my way from the grave to get to you if I thought I could keep you safe. It took me a long time to realize I needed to keep you away from me until I knew I could give you the life you deserved. Lena, trust me when I say I died that day you told me you loved me, and you were the only thing that brought me back." His chest is rising and falling so fast I want to reach out and feel it, to make sure it's real. To feel his heart beating against mine. His words circle in my head on repeat, and I memorize them like my favorite tune. With each moment that passes, heat rises within me, starting from my toes, going up to my eyes, until my whole body is burning for him. So, I do the only thing I can think of. I lunge at him, my arms wrapping around his neck, and crash my lips to his. I kiss him with love, with anger, and with five months of grief.

41

Artyom

Warm fingers circle the scars on my abdomen. I look at her and see that her brows are drawn. She's doing that thing again where she blames herself. I take her hand and kiss it, bringing her back to the present, back to us in this bed. It's been a month since I came back from the dead, so to speak. Every day, she looks at me as if I might disappear again, and every night, we make love like there's no tomorrow. All of this is my fault, her grief, her guilt, and I wish I could take it all away. I spent the last five months hiding from the only person I love, letting her think I was dead, convincing everyone I was gone so we could blindside Viktor and take him out for good. There will be consequences with the council later, but right now, I'm glad I was able to put him in the ground. He never even saw it coming. He thought he had us, had my home, me, and my girl in the palm of his hand, but what he didn't know was that I can't die. Not now, anyway. I'm too selfish. This is my home, and letting go of Lena has never been the plan.

Living without her has been complete torture. I've almost

killed Alec twice because he refused to take me to her. I've thought about kidnapping her more than once, but I knew the police would be involved. Since I needed to be dead, my men on the inside couldn't help me anymore, or Viktor would know it was me. Alec was right every time. They needed to see I was dead, and only my *kroshka* could make them believe.

I look into her eyes. "I'm here," I say, smoothing the crease between her brows. "Even death can't tear me away from you." She smiles. God, I missed her smile. Her scent and the way she feels just lying next to me. It's what I want for the rest of my life.

She's going back to Arizona in the next few weeks to hand in her resignation at the hospital where she's been working and to talk to her family. I feel a sense of responsibility for what she's losing, so I vowed to give her more than she's ever dreamed of. I give her a quick peck on the lips and roll out of bed, heading toward my suit jacket hanging on the doorknob. She starts to protest, but then sees the black box in my hand. Her eyes dart to mine as she waits for me to say something. I walk back to her and kneel in front of her, her legs dangling from the bed.

"Lena, let me love you in this lifetime, and when it's over, I will love you in the next. Not even death will keep me from you, *kroshka*." I open the box, and tears begin to roll down her cheeks.

"How did you get it?" she asks, still in shock.

I smile. "The moment you told me about your grandmother's ring, I sent Alec to get it."

She laughs and cups my face. "I love you, Art," she says between kisses.

"Say you'll marry me." She looks into my eyes, and I can see the light in them flicker and dim. A knot begins to form in my stomach. Something is wrong.

She looks down at the ring, still in the box, and says, "I can't."

Acknowledgments

To my family, thank you for supporting me in ways big and small, and for always believing in me, even when I doubted myself.

To my husband, who has been cheering me on since the very first sentence and never stopped reminding me that I could do this.

To my best friends, who kept me company through this journey with late-night chats, laughter, and feedback that always managed to hit the heart of what I needed to hear.

And finally, to everyone who picked up this book, thank you for giving these characters a place to live outside my head. Your time and your hearts mean everything to me.

About the author

Milana Robertson is a debut author with a love for all things romance, especially the dark, brooding, and beautifully complicated. Raised in Queens, New York, and now living in Phoenix, Arizona, she draws inspiration from her Russian roots and a lifelong fascination with stories that blend danger, passion, and heart.

A new mom and full-time romantic at heart, Milana began writing as a creative escape during early motherhood and quickly fell in love with the process. *Angel in Black* is her first novel and a tribute to the kind of sweeping, emotional narratives she's always loved to read.

When she's not writing, you can find her curled up with a good book, chasing after her daughter, and always dreaming up her next story.

Author's note

Writing *Angel in Black* has been one of the most challenging and rewarding experiences of my life. This story started as a whisper, a dream that would not let go, and slowly grew into the world you just stepped out of. Along the way, I wrestled with characters who did not always do what I told them to and with themes that tested the balance between love, power, and survival. What kept me going was knowing there would be readers like you willing to walk into the shadows with me.

Thank you for giving this story your time, your emotions, and your imagination. Every gasp, every laugh, every late-night page turn means more than I can say. If you felt something while reading, whether it was heartbreak, obsession, or hope, then I did my job. And if you are ready for more, Lena and Artyom's journey continues in *Devil in White*. I cannot wait to share what comes next.

www.ingramcontent.com/pod-product-compliance
Lightning Source LLC
Chambersburg PA
CBHW021043310726
48969CB00006B/1792